THE
MHARISAIG
MURDERS

DAVID CLARK KEACHIE

ISBN: 9798655114753

Published by Amazon KDP Copyright @ David Clark Keachie 2020

~

For Jessie

With great thanks to Gordon Heaney and John Young

Serial Killing for Beginners

It was a cold, damp Shrove Tuesday when he first decided to murder someone.

He had long struggled with a gut-clenching hatred of powerful people, their impact on others and recently, him. Not long ago, in a moment of exquisite clarity partly brought on by his own personal stresses, he resolved that these frustrations could no longer be endured.

Prior to this epiphany, he had no intention of ever carrying out a serious crime, heinous or otherwise. Yet after he had resolved to do so, he became pleasantly free of any doubt, misgivings, or even a hint of concern over guilt yet to come. He became obsessed with the method, deciding that he would include homages to killings of the past. Reinterpreted, they would become his trademarks. In the preparation for the murder, no risks could be left unmitigated, as he needed his freedom to continue, although his life was imperfect indeed.

His primary target would be selected from a list of miscreants whom he considered potentially deserving of punishment. In the act of building this catalogue of creeps, his sense of moral righteousness rose with each new addition. They included a nasty selection of politicians who indirectly caused misery and premature death. He added several wealthy, powerful people whose businesses were spectacularly crooked, and to complete the list, quite a few individuals whose heinous crimes had been treated too lightly by the courts.

The filtering down to a shortlist caused him great annoyance, particularly because some of the most suitable targets' security arrangements and locations meant they were beyond the reach of his justice. Nevertheless, he carried on with his quest for a suitable candidate.

After much analysis and online research, a viable and deserving subject shone brightly above the rest, an Edinburgh-based businessman greatly deserving a deep slice of retribution.

He watched him, cautiously and from a distance. Notes of habits and routines were made and distilled until certainties emerged. The subject was ordinary in most outward respects, a steady citizen of the capital. He was a respectable man who had a successful career, and showed all the signs of being a prime example of the capitalist dream. He drove a dark grey, top of the line Range Rover and parked it in the driveway of his executive six-bedroom home each evening after work. He had accumulated wealth far beyond what most of his fellow countrymen could ever expect to earn, honestly at least. His fortune had been garnered through investments, mainly stock-based these days but earlier – not so long ago – his subordinates headed up various companies on his behalf, selling payday loans hard, insurance policies sometimes and cold-calling the vulnerable, promoting his gamut of scams and unfulfilled promises. Most annoyingly, and thanks to some well-advised legal distancing and by the use of others as company directors in his stead, he had avoided prosecution while greedily extracting the financial benefits of these scams. These tricks the businessman had learned, from his father, from his expensive education and his advisors. He knew how to make money and stay clean, and damn those who didn't.

It was on the third period of surveillance when a plan of how to get access to this odious businessman unfurled. Monday to Friday, a fully-staffed office precluded opportunities daytime. His full household of wife and children meant that weekends and evenings were impossible at his home. The only option was to catch the target in the evenings before he returned home. That meant the late-night time spent each Tuesday evening with his lover, at her apartment in one of the most douce and sought-after pockets of the capital.

Given the nature of the relationship, it was unlikely that anyone else would know where the target would be. Perhaps his wife would only worry if he was away for an extra hour, perhaps even two or three after his normal home time. Using these assumptions, he did some online research, finding the woman's name, employment and all but confirmed her solitary residence. From this framework, he settled on a date and time. After the fourth reconnaissance, all was finalised and materials were readied for a week later.

Arriving at the apartment approximately thirty minutes before his target would, he rang the doorbell and forced his way inside, pulling the young woman towards him and covering her mouth with the pad. The chloroform acted even quicker than he had hoped. His collateral witness disposed of temporarily in her bedroom, he wandered around the bohemian flat, taking in the eclectic mix of the décor. It was all a muddle of continental curios, masks and scattered rugs, the air thick with the sickly smell of sandalwood incense. The anticipation was heightened by this act of inhabiting the house and controlling the surroundings like he would take control of the victim. Taking care not to touch anything, he admired the personality of the apartment, the louche yet expensive décor somehow fitting for a place of assignations between two very different lovers.

3

Perhaps he would like to have a partner with this taste, this style, someday.

He spread his tarpaulin inside the broad, rectangular bathroom and donned two layers of hazmat suits and mask, ensuring that his sight remained unhampered by the goggles. He hadn't touched anything else in the apartment. All other items he needed were taken from his rucksack and placed on top of the tarp. Final decisions made on the instruments, he sat with them on the tarpaulin until nearer the time. The last five minutes, he stood behind the front door, helping build his adrenalin, his pulse racing until the bell rang. He opened the door unseen to the target, who entered and looked straight at him, uncomprehending for the briefest of moments until the dart hit his chest and the door closed, the street ignorant to the drama playing inside.

As with the chloroform, he was delighted with the efficiency of the tranquiliser. A veterinary product of American origin, he had taken delivery of it some days before from a supplier who operated in a part of the web where prying eyes could not easily see. Almost instantaneously, the target had fallen without resistance, except to claw the dart from his chest and drop it conveniently at the feet of his attacker. Lifting the spent dart and placing both it and the pistol back in the case in the bathroom, he checked on the sleeping woman and then back to his target, still spread-eagled on a multi-coloured rug beside the door. He pulled the rug and the man along the few metres of the corridor and into the bathroom to begin his work.

Adam Retreats

The prospect of returning to my home village was not filling me with eager anticipation. I'd been away now for a couple of years, barring one or two flying visits during which I had gone to some lengths to avoid my presence becoming known. I'd been busy with my career and then getting out of said career before it became the death of me. Falling in with bad company, my mum would have called it. Not the worst, as experience had taught me, but still bad enough to remake me as a criminal, thanks to my two-year-long stint as enforcer and director of the Portfolio, our narcotics distribution organisation. This is now thankfully over and disbanded, our capital invested in more legitimate immoral investments.

I'd survived shootings, stabbings and more insanity than my younger self could have countenanced since I innocently left Glasgow University for what I imagined would be a career as a trainee journalist. Instead, I found myself inadvertently drawn into a lucrative narcotics career where deadlines meant 100-kilo deliveries. My new mentors then reached a career point where their money was made and age had caught up with them, so my early superannuation was more of a happy coincidence than down to any Machiavellian genius on my part. My services are still valuable to the Portfolio, shifting our liquid cash reserves into new areas, global projects and so forth, with me and my superiors, the Allantons, now comfortable captains of the investment world and enjoying the safety of having departed the narcotics trade forever.

Thus, my last unlawful duties completed, I had left our erstwhile drug route base, Inverannan, travelled south and away from the wilder scenery of the far north, back to my home village, Mharisaig, as the spring season threw verdant bloom across fields and forests. Intending to avoid contact with my old friends and neighbours until I had time to process my thoughts, I had picked up a few bags of supplies in Ullapool on my way home, making me self-sufficient for a few days at least. On arrival, I painstakingly manoeuvred the car as far as I could along the overgrown driveway until it was almost behind my parent's vacant cottage, hoping rather than expecting that I would remain unnoticed.

A preliminary look around the cottage left me with more than an impression that the property was showing distinct signs of abandonment. No broken windows thankfully, but the paintwork was ancient and flaked, the grey wood of the windows showed through and the ivy and other intrusive plants seemed to have partly consumed the left side of the cottage. Inside had fared little better, the doors now warped and, after staying mostly in high-value London flats for the past two years, the whole place looked even more appalling than I remember. I then spend a long time cleaning, taking the whole of the first two days, throwing out everything that was lying about, including many black bags of moth and mildew-ruined clothes which my parents had left behind when they relocated to sunnier climes. There was a sentimental sadness in the act, clearing out a past family life which carried with it my long lost childhood memories. Breaking up almost all the furniture, I used my father's ancient sledgehammer and rusted saws to reduce them to sections which I could lift and pull from the cottage. The foul carpets followed until eventually the removal part of my work was done and all the detritus was disposed of, temporarily at least, into the badly-sloping timber garage which would also need attention at a later point.

I then set about clearing the bare rooms, therapeutically scraping the decrepit single layer of wallpaper until the undulating and cracked plaster of the walls was revealed. There, some scribbled records had been made, pencil marks telling future generations the names and dates of those who decorated and painted this home before me. The most recent name I recognised was the man who owned the house before our family, confirming that my dad was indeed a spectacularly lazy bugger who hadn't decorated in all the years we lived there, which lifted my mood and gave me my first smile since I had arrived back at Mharisaig. It took me a full day of constant effort to scrape the wallpaper from the downstairs rooms; by then my enthusiasm for DIY had not just waned, but completely dissipated. That night, I decided that my efforts may well be better spent on procuring assistance and fell asleep with plans of my next steps.

~

I wake to a cold and no longer attractive renovation project and the realisation that my father's laziness is genetic and that any further work will be delegated to someone more capable. As I've now spent three days in the cottage, working constantly until the spring light faded, and sleeping upstairs in the single bed of my childhood, I finally have no option but to engage with the outside world. Besides that, I have run out of milk and can't justify driving forty miles to the next shop just to avoid going into the village. So, with forlorn hopes of my anonymity continuing for just a little more time, I drive down to the crossroads and towards the village shop for supplies. Everything that is Mharisaig seems unchanged and I survey it as I drive, taking in the familiar houses and lanes that line my route. I park outside the shop, waiting until a customer leaves, a woman who lives in the street just along from me and who would undoubtedly wish to engage me in conversation. The way clear, I slip into the shop and pick up a couple of bottles of milk and some chocolate, which I have hardly eaten since I left Scotland but somehow feels like the right thing to buy today.

The shop attendant, a youth perhaps still in his teens, takes the items from me silently and gives me change in the same sullen manner, which is ideal. I don't recognise him and the opposite seems true, so I begin to hope my profile may just remain low after this. The door opens with a slight clang of the bell and I turn to face Niall McRae, my oldest friend and one of many who I'd have much preferred to avoid, for a few days yet at least.

'Don't think you can fucking well hide out in that cottage and sneak down here for your messages ya bastard!' He shouts, grabbing me in a clumsy Highland approximation of a bear hug.

Niall has grown wider than he had been two years ago, the metabolism of youth clearly unable to keep up with his diet. I return the hug and manage to disentangle before it feels even weirder than it started.

'How's it going Niall? You been hiding in the bushes waiting for me?' I smile at his grinning expression.

'Seen your big motor passing the house, mate, cannae miss that thing'. I now slightly regret turning up here with my London car, which I'd had one of the guys bring up a couple of days before. I had considered keeping my hire car or taking an old Land Rover from Inverannan but preferred the comfort and luxury option.

'Yeah, just got back for some rest, was going to give you a shout when I'd settled in.' I tell him.

8

He looks at me suspiciously. 'Your arse, you just knew I'd annoy you and want you to buy me beer now that you're rich.' I shake my head to deny it but I wish with all my heart that I had indeed managed to avoid him.

'Anyway, see you at the pub at seven after you've finished your Maltesers. What fucking age are you?' He leaves, laughing as I follow him out, the store attendant looking fecklessly after us. I jump into the car and return Niall's wave. He walks through the gate of a house just along from the shop. Something has changed, at least, as Niall certainly didn't stay there two years ago.

I sit in my car for a while when I get back, thinking over the tasks I can now initiate that my presence in Mharisaig is known. I'll get some locals to do the windows and doors, painting and all that, and see where to buy furniture, something I have as yet never done. The only untouched room in the house is my bedroom, so I also need a new kitchen, bathroom and basically every room in the house fixed. Pathetically, I think about getting someone else to design the whole place on my behalf, but I don't really have a "someone else" at present and I don't think Mharisaig is likely to over-encumbered by interior designers.

Leaving the car, I force the front door open again and look at my handiwork. The living room is completely bare although still musty and with marks of dampness on the ceilings and the lower half of the walls. The floors creak as I walk along the hallway and into the time-travel kitchen, which I think was installed in the 70's or earlier, and not in a classic country-cottage style, more of a yellowy plastic-edged and decrepit theme. There is no doubt, I need someone to fix this shit-hole up and it won't be me. I chill out for a while, swallow some medication as proscribed by my now-disengaged psychiatrist and then order my thoughts as she recommended. I shall meet Niall, do my best to be normal and see if he has any contacts in the building trade who can help with the house.

Just after seven, I head down to the sole pub in Mharisaig and in to meet Niall, who is sitting alone in the near-empty bar reading a newspaper.

'Still reading that shite?' I point to the red-top he is gazing at.

'Just the football and you can stop being a posh twat. I suppose you are reading the Telegraph or the FT now?' he counters.

'The fucking Beano would be better than that.' I tell him as I head to the bar.

I order two pints and two 18-year-old malts, the better to prevent Niall from winding me up about being mean. He doesn't take that tack but instead has decided that he'll focus on me being a rich show-off.

'Last time a round like that was bought in here was the royal visit'. He tells me. 'I wish the old Adam Darnow was here instead of this replicant'. I again tell him to fuck off and he seems satisfied to move on to a different conversation.

'So, my long-lost pal, what have you been up to since the last time you rode out of town? You left here on a number 62 bus and came back in an eighty-grand motor. Won the lottery?'

He raises his eyebrows and I wish I'd thought through a better cover story than I have.

'You know what I've been doing, making loads of dough in the property game. I got offered a job in

London and the rest is history.' I give him one of my cards for the Allanton Property Portfolio, embossed and expensive, he glances at it and immediately afterwards starts to pick his teeth with the corners.

He takes a drink of the malt and then a quarter of his pint disappears down his wide neck.

'Aye, if you fell in the river you'd climb out with a salmon in your pocket, you lucky bastard.' We clink glasses and my pretence is guaranteed, I trust.

'So what have you been up to, apart from not going to the gym?' I ask him, looking meaningfully at his significantly expanded abdominal area.

'Aye, it's Liz, she's a chef. Brings home the leftovers every day and they are fucking awesome. It's no really my fault Adam. I am helpless before these plates of wonder.' I laugh at his expression but tell him he needs to stop being helpless before he can't get through the door.

'It's easy for you to slag me, sitting there like a fucking behemoth. Are you still boxing or whatever?'

'Not right now, but I kept on at it when I was down south. Went to a gym there and the guys were top notch. I didn't know many people socially in London, so that was ideal when I was bored.' Niall shakes his head.

'You're making me feel bad anyway. At least get a pie from behind the bar and some crisps, start putting on some weight for me.' I shake my head and he starts to tell me what's been happening to our pals since I was last here. The usual tribulations of Highland life mostly, but a few sad tales too which actually make me feel an unexpectedly genuine pang of melancholy. Since I became involved with the Allanton's business, my emotional range had only gone between numb and angry, so I am more than slightly surprised at the recent return of these feelings.

'Aye well, other than that everything is much the same. Look, here's some of the chaps come down to see you. Thought I'd phone round and see if we could get all your shyness out of your system in one go.'

I turn to see a cabal of my old school friends entering the bar, whooping as they arrive. Me, I wish that I'd stayed hidden in the cottage.

Four hours later, for some reason I'm standing outside the pub with Niall while he smokes and continues a mini-rant about some grudge he has with one of the local businesses. This reminds me of my own need for a builder, so I ask him if there's anyone good local.

Niall smiles at me, beatifically through the alcohol fug and says 'Mate, you've come to the right place. I will do the work myself, with the help of my able men inside'.

I look at him with some scepticism as he tells me that he and three of the reprobates currently in the bar have indeed constituted a building firm, which I remember vaguely that they had threatened to do years ago.

'Correct me if I am not remembering things as I should, but weren't you useless at all that?' I ask Niall as he rocks lightly backwards and forwards, trying to relight a damp cigarette.

'Aye, I am inflicted with a lack of practical skills Adam, you are correct.' He nods sagely. 'However, I am a jovial salesman and a damn fine planner and driver, so those monkeys do the work while I run the show and bring them the stuff they need.'

12

This is better news, as the cottage is in bad enough condition without Niall inflicting his cowboy woodwork ineptitude on it.

We head back inside and I get another round in, I feel I am subsidising these sponging bastards somewhat. At least I can afford it now, although I don't want to make a habit of this.

Niall leans in towards me when I get back to the table and I think that the cold air and cigarette may have triggered a deeper level of drunkenness than he had five minutes ago. The others are talking about football and not listening, so I'll let him divulge his secret.

'Did anyone tell you that Anna is back too?' My heart sinks. My time with Anna is one of well, all of my relationships which I did not handle particularly well. I shake my head and he goes on.

'Was engaged to some guy in Aberdeen and she dumped him. Dunno what he did but Anna chucked her job and moved back in with her mum. Her dad died last year too, so she's not had it easy.' I feel nothing but guilt now, as I certainly hadn't added to Anna's enjoyment of life. We had been together just before I went to London, but I broke it off rather abruptly when she visited me there. I had no choice, really, given what I was doing for a living back then, but I could have been well, less of a dick about it.

Niall tells me that his partner, Liz, is friendly with Anna and then moves on to another subject, thankfully. I've not been drinking much whisky, just bottles of session ale while the lads have been throwing down everything they could let me buy. Last orders are shouted and a long half an hour later I'm able to say my goodbyes and leave them to stagger home, Tuesday night in Mharisaig finally over. My head is more than a

13

little fuzzy but I'm probably in better shape than the others. The cottage is in the opposite direction from them so I walk there alone. One car passes, heading towards the village and it slows to let me move off the road and onto the verge. I see a surprised expression on Anna's face as she glides past, but does not stop, unsurprisingly.

A Perfect Culling

Each cut he inflicted vented his suppressed emotions on the juddering carcass of the former businessman. The deep, bloody incisions were an exact balance between rage and control following a ritual which he had designed, following the methods once used in other unsolved crimes, long ago. The target died quickly, never having wakened, almost an aside to the butchery that was being wrought upon him. After it was done, the killer felt better than he had in years, his impotence no longer constrained but vented, released, leaving him sated yet somehow needing more.

Almost an hour later, after his protective suits, boots and mask were stowed back in the rucksack, he glanced around the bathroom with a sense of deep gratification. After all, the man's innocent family would still be wealthy, his lover unharmed, just the guilty party having been surgically removed from the land of the living. His death would surely become a memorable reminder to the world, of the restitution that must be made by all such creatures.

After checking out the side street both ways, he closed the door with gloved hands and after attaching a blood-stained notice to the railings, made his departure from the scene, unmarked and unseen.

Almost an hour later, a neighbour stopped and read the notice. She recoiled at the content and after a wishful moment that it may be a hoax, dialled 999, waiting outside until the sirens became louder and the police arrived at the hitherto quiet avenue. She watched as ambulances arrived in short order, more plainclothes and uniformed police, and scene-of-crime officers aplenty until the area was a cordoned subject. No more douce respectability, but now the main subject of the Scottish national news. She was taken aside and her statement carefully recorded, then left to watch the unfolding event develop from her upstairs flat. News teams arrived to form a second perimeter around the front door of her neighbour, the lassie whose name she did not know but who always dressed flamboyantly. She hoped that all was fine with her, gasping when she was brought out on a stretcher, face uncovered but for the oxygen mask. Having had enough of this disturbing spectacle, she closed her curtains and wept, long and deep for whatever had gone on.

The Major Investigations Team had incrementally arrived, taking charge over this appalling bloodbath. The bathroom was where the victim lay, however, it was unlike any case they had worked – and the team were not callow, counting over two hundred different murders in their collective experience. Their usual workload comprised of bog-standard homicides, typically carried out by someone the victim knew. They knew how to build a solid case with their now-advanced police processes, forensics, DNA and data analysis. It was commonly and increasingly linked to organised crime, often the victim would be known to them in some capacity or other, but this one, this was off-the-scale. A few of the team had been on major incidents on traffic, seen some mangled shit that would lead to nightmares, but at least those had been accidents. This was someone's deliberate act, an appalling murder that would haunt their quiet moments and one which could perhaps never be wholly erased from memory.

The corpse was removed, eventually, and the forensic work would continue overnight and all the next day. Record amounts of photography, blood splatter analysis and testing were taken and the team were determined

16

that the deceased and his family would have justice, no matter what they had to do.

The victim's wife, devastated at his murder, showed little surprise when told that he had been found in the apartment of another woman. She suspected several affairs in the years of their marriage. Distraught nonetheless, she could shed no light on where they should look next, so they shifted their attention to his business.

Additional officers were transferred into their investigation as the questioning exposed a clear divide of the opinion of former employees. Some stayed broadly loyal to his memory, perhaps having previously shared his thrusting imperative to make money and had done well from hanging to his coat-tails. The others, those who damned his name, had been mistreated, lost their jobs, been bullied to meet targets or just had enough moral decency to escape whatever branch of his malign business empire they had found themselves in.

In their experience of the senior investigating officers, a list of suspects was often initially viewed as close family and friends. For criminals, it was typically extended to who their enemies were and, despite the natural unwillingness of their peers to talk to the police. Information could usually be gleaned from somewhere. This guy though, he had by far the biggest range of enemies of anyone they had ever come across. Their investigation into his myriad business activities had revealed more scams, frauds, cheats and crimes than they could have imagined. On a personal and professional level, confirmed by many ex-employees, he was pathologically duplicitous and unpleasant. The phrase "more faces than the town clock" along with often more bitter condemnations were routinely and vigorously put to them. He was also noted as having an almost complete lack of empathy to those who worked for him and indeed towards the tens of thousands of individuals whom his companies had fleeced.

From a purely legislative aspect, three major investigations had already taken place in the past several years, during which eleven former directors had been convicted on crimes which could not be legally attributed to the victim, but were certainly directed by him. Motives, it seemed, were many and varied, in this murder enquiry. This contrasted utterly with his family life, his social life and most sharply with his public image, which projected near-paragon status for his charitable works and open-handed munificence.

Weeks of investigation rolled along into months and the media soon drifted off to matters anew, the case not forgotten, never would be, but after a prurient few days the public soon gets bored and new stories are needed. It was in the third month when the team started to wind down, leaving a few dedicated officers to keep it going, the trails all cold now and not a hint of the monster that carved and slew the victim. At the end of the main investigation, all they knew was the height of the assailant, that it was certainly a male, right-handed and they had a profile which was of bugger all use to them as there were no leads whatsoever to anyone who remotely resembled a viable suspect. Even the note, with it's Old Testament quote written in perfect script and covered in the victim's blood, offered no leads.

The remaining investigations team could hardly muster great sympathy for the victim but, being the professionals they were, kept on doing their job as no-one, not even a corporate criminal like him deserved to go like that. The list of persons who had a motive to kill him was longer than the intestines they had found wound out around the bathroom, yet not a fingerprint or a microdot of DNA had been found. Even with their forensic understanding of the murder act, the scene itself, with photos of everything and analysis as deep as the scientists provided, even after that, the team had not one person who could be considered their prime suspect.

Niall the Builder

I don't know how bad a hangover the others have, but I am in severe discomfort when I waken. There are no helpful painkillers in my now-empty cottage, so I drink as much water as I can and go back to my pathetic single bed until I feel better, which takes me almost to lunchtime. This gives me time to think about last night, trying to remember what the guys told me about the denizens of Mharisaig, who had left and what had happened to those remaining. My memory for names has not always been reliable, so the unimportant acquaintances just linger as faces in my mind. Anna, on the other hand, makes me worry.

She had visited me a couple of times in London before I broke up with her, two years ago and at the start of my tenure as a co-ordinator and occasional enforcer for the Allanton crime family. Anna had been in my apartment, had dined with me and certainly asked me how I became almost instantly wealthy, which was a substantial reason for me to terminate our relationship. I was in a dark place back then and I am ashamed to admit to myself that I considered an even harsher ending for Anna, to prevent any chance of her suspicions reaching a wider audience. Thankfully I had not done anything extreme, but now am in a situation of my own making, back here in Mharisaig with someone who almost certainly figured out that back then, I was indeed a "right bad yin" as my mother would often refer to criminals.

So, I'm torn between leaving Mharisaig again, ignoring the situation or speaking to Anna about it. Typically for me, I decide to take no action whatsoever and just see what happens. If she just wants to avoid me, that's fine. If not, I'll see what happens. I'd spent a lot of effort, time and risk getting away from my criminal life and above all else, I cannot fall back into it, or indeed let it catch up with me. Here I am the original Adam Darnow, resuming my life after a rude interruption by gangsters, along with dealing with the resultant and persistent psychological issues and with an ongoing determined focus on not getting caught, ever. Tricky, but I have managed it so far and I don't need any rumours starting about me, especially not here, my home town.

The cottage phone is long disconnected so I have a few things to deal with which requires me to drive to somewhere my mobile works, the far side of the village now being proudly within range of a mobile phone mast. I get a shower, put on some respectable clothes and drive down to where the pub advice has it, my mobile phone will work. I call Gillian at Inverannan first and we talk for a while, she tells me about the ongoing work and plans there and that she misses me. Resisting the urge to chuck my cottage restoration project and head back up there, I tell her that I'm getting someone local to work on the building and close the call, promise her another one soon and wish I was with her. I know that I need to be wary of my behaviour with Gillian as I have made what Niall last night referred to as a "serious arse of every relationship I ever had". It made me laugh at the time but is probably not something to be proud of, if there is ever to be hope for me.

I call the offices of the Portfolio where I have left my team in charge of our now-almost-legal activities and afterwards John Allanton for a quick chat, fulfilling my role of updating him on the business while not actually having to do anything myself. I then call my parents abroad, my first chat with them in a long, long time. All

21

is well with them and I have done my duty, made contact with those I should, and now can completely forget about them all for another while.

The last thing on my list, I call the number Niall gave me for his partner's home and after some time, hear his croaking tones.

'Are you actually a builder or were you just talking shite last night.'

'Both.' He takes a moment to cough his lungs up.

'Jesus, you need to stop smoking. That's a sign, that cough.'

'Aye, never again. Where are you?'

I tell him that I'm at the mobile hot spot he told me about and asks me to pick him up, he'll come round to the cottage with me and price up what I need.

I sit outside his house after sounding my horn, then I realise I'm at the wrong one. I get out of the car and through the gate and knock on the door of what I hope is now the right property. Liz comes to the door and invites me in. She has a lovely smile and is petite, her frame like a long-distance athlete and absolutely unlike her partner Niall, who is sitting on the sofa like a lardy zombie. He turns face –up when I enter the living room and introduces me.

'Liz, this is Adam, Adam, Liz.' Perfunctory and accurate.

'Hi Liz, how do you put up with him?' I ask.

She snorts, 'I won't for long if he keeps coming in like last night. You smell like a distillery threw up on a cigarette factory.' She shoves the side of his head as she passes the sofa and he groans and tells her to leave him alone, he's not well. This seems to be correct as Niall suddenly leaps up, runs upstairs and we hear an extremely loud and unpleasant vomiting noise from behind the bathroom door.

Liz shakes her head.

'That might have been my fault. We were catching up after a long time.'

She looks at me and shakes her head. 'Nope, he would have been fine if he'd come home after the pub. I think they went to one of their houses and kept drinking, I heard him coming in about 4 in the morning.' That explains his condition and also makes me wonder if the building contract is in safe hands with a group of young men who drink to that time on a Tuesday. I make a mental note to talk about this with Niall, who will ideally never know that much of my past two years have been taken up with these types of discussions.

'So I hear that you are a chef?' I change the subject with Liz.

'Yeah, over at the Roshven Inn. Bit of a hike to get there so I stay over some nights and get some peace from Niall. What are you up to now? Mharisaig will be a bit dull after London.'

'I'm fixing up my mum and dads place. They are living abroad for a while and I promised I'd keep the place in good order, which I haven't. Niall and the lads have offered their services.'

'Cool. They are good workers, except for Spewy upstairs. He's competent at arranging things though, they've fixed up a couple of extensions and garages, so I'm sure they will be fine.' I can tell that she wants to speak about something else, and I hope to god it's not about Anna.

'Anna phoned this morning to say she'd seen you.'

Oh great.

I nod, but don't know what to tell her.

'She's had a pretty bad year or so. Don't know if Niall told you. She was engaged to a guy who worked on the rigs, but he turned out to be a bit of a junkie every time he got back home so eventually, she packed him in. Her dad passed away too so it's just her and her mum now.'

Still, I don't know what to say, so I just nod sympathetically.

'Anna got a bit of a surprise when she saw you. She spent a bit of time crying, so maybe keep away if you don't want to upset her.' I'm now thinking that Liz is rather a prying type and suppress the urge to tell her that everyone in Mharisaig can go take a fuck to themselves, but best not.

'Look, Liz, I made a mistake with Anna and the last thing I want to do now is upset her. I'll only be here for a couple of weeks and then I'll probably leave forever. Unless Anna wants to talk to me, I'll just keep out of the way.' She nods approvingly and I pat myself on the back for not reacting. All that therapy wasn't wasted after all.

Niall re-emerges, looking pale but no doubt feeling improved. 'Ready to go?' he asks.

'Maybe after you brush your teeth.' I tell him.

He breathes into the palm of his hand and nods, walking back upstairs to apply toothpaste to the problem area.

Liz shakes her head and I have more than a degree of sympathy for her. I do wonder how anyone puts up with Niall.

'Twat' she says under her breath as she leaves for work.

Niall and I go to my place and spend about an hour walking around the cottage, he with his clipboard and taking notes of the many and various tasks required to make it habitable. Of course, I realised that it was an unmaintained shambles, but when presented with a proto-builders list it appears much worse. A climb up a barely-usable ladder confirms to Niall that the roof is also "totally shagged" and that the chimney is "a fucking death trap", as well as multiple sources of water penetration and the resulting dampness. Three sheets of A4 of problems are the result of his initial overview and he opines that no doubt he'll find more when he removes the moist and stained plasterwork.

It is, in Niall's opinion, better to knock it down and build a new house, rather than fix up what would only ever be a small cottage on a roadside plot. I, however, with budget not an issue and sentiment at the forefront, tell him to get me a price and not to take the piss with it. He lumbers off back to the village on foot and I drive in the opposite direction to find a bank, for a down payment will no doubt be required and these boys are keener on cash than a cheque.

A long drive later, my car is full of food and general supplies again and I have a few thousand pounds on me, with more on order. While I am away and in reach of a mobile signal, I read through my emails on my phone, ignored these past few days. I have several from the Portfolio office, too many in fact, so I reply to last one, specifying that I need now only be contacted under critical circumstances and that I will require a weekly summary, rather than daily emails. When I left London, I discussed with the Portfolio team the consequences of any misdeeds. So long as they hold the memory of our meeting on the subject, I have no worries of fraud in my absence.

I drop some of the money in for Niall and demur on his invitation to the pub, possibly helping extend his relationship with Liz by doing so. He's back on his sofa for the evening and again, I think that Liz could absolutely do better, although it's a small pool of talent here in the Highlands and at least his patter is generally good. Niall promises to make a start the following morning, although I am uninspired by his demeanour and tell him before leaving that he is a lazy fat bastard, by way of encouragement.

When I get back to the cottage, a small dark blue Citroen is sitting outside, but there's no-one inside. I shoulder the front door open as usual and have a look around, no intruders so it must be someone just out for a walk, leaving their car in the slight widening of the road out front. I stand in the kitchen and look out over the evening gloom of the unkempt back yard when a face looks in straight at me through the window. I yelp and jump back and there's a scream from the other side of the window as Anna falls into the overgrown weedfest that is my garden. As I open the wonky back door, she is extricating herself from a tangle of long sticky weeds and trying to suppress rampant blushing, which I can't help but smile at.

'Need a hand?' I ask, trying to look genuinely concerned.

'Fuck off' she replies, although I'm not clear on whether this is the message she came here to deliver or just a response from someone with plant life in their hair.

'I can't, this is where I live.' I tell her with a faux perplexed expression.

Anna goes to run around the side of the cottage and away, but I follow, grasp her arm and stop her, releasing her immediately in case she thinks I am being aggressive.

'I'm sorry; I was just trying to be funny.' I tell her.

'Don't fucking start doing anything witty, it's not your forte.' she hisses at me.

I'm wondering if she just turned up to give me abuse but in the interests of finding out what she wants, I decline to proffer another reply. Gesturing for her to enter the cottage, I stand back and she does, with me following. She washes her hands in the sink but there are no towels so she dries her hands on my jacket which is hanging over the cupboard doorknob. I don't think she's entirely friendly towards me. I follow her into the living room, which is devoid of all but a summer folding chair with orange floral material. She sits down and looks straight ahead, ignoring me and giving no further clue as to her intentions or the reason for her visit. Leaving her to it, I walk upstairs to put my phone in to charge and by the time I return, she seems to have recovered from her fright and fall in the garden.

'So what are you doing back here Adam?' She gives me a look which is hard to read but perhaps implies half anger, half sadness. I sit on the floor across from her, resting my back on the cold bare wall.

'What it looks like. Fixing up my parent's house, nothing more.'

'Not selling drugs or whatever you usually do in Mharisaig then?'

There it is; my career very much in the open. I look at her and she can't meet my gaze. I calm myself and gather my thoughts.

'Look, I don't know what you think you know about me, but I am not involved in anything illegal. I promise.'

'What does that mean from you, a promise? Not fucking much in my experience.' She may well have a point here, but I'm still unclear on what she wants from me.

'Why do you think I am involved in drugs?' A question which may mean one of two things to her, and I wait while she considers her answer.

Anna pulls her fingers through her straight dark hair and then looks at me accusingly.

'Don't give me your bullshit Adam, in two months you went from being a cub journalist to living in a fucking Knightsbridge flat and your personality turned from what you were, into some dark-hearted cold bastard. Remember how you broke up with me? Even your eyes were different, you sounded like a fucking robot and I couldn't detect a hint of emotion. You're no fucking Estate Agent or whatever you pretend to be and I hope you're not back here to peddle whatever the fuck it is that you sell.'

This tirade, while unexpected, is fairly accurate regarding my state of mind and employment back then. Anna was an innocent, and I had just started working, albeit not entirely of my own volition, for the Allanton crime family. I just withdrew into myself, couldn't cope with anything from my previous life and Anna was absolutely the best thing before it happened, but not afterwards. I had dismissed all thoughts of the people I knew before my narcotics career, partly in case they became involved but mainly to help me isolate, insulate myself by becoming what I had to be. I'm not sure how much to admit to her, she could go to the Police with whatever I tell her, maybe even be recording me now. I shake my head to clear the suspicions and decide on a middle of the road explanation for her.

'Anna, I am back to fix up the house. That's it. I'm not involved in anything illegal anymore and I have spent the best part of the last two years trying to make that happen. Back then, I got involved in something I couldn't stop and I had to keep away from you, from mum and dad, from anyone who knew me before.' As true as I can tell it without saying anything tangible, just in case my paranoia is genuine.

She snorts. 'So you were protecting me, were you? Arsehole.'

I shake my head and go into the kitchen, get two beers from the decrepit fridge and hand her one, which she accepts wordlessly.

'I was protecting me. The people I worked with were serious. It's all over now and I have a proper job, sort of. I'll be away from here soon after the cottage is finished - Niall and the lads are fixing it up.'

Her laugh, loud and genuine, rings around the empty room.

'Those clowns couldn't fix up a tent.' This wasn't quite what Liz had told me earlier but then she is Niall's partner and may have an interest in them getting the job. Fuck.

I put my head down and scratch my hair in annoyance. 'I've just given Niall an advance to let them buy some materials.' This time, we both piss ourselves laughing. Although I'd prefer that it wasn't at my expense, at least Anna has paused being furious at me.

'You never know, they might do a good job.' She sniggers and I smile at her, suppressing the fleeting thought that I could take my money back and break their legs if they don't. Anna is still innocent, after all.

After a period of silence, I go fetch us another beer and we sit, the anger hopefully dissipated, perhaps ready to return if I say the wrong thing. I don't want to ask anything personal as that might make her flip at me again, so I keep quiet.

'OK, so you are the strong and silent type now are you?' Anna seems to have noticed my reticence. I nod and smile.

'I thought if you wanted to tell me about anything, you would.'

She looks sharply at me. 'Like what?'

'What brought you back here? We've both found our way back to Mharisaig, maybe licking our wounds.'

She sighs and takes a swig of the beer bottle. 'I'm back because mum was lonely and I was hurt. I'm sure Niall told you about Robert.'

'Was this the guy in Aberdeen?'

'Yeah, I seem to have formed a pattern where I meet nice young men and after a while, they get involved with drugs and turn into monsters.' Another nice dig at me.

'Is that what happened?'

'Pretty much. He hadn't seen his pals much when we started going out, but after New Year they had a social thing going when he was home from the rigs, just poker nights and stuff he told me. He always liked a drink but then he got into all that other shite. I'm sure I don't need to go into the details of what happens next to someone in your line of business.' Fuck me. The sniping is never going to end.

Anna takes a deep drink from her bottle and goes on. 'Dad died around that time and Robert got suspended from work after a drugs test. I couldn't cope and had to be with mum, so I took a career break and came here. I'm three months or so into my year out and looking forward to spending my summer with the midges at Mharisaig. You turn up like another ghoul from my past and here I am, drinking beer with the bastard who broke my heart.' Her voice breaks and she turns her head away.

With that, she abruptly puts the beer bottle down, walks out the back door and I hear the car drive off. That could have been worse, I think to myself.

A Country Murder

For his second expedition into his career as an avenging serial killer, he sought his target using an online journalism blog, which uniquely for the world of the media seemed to him to honestly expose the filthy and grasping behaviour of establishment criminals. When he was not working and had time to sit alone at home, this was his new pastime, and most interesting it was too. There was no shortage of politicians on the blog to contemplate, each using their lofty position to enhance their already considerable wealth, putting selfish concerns above the lives and livelihoods of the miserable proles. He had never been much interested in politics, but now he felt that there was a role for him to fill, to make an impact, even.

After much analysis, his thoughts coalesced towards one particular architect of misery, one with a long record of immoral behaviour towards the poor of the country. This individual sat on boards of companies which routinely asset-stripped companies and sent others to liquidation, casually damaging lives and made this particular swine vastly wealthy along the way. In his political capacity, he was a key part of the reduction of public spending, and there were many heartfelt speeches online where he expounded the benefits of the free market while disparaging those who needed help from the state. This was a clever, well-educated gentleman of good breeding, who despite all his wealth and high position was 100% an absolute cunt of a man.

He hesitated to settle on him though, as he had a young family, but so did those he ruined, so that excuse was moot. In any case, this bastard has more in his negative column than could be outweighed by any familial misery which his premature death might cause. They would all presumably inherit his wealth anyway, so any last vestige of empathy was washed away by the statistics and stories of misery this man had already wreaked in his abhorrent career. Indeed, much of the motivation to murder this particular gentleman was to prevent him from doing further damage to society, surely an admirable aim.

This man would be guarded, certainly, so to spend any time on him, working with blade and tools, would need great planning and some good fortune. There was also the problem of getting to the south of England to scope the target, and then to carry out the act, but he had enough free weekends to make it a viable proposition. After settling on him as the target, it was all he could think about, no matter what else was going on, this guy was embedded in his mind. He soon found out where the target lived, an accidental online publication of a list of public figures and celebrities happening fortuitously not long before his search commenced.

On the appointed weekend, he flew down south, late Saturday evening and made his way by hire car to the address, all the while hoping that there hadn't been a recent relocation, or that he would be spending the weekend at another bolthole. On his arrival, it became apparent that the house was guarded by at least two security men, however, that evening a party was being hosted, so the cars and taxis which disgorged wealthy friends meant that all was a hubbub. After some scrambling around in the undergrowth, he found a spot to overlook it all, unseen in the lee of a ruined farm building across the road from the main property. There were four CCTV cameras in his line of vision, three of which were covering the road and driveway and one pointing at the front door. Unless there were other cameras which he couldn't see, the garden and side of the property were not covered. He watched the garden party all evening and into the early hours. His night-vision binoculars came in particularly useful as he watched the target's wife being casually unfaithful in a quiet part of the garden. The security men drank a few bottles of beer before they drove away at 2 am when their shift ended, and all was unguarded. The stragglers, even the most drunken and vocal guests were gone not long afterwards, amidst great braying and heehawing.

Around 5 am, his heart pounding and palms sweating inside medical gloves, he left the sanctuary of the undergrowth, clambered over the garden fence and entered the house through unlocked French doors. He stepped unchallenged into the lounge, still strewn with the detritus of a party well enjoyed. His target, either as a result of marital discord or the volume of alcohol he had consumed, lay snoring on a broad, cream leather sofa. As he carefully surveyed the rest of this part of the property, he realised that a bundle of blankets on the other sofa in the room was actually a sleeping child.

He paused, and felt disappointed as he knew that his conscience would not allow a child to waken and witness his handiwork, nor could he reasonably chloroform an infant. He dismissed momentary thoughts of carrying the daughter into another room and tying her up while he worked. It was just bad luck of having the child fall asleep in the same room, he supposed. Standing above the target, he looked down at his bald head, circled at the back and sides with a well-groomed inch or two of silver hair, his features youthful for his age and untrammelled by lines. Leaning over him, he wondered if it would be better to simply slice the knife along his throat, imagining the glorious ending of life as the eyes opened and closed in despairing panic.

No, his backup plan might be a less satisfying approach, but it would allow him to leave the incident unsuspected, which in this particular high-profile case may be advisable. His research had shown that the victim had a penchant for British Sports Cars and was a habitual Sunday morning driver along the steep lanes of this green and pleasant land, in his precious Morgan Plus 4. Old cars are notoriously prone to developing faults and with the help of an online workshop manual, he knew exactly how to loosen the brake pipes just enough to let them function until the vehicle went over a bump, quite a precise piece of automobile re-engineering but eminently viable. Disappointed at having to discard his more tactile murder method, he left the sleeping rodent and his daughter and entered the garage through a connecting door from the kitchen to begin a minor brake adjustment.

There was nowhere near the house to hide confidently unseen in daylight, so he returned the same way he'd arrived, back further along a footpath to the side road where he'd left the hire car. There, he donned suitable hiking attire, sunglasses and a lightweight tammy that he'd brought. After breakfasting in his car, he set out along a right of way and watched from the riverside path to wait for the show. Two hours later, he heard the burble of a well-tuned four-cylinder engine and watched as the British racing green classic took to the road, his hungover target at the wheel. As his information told him, he was a driver without caution, enjoying the adrenalin of fast driving and skilful cornering. He jogged along the path to watch as the car sped down the straight incline and towards a tightly angled approach to the stone-built bridge. Unable either to brake or to avoid the structural pillars either side of the bridge, the stunning example of British automotive engineering plummeted down the side of the escarpment and into the deep brown, rushing river flow.

He ran downhill towards the bridge and saw the target in the left centre of the river, neck-deep but still in the car and struggling to release his submerged seat belt. Running down the tracks of the car to the riverside, he waded out to the car, stopping the man's efforts to escape the seatbelt by pushing down on his shoulders. Panic caused the driver to immediately breathe in water and within a few frantic moments, his life was ended. There was no-one else around, so he struggled back to the shore, up the incline and off along the path to his car and away from the scene. Half an hour later, he discarded every item he had worn into a roadside bin, donned his dry clothes and left, airport bound.

The next morning's newspapers carried a range of headlines, all of which made him feel most delighted that all had gone well, but still tinged with the disappointment of not having used his knife on the subject. It wasn't a success, not really, but at least the world had one less shite of a man in it. The police wrote off the death as an accident and the obituaries gave the impression of a better man than he had been, but that was just the way of the world. His killer was the only person who knew the truth, and he was already thinking of his next victim before this one was cold in the ground. Next time, it must be a more personal matter, with time for him to work on his subject properly, like in Edinburgh.

The Crags

I am wakened at 7.30 am by the sound of a badly-exhausted diesel vehicle reversing along my driveway and the loud voices of Highland louts. I shove on my jeans and go downstairs as Niall comes along the hall, dressed like a professional builder right down to the hard hat and ill-fitting trousers.

'Morning Adam, it's time to get this shit-hole out of the 19th century. I'm going to leave the guys here to clear space around the back to put the materials. Don't worry; we won't mess up all those lovely flowers and borders out there.' He looks into the living room and sees the beer bottles still sitting where Anna and I left them.

'Had a visitor last night then? I heard Liz on the phone to her, thought you were the topic of conversation. If she had a beer with you it's friendlier than I thought. Any time they spoke about you they both sounded a bit angry and stabby'.

I look at his grinning moron face. 'Thanks for warning me. I must remember to do you a favour like that one day.'

'Ach, I knew you'd be fine. Just show her that six-pack and she'll be putty in your hands. She's not still upstairs in her jammies is she?'

I don't deign to respond to him, just walk into the kitchen and put the ancient kettle on. 'Are you making the tea then?' Niall asks, hopefully.

I turn to him and gesture towards the others outside with my mug. 'Are you actually builders Niall? I wouldn't want to be in a position where you make an arse of this and start offering excuses.' I don't want to threaten him, I mean he's a pal but I've just left a business where you get killed for turning up two hours late with a payment so my tolerance levels are not quite calibrated to receive bullshit from dodgy builders, even one that I have known since school.

'No, we are fine. Well, to be honest, we are better at the rougher bits. We will get someone in for the finishing work if that's OK?' There it was. The lads are labourers and nothing more. Fuck me.

We spend ten minutes teasing out the limitations of the Mharisaig Building Crew, after which it is apparent that most actual qualified trades are not represented by my old friends. I remit Niall to hire the necessary skills and for his guys to do the fetching and carrying for them as required. They will still get paid, but I leave him with no doubt that they should stay away from anything structural, expensive, electrical or water-related. He agrees to refocus their activities, starting in the meantime by clearing the hideously overgrown garden, the garage and its contents, for the next few days or until craftsmen can be procured. I'm probably glad that Anna turned up now, albeit I could have done without the anger and negativity about my career and personality. Still, she did save me a lot of hassle with builders, so on balance, well done Anna.

I put on shorts and an old t-shirt and set out for a run, through the village and upwards to the roughly-cut tracks which criss-cross the oldest part of the forestry commission land, north and west of Mharisaig. It's a bit boggy in places as it's meant to be only occasionally used by the forestry vehicles which bump up and down between the plantings, but I always liked cross-country running although it's been a long time since I did it. Through the midge-clouded lower portions, up and out of the tree line and onto the mountain, keeping now to the sheep tracks which undulate along the side until eventually I get back down to the trees and reach a sheltered flat section beside the crags, looking back down to the village about two miles from where I started. The sweat builds on me as soon as I stop, the running breeze no longer cooling me and the midges start to swarm, making me wipe my face with the bottom of my t-shirt to clear them away. Looking down with teary bug-irritated eyes from my elevated position, I can see a pile of clothes lying on a ledge far below, strewn at an angle. I wipe myself again and take a look at what lies there. It certainly isn't just a pile of clothes and I curse my bad luck for seeing what I do, a body fallen from a high position.

This is something of a quandary for me. Do I keep running and deny seeing anything or do I report it and accept getting dragged into a police investigation. I don't have a criminal record but fuck knows what some other government organisations might have on me, or the Allantons or anyone who commits crimes which we hope are under the radar. That said, someone is bound to have noticed me out running towards here, you can't do a bloody thing in Mharisaig without someone seeing you. There are probably several old biddies in the tea room right now talking about Adam Darnow out running and him meant to be fixing up his parents' old house. Shame they left him all alone but he seems to have done well for himself blah blah blah.

After considering my options, I have no option but to report the bloody idiot who fell. I figure that the chances are it was a while ago, weeks even with luck and the police, even if they are thick as fuck, will quickly realise that I am not a suspect. Fingers crossed.

I run back the way I came to the village and into the pub to make the call from the payphone, borrowing the change from the barman, Scottie. I don't tell him what happened as he is the biggest gossip in Scotland and this would be all round Mharisaig before I finish my 999 call.

The Police take about thirty minutes to arrive and I get in the back of their car and take them to the nearest point we can drive to. Another twenty minutes walking and we are looking down from my earlier vantage point to what I see now is definitely a body. There is no easy way to get down to it, so the cops call in for a helicopter along with some climbing support staff and I give a statement, leave my details with them and thank fuck I've done my civic duty without further suspicion. I run back to the cottage and find just Niall and Euan there, finishing their lunch, and I tell them what happened.

'Bloody hell, who was it?' Said Euan, pointlessly.

'Euan, I told you it looked like a load of old clothes about a hundred metres away. Since I had left my running telescope in the car, I couldn't quite make out the identity of the poor fucker.' He nods wisely, which is quite the opposite of his actual understanding of most situations.

Niall closes his rucksack after disposing of several no doubt Liz-made sandwiches. 'It could be a suicide. It's some fall from up there, usually it's sheep that wander over in the dark. I can't imagine anyone local would go up there for a walk. We used to throw stones over and count how many seconds it was till it landed right at the bottom. Don't remember how long it was, but a few seconds.'

I'm looking at them and wondering if all the exposure to fresh air up here rots the mind.

'Yeah well, the cops will find out I guess. Once the Mharisaig rumour mill gets going, we'll have plenty of suspects, probably me amongst them. Anyway, you should get back to work chaps. Where are the other musketeers?'

Niall rises with some difficulty. 'They're away getting me a hot pie from the shop. Hold on, what's that with the musketeers? Does that make me the fat one?' I smile innocently at him and close the door, away upstairs for a shower, away from that shower.

About two hours later, the same cops pull up outside the cottage as I'm sitting with Niall and the guys having some tea. I walk round to meet them, asking them to follow me inside as I shoulder the front door open.

'You should get that fixed.' The first cop tells me and he's right, although the presence of a builder's van might have suggested to a sharper mind that I was already handling that situation. I nod and smile and put the kettle back on, make the two lads a cuppa and give them some biscuits. In general, I prefer to avoid the Police, however, in this unusual instance I find myself innocent of wrongdoing and have a fair degree of confidence that this is just a visit to finish my involvement.

'We confirmed that it was indeed a deceased person down at the crags. The body has been taken for further examination however the initial appearance suggests that it is a male and that he had been dead for some time, perhaps several days.' This is good news, obviously not for the deceased, but never mind, I'm not in any trouble, so happy days.

He goes on. 'You mentioned that you had been working away for the past while. Can you tell me when you got back?' I do and they write it down, I never knew that helping the Police could be such fun. If the poor dead bugger met his end a couple of days before I got into town, I'm off their radar and need never speak to them again.

'Where were you before that?'

'I was at a place called Inverannan Estate, one of the properties owned by my company. I was there for a few days. Before that, I was working in London for a while. I haven't been back to Mharisaig for a long time, until now.'

'What is your business Mister Darnow? You mentioned properties.'

'Exactly that, I am a partner in a global property investment business. That's why I'm rarely here. I live mainly in London now, unless I am abroad on business.' I smile beatifically at the cop, who looks slightly annoyed at me and I realise that my explanation may have sounded boastful about the whole partner / multi-national thing. Anyway, he asks for the name of the company and I tell him, he jots it down, asks my address in London, which I make an excuse that I have to check my phone to get the postcode, as I moved there recently and I'm shit at remembering details like that.

He closes his notebook and thanks me for the tea. 'Are you doing the place up?' He asks, confirming that he's a detective with a bright future.

'Yeah, just waiting on more tradesmen, they need to do everything from the damp course to the roof and all points in between. My parents are abroad enjoying their retirement so I get the job of making the old place habitable.'

'Good for you.' He tells me, somewhat needlessly as he heads out and off, leaving me and the Highlands worst builders to continue the redevelopment of the cottage.

Railway Terminus

His third foray into the world of disposal-by-murder was, by necessity, an act of opportunism with a sprinkling of luck required to make it happen, and especially to get away unchallenged. The target, this time, was a gentleman who had protection, was cautious and above all else, was guarded to the point of being untouchable. His tentacular business interests were promoted as separate entities, seldom if ever linked to a core individual, his face absent from a thousand heavily-marketed promotions. There weren't two in a thousand people in the country that could identify him from a photograph. Such was the breadth of his commitment to his own personal safety, and the wealth which was his lifeblood. His interests, funded firstly through paternal crime then design and luck, albeit with acumen, meant that his exponential growth spread in every direction, but rarely to the taxman and far more often to the predictable trappings of a multi-millionaire.

At the outset, this man had been discarded as an achievable target. There was little opportunity due to his security-aware lifestyle, and few occasions where he could be reached in an unguarded moment. Then, by fate or by whatever hand guided him, an opening appeared in front of him which allowed him to be close to his victim. It was the occasion of the opening of a railway station-based new outlet for his fast-food chain, named for the memory of a long-gone but apparently much-missed grandparent. Such was the strength of this personal connection that it mandated a rare public appearance from the man himself.

It had taken a significant degree of planning, but the advance notice he had was just enough to carry out his research. After taking a paid tour of the railway station to help visualise the layout, and obtaining detailed layout plans online, he knew about as much as the workers themselves about the building. The uniform and ID were fairly easy to purchase and replicate after the tour and after taking off his light waterproof, all he had to do was walk into the station with the hundreds of others, pouring in during the rush hour and readying for his work.

Surveilling his target from a distance, he stood along with the throng of onlookers as the normally reticent figure smiled, cut the blue and white ribbon and stood while flashing cameras deluged him with attention.

'It gives me" he announced with all the warmth of an automaton playing a recorded message, 'immense pleasure to announce the opening of this high-quality takeaway, using recipes passed down in my very own family. Let's hope that we see one of these guys on every main street, brightening up all our lives and giving us something to enjoy even on a rainy day like today! Thank you, Glasgow, for coming out to see me in this weather! I hope you will enjoy the wonderful, traditional food and don't forget to use the vouchers!'

Screeching cheers of the mainly adolescent crowd rebounded and echoed like high-pitched Gregorian chants back from the high glass roof of the station. He watched as the security men kept the press well away from their boss, making sure that distances were maintained and niceties observed.

The target gestured encouragingly towards his team of uniformed restaurant staff who instantly joined the throng, handing out tickets, scratched to reveal a free item or money-off amount. The entire concourse was flooded with hungry, keen customers, already fired up by a carefully constructed social media campaign and thus a new, vastly profitable arm of his burgeoning empire would be launched successfully. A cordon of security guards was left to facilitate the great man's exit from the launch however one motivated individual had already deduced the route and moved accordingly.

The insipid morning light of a wintry Glasgow shone brightly enough to make their departure towards the service ramp easy to negotiate. The two security men and the target then walked downhill, away from the concourse and hubbub towards a waiting limousine, and a journey to the airport, some eight miles almost directly west. The guards went before their boss, ensuring that no media chancers or the Great Unwashed Masses, as he sometimes called them, got within touching distance. As they went lower, towards the street level doorway, the light dimmed to a shadow, only broken by occasional dim strip lights, their glow reduced by years of dust and neglect. Their footsteps were audible in the silence of the lower service corridor and the stale scent of metallic railway dust hung heavy in the dank air. Reaching the end of the walkway, a Scotrail attendant who had waited patiently to aid their departure, nodded and unlocked the external door. As they had been trained, the two men, one after another, stepped outside to ensure that the chauffeur and their Range Rovers were in place. Once their feet hit the pavement, they heard the clank of the steel door clanging shut behind them, alongside the simultaneous, awful realisation that their boss had not joined them outside.

Inside, the tall, bespectacled figure of the target was looking in considerable uncertainty at the anonymous, uniformed attendant who faced him in the gloom of the corridor.

'Open the door son.' He instructed the attendant, with just a hint of fear cracking in his voice.

Instead of an apology and an open door, he watched in horror as the man drew a long, chef's style knife from behind him. Turning, he strove to get his lean frame as far away as he could, but only a few metres later, he felt a punch in his back, then stopped and turned, his attacker within arm's reach and still holding the knife, now dripping blood.

The target felt faint, tried to shout but nothing came out, his mouth dry, he was all but lost, yet found the energy driven by fear of his life to rise and stagger away before falling again to his knees, his back now aflame with pain. Two more excruciating blows fell onto him, thrusting him face-downwards with tremendous force and leaving him lying straight, arms to his side on the cold, grey concrete. The last thrust was so powerfully vicious that the blade was driven in to the hilt, there to remain until the autopsy.

He stood beside his victim, just for a moment's pleasure, and then walked along the corridor some ten paces until he reached an alcove on the left, which hid a slim, metal-panelled door. He'd broken the lock earlier when he'd arrived and made his preparations with his accustomed care to detail. If the situation hadn't gone to plan, he had intended to simply leave by that exit and make his way home without fuss, however not now, the plan was live. As he closed the door behind him and stood in the alcove, the shouts and the sounds of the security men inside were just audible, as they ran down the ramp towards their dead boss.

The route he had chosen was fundamentally challenging as it started in the city centre, with CCTV cameras at all points and no easy escape. Understanding the difficulty of the situation, he had planned three possible routes and started on his optimal choice. Removing his jacket and hi-viz vest, he stowed them in his rucksack, extracting a cap and black hoodie and donning them before leaving the privacy of the recess. Joining the crowd of shoppers, he walked unnoticed until the underground station, where he used the ticket he'd bought earlier and after a three-minute wait, took his seat and after a nervously endured journey, disembarked at Hillhead and walked towards the university buildings, where he found a bin for the hoodie and the cap, replacing them with his green waterproof jacket. He took a turn back north and after a fifteen-minute walk through tenements and leafy streets, was back at the car. He drove along a pre-planned circuitous route, the monitored main roads avoided until he was confident that he could not have been tracked or traced by CCTV.

It took a further half-hour to get onto to the main road north, home and safe, hopefully unseen and unsuspected.

The profile of the murder was far greater than he could have imagined, although he had known that a media circus was inevitable. As he hoped, much of the attention was directed to valid enemies, of whom the target had in untold numbers, considering his family background and often muscular business approach. The opinion was that a professional hit had been carried out, the investigation unable to identify the killer, but the authorities seemed to have no inkling that this had been the work of a skilled amateur.

Still, the feeling returned that the killing was not personal enough. It was lacking his preferred intimacy and could not form part of his body of work, perhaps his magnum opus, if that was the objective. On the plus side, he was again unconnected to the investigation and had left no evidence. On the minus side, it was no more than an assassin would have done. No artistry, and thus an absence of any message or personal touch. Most importantly, it had not assuaged his gnawing desire to spend time again with a victim, to write on their body with his blade and free their innards. His thoughts developed on how this would require a lower profile target, someone who had the same credentials as the others, but was little-known and perhaps unguarded. Then he decided that it was time to address a personal matter, one which had increasingly crept into his waking thoughts over the past months. This target would indeed be perfect for a more tactile murder, one which needed a great deal of planning to make sure that he had time, face to face, to satisfy the urges within.

Rab the Tab

Robert McBride had endured an unpleasant, stressful and generally shitty last few months, during which his previously settled and optimistic life had nosedived badly. It all started, as many disasters do, with a drunken night out in Aberdeen city centre. Robert had been in a pub for a quick pint and run into a group of former school pals that he hadn't seen for a while. They didn't recognise him with his beard and slagged him off, good-natured though, for being a fucking hipster. One drink turned into ten and he started smoking after five pints too, despite not having even had one in the last six months, so his self-control was dissolving as drink after drink went down his neck.

The group were a great laugh, always had been. Some of them were still into having fights at the football, Robert had been like that too when he was a kid but the lads had kept it going into proto-adulthood. He wasn't really the fighting type even then, too good-looking and didn't want his face getting the scars that some of the others collected. The boys had some great stories right enough and Robert hadn't laughed as much in a long time, the tears were running down his face when Gowrie told his story about being chased, drunk as a ferret, by Hearts fans outside Tynecastle all the way to Haymarket, where after a major scuffle, he got on a train and ended up falling asleep until Berwick-on-Tweed, where he found himself stranded on a Saturday night with two pounds fifty, no phone or wallet and nowhere to stay on the coldest night of last winter. He'd saved himself by breaking into a caravan in someone's driveway until the morning light, when an irate father of the house found him and a fight ensued in the confines of the small space. Taking the man's wallet and car which sparked a police pursuit, Gowrie eventually got back to Aberdeen via another stolen car, a bus to Fife, hiding in a train toilet until pursued by the authorities through Dundee and lastly, by hitching a ride from the outskirts of Dundee with an amorous truck driver.

Robert and the lads moved from the pub to someone's house, to let him swap a pair of shoes for his trainers, which were not permitted in their nightclub destination. When the lads got to the club, Robert was in his element, despite almost being refused entry for being somewhat incoherent. He accepted the offer of some coke to sharpen him up and that was him back on track, loving every minute of it. He'd phoned Anna to let her know he'd be late and she was cool as usual, told him to have fun, and he was definitely going to comply. There was a woman too, but he left her about 4 am and went home by taxi, still a decent time to get home from a club and Anna would be fine. He slept on the sofa, snoring and still with a barely noticeable trace of white powder just inside his right nostril.

Anna wakened him cheerily, but after she went out he was noisily sick in the toilet and spent the rest of the day shivering in bed, the noises of the passers-by from their flat intermittently bugging him. The apartment wasn't great, but it looked right onto the river, across a busy road but still a better view than where he had been brought up. Anna was a real catch for Robert, who had always been known as Rab until she insisted that it sounded coarse and that Robert was a name to be proud of, so he should bloody well tell people to call him by his proper name, so he did.

He'd joined a WhatsApp group with the lads last night and the patter on it was outstanding, non-stop pictures and videos giving him a right laugh every day until he left for the rigs and the phone lay unattended while the long shifts took over his time. When he got back, he caught up with the guys a couple of times, then on his next rotation Anna was back in Mharisaig helping her mum when her dad was right not well, Robert having missed the first news of his illness before, as he was on the rigs and when he got back, he was having too much fun to care about a sick old man. His pals loved their cocaine and Robert had plenty of money so he did too, and more. Soon after that, he was on the heavy stuff and Anna was losing her shit all the time about the state he came in like, wouldn't fucking stop nagging him. They had been saving up a bit, maybe for a better flat or maybe a wedding but Robert had skooshed most of it away without telling her. She didn't believe he would replace it but he promised, so she stayed. Then he had a big night before going back on the rigs and the bastards pulled him aside and done a drugs test and he was back home that day, suspended and embarrassed. The worst thing was that Anna didn't even shout at him. The cops came and interviewed him but just gave him a caution or something and he just wanted to press rewind and start the past few months all over again. He was skint but found some cash in Anna's top drawer so he headed out to meet his pals and get their patter, try to feel better for a wee while.

Rab got back the next morning, sheepishly opening the lock to find an empty flat with no television, no ornaments, no photographs except those of him and most importantly, no Anna. She hadn't left a note, but her clothes were all gone and only a couple of cardboard boxes still sat in the hallway. He was looking inside them when the door opened and it was Ruaridh, Anna's cousin who stayed in Stonehaven, letting himself in and standing looking pissed off at Rab.

Ruaridh told him that he was getting the last of Anna's stuff and took the boxes out to his car, parked around the back. Rab asked where she was but was told to fuck off, so he pulled Ruaridh by the shoulder to turn him around and make him tell, but Rab was punched a few times until he fell over on his back and couldn't focus properly. Ruaridh told Rab to stay away from Anna and, after making a very specific set of threats, left him there, the blood running from his nose and down his face to the grass beneath. Once he had composed himself, Rab went inside, had a shower and tried to see if there was any money lying about. He found a twenty in a jacket and almost another ten in change from drawers and jeans which were lying at the bottom of his wardrobe. Rab was good to go, so out he went with the last of his cash.

He was suspended on full pay for four weeks before his disciplinary meeting, which he went to with a union rep he knew well. The rep told him to ask for treatment and say that he was an addict, so he did that but still got a final warning, counselling and put on an abstinence monitoring programme, whatever the fuck that was. Rab was told this was a one-chance thing and he promised that he was clean, sorry for causing the hassle and all that. Inside, he was sad about losing Anna but he had his pals now and they were a great laugh, so he just had to keep his head and make sure he was testing clean before he went on shift - that was all.

He had his next shift on the rigs the following Monday, but there was a great Sunday of football on the telly and he went to the sports pub with his mates to watch it. Rab was drinking bottles of beer so that he wouldn't get drunk, but he had quite a few, then someone bought tequila slammers and Rab loved it. He wakened up with no memory of how he got back to the flat and a partially eaten lamb kebab on the coffee table beside him. He was sick, got himself cleaned up, got a taxi to the airport and then tried to keep his stomach clenched during the helicopter flight to the rig. They took him aside as soon as he had left his bag in the locker room and did the drugs test and, even though Rab didn't remember taking anything the night before, he well and truly failed the test. He left on the same helicopter he arrived on and was back in the flat just a few hours after that, spending the next few days in a depressed state until the food and milk needed replenishing. He went to the shops and got what he needed, missing having a car as it was Anna's and she had taken it when she left. When he got back into the flat, letters awaited him, and they told him that he was back in the disciplinary process, although Rab knew full well that he was fucked this time.

The date of his disciplinary meetings passed, he always ignored his phone when it rang and left any official company letters unopened, knowing that they were just invites to a hearing or something. After a couple of weeks, he finally opened a letter and it told him that his employment had been terminated, listing all the dates he hadn't attended and all the attempts they, as thoughtful and well-advised employers, had tried to make contact with the problematic Mr McBride. Rab went to the cash machine and found that his last salary had still been paid as usual, so he was fine for a bit. He needed cheering up, so he messaged the lads and took it from there.

It was nearly five days before Rab ran out of money. He'd been clubbing, met a woman he liked, took her out, did every drug he could get with her and forgot about his troubles until he got back to the flat and couldn't get in. Rab didn't realise that a lot of the letters he hadn't opened, the knocks at the door he ignored and the calls he didn't take were from his landlord. Anna had dealt with all that, before, so he didn't even know what account the rent was paid from and maybe hoped that Anna would have come back and they could sort it all out.

The landlord was well aware of his legal obligations, what communication he rightfully had to do and the challenges of handling errant tenants, however he did not really give a fuck about any of these. In the real world, he would briefly try and give the defaulter a chance to redeem themselves before either changing the locks or, if the tenant felt strongly about their case, sending his two sons down to intimidate and/or batter the problem person. Rab was out when the men arrived, so locks it was. They had emptied his clothes into two black plastic bags and left them at the door, so at least Rab had that. Hefting them onto his back, Rab made his way to the Council offices to tell them that he was homeless, skint and needed somewhere to stay.

Another week or so went past before Rab really fucked up. The woman that he had met had phoned his mobile. She thought that he was not only quite a handsome bloke but was under the misapprehension that he had plenty of disposable income to entertain her with. He arranged to meet her despite having something of a quandary on the cash front. Rab tried borrowing money from his pals, but unfortunately he had already told them his work story and they knew they'd never get the money back, so to a man, they told him to fuck off. He left the WhatsApp group in disgust and tried to think where else money could be found. A solution presented itself near the corner shop, which had a small Post Office inside. One brief tussle later with someone who emerged with their pension in hand, Rab was running like a deer, clutching the notes and happy that his finances for the evening were sorted. He cleaned himself up and went to meet the woman in town, bought her a few drinks and got some gear off of a guy he knew, then a taxi back to her house with just a tenner left from the robbery of the pensioner. She told him that her husband was on the rigs too, but Rab didn't know him and hadn't realised she was married, although that wouldn't have mattered anyway.

What did matter was that after he finished his two weeks offshore, someone told the husband that he'd seen the wife and Rab in the pub and that they had left together. Like many on the rigs, the husband was wary of such things happening and had a broad streak of jealousy, along with a known proclivity for violence. Four days later, Rab got a text from one of his pals, giving him some advice to keep his head down as a former scion of one of the biggest crime families in the city, one Ally Quinn, had found out that he'd been out with his wife and was actively seeking revenge.

Ally Quinn's brother, Simmy, was one of the main dealers and money-lenders in the Granite City and in addition to him, their entire social circle was packed with every nasty type and flavour of criminal that Robert was told would be highly likely to wreak harsh revenge on him. Thankfully the homeless flat was well away from where his pals or where the woman lived and he was keeping his head down and his hoodie up after the robbery anyway. This situation couldn't last though, as Rab could no longer walk about the area or the city centre in case he was recognised, so he decided to leave town before anything untoward happened. He was on benefits now, eventually after getting fucked about something rotten, so he had enough money, just, to get away if he could get work somewhere. After searching online on his phone, he applied for a couple of labouring jobs, got an interview in Inverness which would refund his travel expenses so that was sealed, Rab was on a bus and dressed in his best. The homeless flat was left empty and he chucked what clothes he didn't need into a bulk bin and left his home city for good.

He wasn't going back to Aberdeen, not worth the risk of getting a kicking or worse, so he declared himself homeless again as soon as he arrived in Inverness and was shown into a quite acceptable flat in a scheme in the north of the city. The next day, in an office in the centre of Inverness, he told the interview panel that the shifts on the rigs hadn't suited him. He told them he preferred dry land and so forth, a load of plausible drivel which set him up well for the labouring job. He'd worked in forestry before too, after school for almost a year, so the whole thing was easy for Rab and he was confident of getting the job, although they couldn't tell him straight away. Rab headed back to the homeless flat and, after getting the call to offer him the job, started with the forestry two days later. They had accommodation for him and didn't mind if he stayed there even when he wasn't working, weekends and public holidays, the lot. It was all very hassle-free and suited Rab to a tee. It was also working quite close geographically to where Anna lived, an unexpected but welcome coincidence that set Robert McBride to wondering whether this particular career change was part of his destiny to redeem himself and finally take a better path in life.

No Sense or Sensibility

It took another couple of days for the Mharisaig lads to clear debris from my garden, the garage and the decades-old accumulation of crap therein. They found some old garbage which Niall thought might be valuable, despite protestations that my family were always piss-poor and never in a position to buy anything remotely expensive. That Saturday, Euan and Tommy were tasked with driving to Inverness with these trinkets to have them valued at a shop there, although I had doubts over Niall's insistence that they were certain to be worth a right few quid. My suggestion that they wouldn't cover the petrol money was dismissed as negativity and I let them carry on, knowing that if my dad had been in possession of anything worth serious money, he'd have cashed it in long before and added it to his pot of money for retirement.

While they are away to Inverness and Niall is spending some quality time with Liz, the builder, Allan Douglas arrives to give some advice on the future of my crumbling property. He knew Niall from college and is round about same age as us, so I was initially sceptical about his ability, however he has the necessary qualifications and I am too lazy to go find anyone else.

Allan is a slim, serious lad who carries an accent as northern as they come. A Lewis man originally, he tells me that he is working on mainland projects to get some money before building his own place on family land back home. He'd had a project cancelled so had an unplanned gap in work which my cottage would fill. Pleasantly surprised at meeting someone competent, my mood is then dampened when he confirms that a significant proportion of the roof structure is, as Niall had predicted, "Totally Shagged", but this time couched in somewhat more professional terms. The only option is to remove the entire structure and rebuild, which could be done by Allan's firm at short notice due to a cancelled project up north, which is good news for me and probably them too. Less positive is the realisation that I can't stay here while the work is ongoing, so I have to decant, leaving Allan to organise his currently available team to plough straight in and take advantage of the fair weather.

My first and preferred option regarding my accommodation is to head north to Inverannan, however a call to the Estate reveals that Gillian is away with her mother to visit an aunt on Skye, who has just had an operation and required some assistance. There is nothing else for me there and I'd just be farting about up there waiting for her, so I decide to stay somewhere in Mharisaig as I still want to avoid London and aid my mental recovery from the past two years. I am still feeling more or less fine. I have almost no negative emotions or thoughts at the moment and haven't done anything illegal since Sir Mathieson Allanton pressured me into that one last favour before he hopped off to the sun. Better for me to keep away from all that, I know is the answer, however boring it is in Mharisaig.

Niall offers to put me up at Liz's place. However, a week there with him would be completely out of the question. Friend or not, I reckon that I would strangle the annoying bastard within three days. That leaves two options, staying at the rooms above the pub or trying to rent somewhere nearby, a holiday cottage perhaps. Since the pub rooms were largely used by drunken patrons after hours for sexual purposes, I'd rather sleep in a tent with a thousand midges than one night on those manky creaking bedsprings.

So, after some asking around, I am put in touch with a nice lady from St Andrews who agrees to rent her Mharisaig cottage to me for a week, at about the price of a transatlantic return flight. After being fleeced for a west Highland bolthole, I am starting to realise that property is indeed where the money is to be made. That said, when I first visit my rental, I am pleasantly surprised at the inside of the cottage, modern and light with far more amenities than I was expecting. There is a well-tended garden of about a quarter of an acre with a summerhouse and a view to a farmer's field on one side. I bar Niall and the others from visiting and settle in there while my poor cottage is being surgically dismantled and then rebuilt. My temporary home is on the northern edge of the village, the quietest area of an already soporific location. Unknown to me initially, the other side of the garden backs onto Anna's mum's house, which I only realise when I am sitting out in the sunshine of my first evening there, enjoying a beer and reading a book which I'd found in the sitting room shelf.

She looks at me, arms folded and with an expression like an irate mother about to scold an errant child.

'What the fuck are you doing here?' She welcomes me to the area with a traditional Highland greeting.

'I'm renting this place while my cottage roof is off. I didn't realise that you stayed across from me.' She snorts and mutters something derogatory under her breath.

I'm still patient but the constant abuse is wearing thin, even if she is entitled to be angry at me. Still, she sits uninvited in one of the summer chairs across from me.

I decide not to speak, declining to give Anna a catalyst to verbally reaffirm any angry thoughts about me.

A few moments pass until she speaks. 'Got any more beer? I'm bored shitless.' I walk inside and bring out a cooler with the rest of the four-pack of lager and sit it between us. She takes one out and cracks the ring pull, taking a draught of the beer that Niall would have been proud of.

'So, how are things?' I ask softly, hoping not to antagonise her as further abuse would predicate me telling her to fuck off and never come near me again. Thankfully, she seems to be able to temporarily overcome whatever underlying levels of distaste she has for me.

Her shoulders sag. 'Just Mharisaig stuff. I had forgotten what it was like to live here, without any culture, sports, interests, internet or anything resembling entertainment.'

'I agree, but if you are here to lick your wounds and hide from the world, is that not just exactly what you wanted?'

'Is that why you're here too?' She has a pointed tone and her question might have more than a grain of truth in it.

'Maybe. I could have arranged for someone to fix up the cottage without me here, but it seemed right that I did it. I emptied the house myself and that was kinda sad, putting out all the old clothes and garbage we accumulated over the years.'

'Yeah, I know what you mean. Part of the reason I'm fed up is that we cleared out dad's things this week for the charity shop. Mum was holding up OK but me, not so much. You know, it wasn't the clothes, it was the smell. His scent was still on the cardigans and the suits, stuff that weren't washed as often as the other things.'

She turns away, takes a drink and I hear the lager going over the lump in her throat.

There's a long pause and tell him that I'm sorry about her dad.

'Thanks. He only got a year of retirement, which is shit. Mum and dad had plans for holidays and stuff after we all left home and he came back from work, but that's all fucked now. She is OK right enough, maybe just putting on a brave face while I'm here though.' I remember that she has two older brothers and ask where they are.

'They both work abroad now, one in Australia with the firm that my uncle is in and the other in Qatar doing construction. They were back for the funeral but away not long after. It's always the daughter that has to stay behind isn't it, even now?'

I shrug as I've never been in a position to find out, being an only child whose parents sodded off to Spain and didn't really bother much with before that.

'Yeah, I suppose it is. Do you need a hand with anything while I'm here? The cottage is out of bounds for a week or so and I'm just here trying to avoid Niall's invitations to the pub.'

'Thanks but we're OK. You just keep enjoying your downtime from the dark side.' There it is. Yet another mention after all the crap she gave me the other day. I've had enough of her remarks and I have an impromptu outburst at her.

'For fuck's sake Anna, I'm out of it all. It was a fucking nightmare and I had to survive for two years, working with low-life scumbags and trying to get out before some lunatic killed me. I had to cut myself off from everyone I loved to preserve my sanity and I'm still not sure I succeeded. The whole thing was all my fault, but I can't go back and untangle myself what happened can I? Fuck.'

Anna looks like she's going to give me a mouthful back but stops herself and calmly opens another can of lager from the ice-filled tub. She seems to be wrestling with the right words but I don't know if there are any.

'Sorry.' I tell her. 'You didn't deserve that.'

'Yes I did. I'm angry at you because everything turned to shit after we broke up and you made a fool of me. I fell in love, went to you in London, and you just sent me away. We're both older now and that's what happens, people treat other people like shit, even when they love them. End of.'

She has a fair point, I'll give her that.

She breaks the silence. 'Can we change the subject? I'm bored talking about stuff that reminds me of what a dick you are.' This gets an instant snort of laughter, Anna joins in and with that, the matter is closed for now.

We are interrupted by the arrival of Liz, who looks over the gate from Anna's house at us with some puzzlement. Clearly, Anna has vented about me to her, and she cannot reconcile this with the sight of us drinking beer together in the garden and laughing like idiots, albeit about me being a dick.

Anna shouts for her to join us and I go inside and return with three more beers. Liz says hi, what's happening and Anna tells her that's she is trying to forgive me for being an arsehole and that I may have had extenuating circumstances at the time, which perhaps means that she is going to stop giving me pelters every time she speaks to me. Maybe she's just had two beers and is tired though, we shall see.

Liz looks like she has something on her mind and would prefer if she was alone with Anna, so I leave them to it and go to the toilet. I mess about in the house, watching occasionally from the kitchen window and then rejoining them only when the animated hand gestures of Liz seen to have calmed down. To think I rented this place for peace and quiet.

'How are things?' I ask with a smile as I join them and hand out the last of the lager that I brought from the fridge.

'Your old pal is a total arsehole.' Anna tells me.

'You need to be more specific, all my old pals are arseholes.' They both look at me askance when I ask what he's guilty of.

'He's bought a *motorbike* and we haven't got enough money for the rent.' Liz tells me with a strong and heartfelt emphasis on the word motorbike. I imagine that Niall's portion of the advance on the cottage renovations had been burning a hole in his pocket, or the crap from my garage was indeed worth more than I estimated. Either way, it sounds from their conversation that Niall might need to swap his new motorbike for something he can live inside shortly. I let them discuss his lack of sense while I restart reading my book and a while later a still-enraged Liz strides towards her car for a showdown with her disappointing other half.

I put down the book and see Anna watching me. 'What?'

'Want to show me around your holiday home?' Since our mutual antipathy has gone the way of past times, I do just that, until she leaves a few hours later, in case her mum is worried about her. As I watch her from the bedroom window, crossing the moonlit lawn and through the gate into her own house, I have a distinct feeling that I have just overcomplicated my life again.

Robert and the Forest

He found the forestry work quite invigorating, which was a surprise to him. He hadn't done planting before but it was idiot-proof and, as he enjoyed it, soon becoming an excellent worker. The foreman, Geoff, was a decent sort but for the most part lazy. Robert sussed him out quickly, as he routinely made excuses for driving places to fetch things that were patently already in the yard or they simply didn't need. He was just going home, Robert thought, or maybe even doing another job for the middle part of the day while they worked. The saplings were left by another lorry with the stakes and ties, so they just worked their way along the rows, one by one until they were finished each day and Geoff came back for them.

Robert had also successfully kicked his habits after leaving Aberdeen. He knew that the drugs were his main problem, the one that lost him his job, his future wife, his flat and left him dually hunted and therefore unlikely ever to return to the city of his birth. He'd thought a lot about his pals too, the bastards who wouldn't lend him money when he needed it, even after he'd bought round after round and bag after bag of coke for them, when he had the money. No, Robert knew exactly why he had fucked up his life and was taking steps to redemption.

Back in Inverness, he had taken the SIM card from his mobile and flicked it into the River Ness, symbolically and practically leaving the old Rab behind and remaking himself anew. He got a new card and deleted all the numbers stored in the phone, except his uncle Hector, Anna's and her mums and one more, one he might need someday. He put a tenner credit on the phone despite having very little of his benefit money left and made a vow to himself that he would only contact Anna when he had saved his first couple of months wages and could meet her, give her all that he had stolen and maybe then she would see that he was in some ways the victim, not the bad guy.

When he started with the forestry, his new boss had been kind enough to give him a lift to their compound on the west side of the Highlands, only five miles or so from Mharisaig, but with no direct road between the two, there being a range of hills in the way. The compound was about two hundred metres in perimeter, enclosed by high metal fencing and with most of it given over to storage. Their accommodation was rudimentary at best, a Portakabin with mattresses on pallets on the floor and an ancient TV and DVD player at one end, along with an electric stove, microwave and kettle. Robert was initially a bit disappointed at these conditions, but he came to accept them as atonement for his misdeeds, something which had to be penitentially endured before he was ready to see Anna once more.

The other men were a mixed bunch, to say the least. There were five others on his crew, not including Geoff the foreman. Their business contract was for two years and this was the eighth month in, the others have been there from the outset. Two of the group were perhaps what Robert would have called tree huggers, in that they were university-educated and primarily driven by the altruistic motivation of re-greening the environment. They never missed an opportunity to tell him the statistics of what needed to happen to save the planet from destruction, which brought Robert quite in line with their thinking. Another of the team was an older guy, who wasn't able to keep up with the rest of them and seemed to have little else in his life than just rolling along with whatever work he was given like a gnarled automaton.

Of the remaining two, one was a Mharisaig guy, Jimmy Broon as he introduced himself. He had a pock-marked face and a forehead with deeper lines than his young age deserved. Robert kept fairly friendly with Broony as he thought that he might glean some information about Anna once he had settled in. The last of the team and the worst, was Gregor. His personal odour appalling, thankfully he slept in another area of the compound in part of a metal shipping container. This had come about after complaints from the rest of the group, which also caused an altercation between Gregor and the worker whom Robert had replaced. This chap apparently could no longer work with Gregor, and Robert soon felt empathy on that front.

Gregor was a heinous individual on almost all fronts. Hailing from an even remoter part of the Highlands, his family had thrown him out when he was sixteen for reasons unknown, although it could have been one of many flaws. Paramount of these was his viciously misogynistic habits, boasting of aggressive sexual encounters to anyone unfortunate enough to listen. He also seemed to have no moral compass whatsoever, stealing anything he wanted and verbally abusing the others when the mood took him. This meant that he tended to work separately from the others and that they had to keep their Portakabin locked at all times. Since he was a bulky and muscular bloke, it was unlikely that any of the group would be able to physically put him in his place, nor did Geoff the Lazy Bastard seem willing to sack him for his various offences. So it was that Robert McBride just had to get his head down and earn some money, all the while recovering from his addictions and his downfall in Aberdeen.

His health took a dramatic turn for the better too, thanks to the manual work, fresh air and abstention from alcohol, drugs and cigarettes. His morning cough dispersed after a time and with it the worst of the cravings, although some residual urges remained. The food was adequate, no worse than the rigs anyway, so he lost the flab he'd put on after leaving work and was visibly leaner after just a few weeks. The others all went elsewhere at weekends, even Gregor seemed to have somewhere to go, although Robert never even looked his way, never mind asking about his time off. Geoff gave the rest of them a lift to Mharisaig every Friday at 3 pm, Broony lived there and the rest got the bus to wherever they stayed. The two environmentalists lived in Fort William and Robert never picked up on where the others were from. They were generally a functional unit, each aware that friendships with the others were unlikely to form further than they already had, limiting their interactions on that assumption.

It was in the third week before Robert first found himself paired with Broony for a day's work, the rain drizzling over them for the whole day and the lack of wind precipitating the bastard midges to attack them. Broony cursed like a trooper all morning, while Robert kept his own counsel and waited for him to burn his anger out until he had an opportunity to ask about Mharisaig and Anna. It was late into lunchtime before they realised that Geoff was not going to turn up, so they ate sandwiches and drank the water which they had been given that morning in case of that very eventuality. Robert opened the conversation, choosing his words carefully, for Broony was a sulky type with a distinct chip on his shoulder about something as yet unknown.

'So you're from Mharisaig Broony.' He asked as they sat under a tree for shelter. Broony smoked, which seemed to keep the midges at bay, so he sat beside him to share the benefits.

'Aye, worse fucking luck. Nowhere, Scotland, that's what Mharisaig is. Nothing to dae and full o' tubes.'

Robert would have to work harder to stimulate a conversation with this one, so he progressed as he had planned, appealing to his lower nature.

'What are the women like there – any lookers?'

Broony snorted. 'Aye, but no many. You'd have to get in your car and drive a good way before you'd get a room fu' of good looking women pal.'

Robert kept going. 'I met a lassie from around here a while back, over in Aberdeen if I remember right. Friend of a friend sort of thing. Anna something or other, she was really nice.'

'Anna Berkmann?' Robert told him he thought that was her name.

'Aye, I know Anna well. She was the cousin of a lassie I used to go out with.'

Robert doubted this, but it didn't matter if he could find out a little more about her.

'What is she like? I didn't speak to her for long, just remembered her name and where she was from.'

Broony shrugged. 'Nice lassie, bit stuck-up right enough. We all used to hang about together when we were at school, ken, but not anymore. She's too posh for the likes of us me now, that's for sure, although I've seen her in the pub once or twice. Her dad died a while back, I think she's back to help her mammy out for a while.'

He went on about Mharisaig, regaling Robert with highlights of his adolescent misadventures, which were probably real events he thought, but just not with Broony as the top guy he described. For one thing, he didn't have the wit to do the things he described, and for another, he did not have the appearance of the pugilistic lothario he would like Robert to believe he had been. For a good thirty minutes, his penance continued as Broony, for once animated, recounted fights won and women wooed until Robert wished he had a hot spoon and meth on him again.

At the end of that day, Broony offered to take Robert to the Mharisaig pub one weekend and he accepted, telling him that he had to save up and pay off some debts first. Then he would like nothing better. Robert wasn't sure that he preferred the sulky Broony to the new one who boasted of sexual conquests in a manner not too dissimilar to Gregor, albeit both of them clearly inhabiting their own little fantasy worlds.

Robert's weekends at that time were dull but necessarily so. He had the Portakabin mostly to himself, watched TV and Geoff even left him enough food so that he didn't need to spend any money. He had one bank account which he'd given them for his wages, a Post Office account he'd had since childhood and which had also been recently emptied of its paltry funds to fuel his drug habit. Still, it meant that he didn't have open a new account – a problem since he had no home address. It let him build up his wages and wasn't one which any organisation that he owed could get access to, as he'd never told Anna about it either. Two paydays in, after working forty-two hours per week, he calculated that he would have £2,688 in the account, so only one month more until he could go to Mharisaig, repay Anna and maybe take her for a drink, ditching Broony of course. Robert planned to stay on at this work for a while more, it suited him and he felt safe in the compound too, but

71

wished he had used a different name when he had taken the job, just in case. That screwball whose wife he had slept with wouldn't be the type to forgive and forget and there was always a chance he could trace him somehow, even off-grid here.

He looked forward to Monday mornings because of this rolling anxiety. He liked it when he was locked in the compound with the others for company, especially mental Gregor who slept in his shipping container at the gate like a foul guard dog. Nothing could get past him, or fail to wake the others before they could get to Robert and at night, he dreamed that if he got rich, somehow, he would have a nice house in his own compound for just him, and Anna, of course.

The Beat goes on

I am wakened just after 5 am to a chorus of lambs, sheep and cows from the neighbouring field to the side of the cottage. The farmer, whose own house is some distance east, seems to have wisely located his various menageries well away from his bedroom and within clear earshot of mine. I close the window, which helps enough to let me get another hour or two of sleep after pleasantly imagining myself blowing the little woolly creatures heads off with a shotgun.

My guilt at having started something with Anna is weighing on me, so I try to clear my thoughts with a run, which will also burn off yesterday's beer. I don't want to go near those damned crags again, so I take a single-track road which eventually ends up joining a proper road in the direction of the coast. I set my watch and just run, going past the distance I normally go and keeping on farther until I'm about six miles from Mharisaig and at the junction of the roads. I'm tempted to keep running but if I end up knackered, I won't be fit to do the return journey, so I turn and jog this time, planning to finish faster once I get close to home. The fields and hedgerows are getting fuller here, away from the forestry land which all but surrounds my village. It's more fertile land here, farmed by one of a cabal of wealthy owners who collectively constitute the landowning power-people around this part of the West Highlands. There are also a few visiting types who own mansions like Inverannan, dotted about and generally well-hidden from the proletariat, lest they try and burgle them or whatever poor people do. Some of the locals in Mharisaig traditionally worked in the big houses, not quite the old servant/master situation but not far off it. My grandmother was, as my mum called it, "in service" which meant being a virtually indentured slave to some rich twat or other, only ever ended when a marriage proposal was accepted. I muse that it's no different from most people's lives now. We are just better at pretending we're not indentured to our mortgages and loans which are owed to the banks, which are owned by the same fucking rich people. That gets me to thinking about Gillian and her colleagues and their intentions for Inverannan. I am wondering if they are planning a workers uprising to take community ownership of the estate, or perhaps leaving the Portfolio in charge but running the place better than me, either of which is fine.

I give this some consideration as I run, especially since Gillian, my – what would I call her – partner, is about to send me their plans for the development of Inverannan Estate, as part of the property portfolio I now manage. I am probably, definitely in love with her although not apparently enough for me to be faithful, which is a problem, like many, of my own creation. Perhaps I can discuss the situation with Anna and calm it all down, or perhaps I am indeed in deep shit. I get back to mindless running as this isn't exactly something I can resolve with a dose of positivity and a jog in the sun. Eventually, knackered and sweating from the humidity of the warm Highland morning, I get back and shower, then sit outside eating some fruit and drinking water to help rehydrate. Niall pokes his head around the corner of my cottage and asks if it's OK to join me. I wave him over and he seems a little sullen.

'What's up? I heard you got a new set of wheels.' I ask, while he wipes the chair of dewy moisture and sits.

'Aye, briefly. Liz went batshit at me last night and told me to grow up, sell the bike and start contributing to the flat, amongst other things.'

'Did she call you a fat bastard?'

He looked at me in amazement. 'How the fuck did you know that?'

'It was just a guess'.

'Fuck right off.'

'Banana?' I offer him my last piece of fruit, which he takes wearily without a word of thanks.

'So what are you up to today?

'Well, I had to get the bus and then walk here after taking my bike back to the garage, who took it back for five fucking hundred quid less than I paid yesterday.'

'Lesson learned mate?'

'Aye, right, I suppose so.'

'I've to lose weight too. Got any ideas?' He asks me without a hint of self-awareness.

I smile at him and tell him that it's a world of pain, fruit and veg with no booze or crisps. He looks fit to weep, so I stop tormenting him.

'Get some decent trainers, get out a run once a day and cut out the pies and the pub. Liz will have the old Niall back in no time. C'mon, let's see how the roofers are getting on.'

We close up the cottage and drive back down and through the village to my parent's house, which is now roofless and the upper bedrooms are open to the elements. There is a cluster of activity at the driveway where a trailer truck is reversing to allow the new timbers to be unloaded manually. The foreman tells me that the start of the frame will be on tomorrow and then the rest of it and the panels the following day, and then water-tight before any forecasted rain arrives, so he's a happy builder. I leave them to it and drop Niall at Liz's where he has been instructed to tidy up and hoover, both of which I suspect are new experiences for him.

I get some supplies from the shop from the same feckless youth who served me when I first arrived, but when I'm leaving I bump into Mrs Abernethy, who if I remember correctly was in some kind of local charity thing with my mother at one time. She has a tendency to dominate conversations and doesn't let me down on that front. She tells me amongst many, many other things, that I've grown (I have), that she hasn't heard from my mum in ages (that's a shame I'll tell her that you were asking for her), that she sees I'm fixing the cottage up which is good (it is) and several more quick-fire updates on her family and people she thinks I will know from the village.

The only interesting piece of information Mrs Abernethy tells me is that the man who got himself killed at the crags was not a local and by all accounts, it was a suicide. I make my excuses and after she tells me that my car is lovely (it is, thanks), I wave as I take her leave and drive back to the rental cottage to try and speak to Anna about last night.

After I stow the foodstuffs in the fridge, I walk down to the gate to see if Anna is there, which she is, with her mother and doing some gardening. She breaks off and joins me, up to the house for a coffee and a chat. Anna is, unfortunately for me, irresistibly beautiful and we don't make it to the coffee at all. This also makes it impossible for me to have the chat about last night and I'm fairly sure I'm now heading for relationship trouble at some point. Lying in bed with me, she tells me that she saw my house deconstructed when she was out earlier and that it will be lovely when it's finished.

Turning to me, I can sense that Anna wants to discuss something.

'So, why do you have such a guilty look on your face Adam?'

Oh shit.

'No, I don't, I was just thinking about something.'

'Bullshit. I know the face of a man who is cheating on someone, believe me it's not my first. Who is she, a Londoner?'

I decide that honesty is the best policy, especially when, like Anna, she is far more intuitive than me about, well, everything.

'No, she's from up here. Not been going out long but I didn't expect to fuck it up so soon, to be honest.'

'Is that what we're doing? Fucking up your relationship?'

I feel that I'd be better never speaking as it just makes everything worse, all the time.

'No, you know what I mean! Both of us never meant to do this, it just happened and here we are.'

She turns to face me. 'Don't get this wrong Adam, I'm still pissed off at you and right now I don't need a new relationship either, but you should try growing up and stop being dishonest about everything. You're just an overgrown schoolboy aren't you?'

I shrug, still lost for the right words as she dresses and gives me a kiss, which leaves me feeling inherently confused but somehow slightly relieved.

After a nap, I head downstairs and look over to see Anna and her mum back at the gardening and I wonder at it all, the insanity of my life. I am also bored so I drive down to see if Niall has finished his housework and see if I can have a laugh at his expense. Maybe Anna was right about the schoolboy thing, perhaps I'm just still immature at heart. Niall is there when I get to his flat and there is a considerable improvement in the domestic cleanliness of the property.

'Fuck me. You and your wee duster have been busy. It smells like fairies and angels in here now.' I tell him.

'You are literally the last person to slag anyone about having a tidy house mate. I remember that you lost your cat for a month and it was just in the front room.'

'Good try Niall, but still, I'm impressed, you're burning calories and doing exactly what Liz told you. I think you've turned an important corner.'

His glance, weary from housework, suggests that he'd prefer if I ceased my cheery banter. After telling him that he missed a bit on the carpet, he flings down his cloth and stomps off outside, me following, amused at his strop. After a short period of swearing, Niall calms down and we sit on the bench along from the shop, exactly where we used to sit after getting off the Inverloch school bus all those years ago. I tell him what Mrs Abernethy said about the body at the crags and he knows more.

'I know who it was, one of the forestry guys who worked in the season. He was apparently a pal of that arse Broonie. He's been telling people that the guy was coming here for a drink or something. Probably got pissed and fell after a walk, but if he threw himself over the edge it would be understandable. Two days up here would make anyone normal suicidal.'

We are coincidentally interrupted by the passing of a police car, my two pals from the other day, back no doubt to tie up loose ends. We watch them turn right and towards my cottage and I have a sinking feeling that they are here for me, so I leave Niall to finish his dusting and I follow to see if the police are indeed back looking for me at my dismantled cottage. When I get there, they are waiting for me and the builders have left, so we go into the vacant, dusty living room where we stand for want of chairs, and they interview me again.

'The deceased is now known to have passed away approximately around the day you returned to Mharisaig, Mr Darnow. Can you confirm where you were on that day?'

I now wish that I hadn't decided to stay incommunicado for the first part of my homecoming.

'Yes, I was here, clearing out the house before I got the building work done. I didn't want to see anyone yet, so brought food and stuff with me. In fact, I didn't even go into the village so that I could get stuck into the work here without anyone dropping in.'

'So you weren't up at the crags until two days ago when you found the body?'

'No, absolutely not. If I'd went running, someone would have seen me, it's a small place with plenty of twitching curtains. Why are you asking me this, is something wrong?'

He looked up from his notepad and the other cop spoke for the first time, the broad accent of an islander. 'Yes sir, the post mortem showed that he had been beaten badly before he fell over the crags. He had numerous bruises and fractures incompatible with a fall, as well as one knife wound.'

Fuck, I am a magnet for trouble.

'Well I've nothing to do with that, I can assure you.'

'That's fine Mr Darnow, but we have to make our enquiries and you appear to show up on our system in relation to a narcotics investigation.'

I almost have a heart attack and for a moment I think that they have had some kind of surveillance going on with the Allantons and, for the last two years, me. Then it springs into my mind, the overnight in cells, years back in Glasgow when I was innocently dragged into my flatmate Robbie's local drug-dealing activities. Thank fuck they never took my DNA back then and I was forensic about everything I did for the Allantons. If I'd not cleared up after myself every time, these clowns IT system would have blown up when it tried to match my DNA to unsolved crimes.

'I was released with no charge.' I tell them. 'My flatmate was dealing drugs, so my only involvement was that I was unlucky enough to rent a room from him.'

I let them note that down, as if they didn't already know. They are just trying to wind me up, see if I start sweating but I've been in much harder situations and know fine well how to respond to better challenges than these two present.

'Who was the guy anyway? Village gossip has it that he was a forestry worker.'

'We have just made a positive identification after making a wide range of enquiries. He worked for a contractor to Forestry and Land Scotland near here, doing the new planting.'

He seems reluctant to let anything else slip, so I don't press. I couldn't give a flying fuck who he was and my main purpose is to avoid further involvement with these gentlemen of the constabulary.

The younger cop asks me if I've ever spent any time in Aberdeen or Peterhead and I honestly answer that I have only ever passed through Aberdeen and never been to Peterhead. When I worked with the Allantons we did plenty of business there but it was all run between the locals and my guys in Edinburgh, so I never had any call to pay a visit there.

They drop a couple more questions to see if I trip up and then take their leave, no apology for taking up my valuable time. I drive back to my rented cottage and spend the rest of the day in splendid isolation, watching TV and wondering whether Anna will knock on my door.

Roberts Withdrawal

Robert McBride had been enjoying his new life more than he could have imagined. He was off-grid, free from pursuers and with a job he enjoyed and a group of workmates he gradually found less problematic than some he had worked with. He had done some overtime too, since he was there at weekends anyway. He was happy to help Geoff keep on track with his project plan, sorely hampered by the late snow that left them kicking their heels and hunkered down in the Portakabin, colder than Robert had ever felt, even on the rigs. They had to work in at least a pair, for health and safety reasons, so they rotated working with Robert except for the two lads from Fort William, who liked their weekends too much to give them up, even for time and a half or double time. So it was that Robert, with some trepidation, found himself working with Gregor for the first time.

Geoff dropped them on-site at 8.30 am and left to fetch something or other which they knew they didn't need. The weather that day was showery, so they sheltered on and off at the tree line under fir, dense and soon to be harvested. Gregor was slightly better company on his own than in a group and seemed less attention-seeking, perhaps calmer in just Robert's company. He tried to engage Gregor in conversation, telling how he planted in a way maybe different, a bit better than the others technique and Robert thought he cautiously liked the praise. By afternoon, they had spoken a few times and there was no real awkwardness between them, the larger man even initiating conversation once or twice. He had, so far, stayed away from any inappropriate musings which Robert was relieved of, as he had felt rather intimidated by the other man's aggressiveness when they first met. Robert wasn't a natural fighter and Gregor could effectively do whatever he wanted to him, which didn't even bear thinking about.

Finally, they completed their last row of plantings and set off downhill to wait for Geoff and a lift back to the compound, exhausted and damp after the rain had seeped through their ineffective waterproofs. Sitting at the roadside with the spades and leftover containers of rock phosphate, used to help the saplings take root, they waited and talked, Robert trying to fill his time with something.

'So are you working tomorrow?'

Gregor stabbed at the ground with his trowel. 'Nah, I've got some stuff to do. Yon eejit Broony is coming back up with you.' This was good news, Sunday was double pay and he wasn't surprised that Jim thought it worth an early rise for.

'What are you up to, heading to the pub?'

'Aye, mibbe. I'm staying at my wee place at the coast for the time being and there are mair holes in the roof than there should be. I need the money fae here, but after all that snow yon time, the weight of it broke mair of ma roof so I'm away to get started on that.'

Robert nodded his vague understanding and asked if the house was near the water.

Gregor's eyes sparkled. 'Aye, it's right on the front. Down a wee track from the road, away fae the noise. I've a caravan beside it right enough, the hoose is too cauld and damp with the weather for staying.' Robert smiles at him and the bulky man seemed almost human.

'What about ye? Going to stay in that midden down there till you're an auld man?'

Robert told him about his debt to Anna, how he needed to pay it back before he got on with his life. Maybe told him too much, but being alone with someone, even Gregor, seemed to make him talkative.

'You've not spent a penny of your pay and you're going to give it all tae some lassie that isnae even looking for it?' Robert nodded. Gregor looked at him with something approaching incredulity, albeit filtered through a manky beard and a few days of unwashed dirt.

They broke off the conversation, probably just in time thought Robert, as his colleague looked about to tell him what a tube he was. Geoff's van bumped towards them and they loaded up, ready to get back to the compound and let Gregor travel to his coastal retreat.

Soon afterwards, Robert was alone in the compound, Geoff having worked out his pay to date after being asked. He had enough to pay back Anna already, and a few more days would be all that he needed to arrange the money and get it to her. There was a post office in Mharisaig so he planned to phone there from his mobile on Monday, as soon as he could find somewhere with a signal. He spent the next overtime day working with Broony, who was badly hungover from a night at someone's house and if he were to be believed, a night of passion with a beautiful woman. Broony was sick a few times and told him, on more than one occasion, that he would never drink again but Robert knew full well that this is soon forgotten when you feel better, have money in your pocket and remember the crushing dullness of the Highlands.

Robert did most of the work that Sunday, telling Jim that it was OK, just go and rest till you feel better. He worked for the two of them, no stopping and absolutely focused on the rows of mouldings he planted, one at a time, time after time until there were no more to plant and his work clothes were drenched with sweat. That day, as he had on many before, Robert clearly understood what he had to do. He knew that this was his penitence, every bead of sweat cleaning his system of the shite he had swallowed, inhaled and injected. Every act he did was in repentance for all that happened in Aberdeen. He never spoke an unkind word to his colleagues, never missed a chance to help someone who needed it, never shirked and took more work on than anyone. He became the best version of Robert McBride he could be, the closest he could become to the man who Anna loved, way back then. She might never know, never want to see him again but that was OK too, he had fucked up royally and once his slate was clear and Anna was paid, the worst case was that he would just have to start again.

His name would be gone, regardless. He had a criminal past to leave behind and there was nothing to stop him being someone else, somewhere else. The experience of working on the land had made him want to do more, but not here and not called Robert McBride. The lads told him that there was work to be found in a few other places, seasonal but paying enough to see him through the winters. He was still a young man and with luck, he could shed his mistakes at the same time as his traceable name. One of Robert's best friends had died young, not long after they had left school and he had hardly made a mark on the world, had few relatives and no connections remaining up north, so Robert decided that he would adopt his name, become him in some way. Maybe Robert could combine the rest of his life with the days his pal should have had, maybe make the best of both.

The following Monday, he asked Geoff to take him to where he could make a phone call to the post office. Geoff would have preferred not to, as it reduced the amount of time he could spend with his friend who lived eleven miles away and who his wife was unaware of. Geoff had kids, but his heart wasn't in the whole thing, and he and his friend had been an item for almost as long as he and his wife had been married. Still, he helped Robert with this request as the lad was a great worker and didn't ask for much, worked any overtime he was asked and never caused a bit of bother, unlike the fellow he had replaced. So, Geoff waited in the van while the call was made and Robert came back in, smiling and thanking him for his help. He dropped Robert off back at that day's site and watched him jog uphill to meet the rest of the team and get to work. The next day, Robert asked Geoff if he could take him down to Mharisaig at the first opportunity and have a half-day off to catch the post office open. He had an errand to run and would find his own way back, even if he had to walk.

Robert wondered to himself, would that be his last act of contrition if Anna shunned him. He would, if that happened, leave the money with her and say his final goodbye and a last proper, heartfelt apology. He hoped that she would forgive him, maybe let him stay with her overnight, but Robert knew that this was unlikely, so planned his walk back to the compound anyway.

Geoff told him that they were behind schedule and he would see. He wondered what drove this unusual young man, what made him look so intense, so determined compared to all the others. That Thursday night, by which time he had unsuccessfully asked Geoff twice for a day off, Robert realised that he was unwilling to help and, in the spirit of self-reliance, woke early, dressed in silence and climbed onto some timber, over the fence, leaving the compound alone and unnoticed. He walked the unsealed roads for the first couple of miles until he reached a signpost for a path over the hills to Mharisaig, a hikers trail intermittently marked at intervals with emblems of acorns on wooden posts. Robert followed the trail without difficulty, making good time and soon reached a high ridge where he could see Mharisaig below him. In the farther distance, he could see the islands in the sea lochs, his heart leaping at the splendour laid out before him.

The downhill walk took another couple of hours and soon he was in sight of the village, the trail taking him downhill past well-separated cottages and some larger houses, down towards the shop and Post Office. It was quite a well-stocked General Store, with a well-hidden postal service in a slim glass-fronted cubicle at the back of the shop. It was unattended, so after a short wait, the young man he had spoken to on the phone went behind the glass counter, opened the safe and handed him his thick package of cash, counting it slowly and ineptly in front of him. Robert tucked the envelope of money away, bought a sandwich and some water and asked the boy if he knew where Anna Berkmann lived. He seemed not to know, or perhaps he didn't want to be involved in whatever Robert was doing, so he smiled and thanked him anyway. He left the shop and walked to a bench, where he sat and cooled down after the walk, feeling the heat of the day on his weather-browned, bearded face and hoping to god that Anna would love him again.

Anna, it ain't easy.

My morning chorus of farm animals reprise yesterday's performance, but after I surprise them by shouting 'Fuck Off!' from my window, the sheep retreat from close proximity and I manage another couple of hours of sleep. After visiting the cottage renovations to see how progress is going, I get some bread at the shop and drive back for a late breakfast. Passing Anna's house, I notice another car outside but think no more of it. Perhaps the more time I spend in Mharisaig, the more inquisitive I become until I ultimately progress to the village gossip First XI.

The sun is out and I eat my breakfast in the garden, wiping the dead midges from the tabletop first and enjoying the slight cooling breeze that is enough to keep their living relatives away. I hear a car driving off and see Anna sitting on the back steps of her mother's house, so I walk over, not wanting to appear that I'm ignoring her. As I get closer it's obvious that she's crying and for a moment I wonder if it's feasible for me to backtrack before she realises I'm here.

'Hi, are you OK?'

Anna looks up and her eyes are filled with tears, hopefully not because of anything I have done.

'Robert is dead. That was him at the crags, the one you bloody found.'

Oh fuck.

'The police told me that he was working at the forestry now. I didn't even know he had left Aberdeen, never mind over here.' She faces the ground and a teardrop splashes soundlessly to the ground.

'They asked if I knew you.'

Oh fuck.

'I told them that we used to go out and that we had started seeing each other again.'

Oh fuck.

'Did you have anything to do with this, with him?' She looks at me accusingly and rather unfairly.

'No, of course not. I've never met him, never heard of him till you told me. I'd nothing to do with this, for fuck's sake.' I tell her, perhaps too sharply and inconsiderately.

I'm much more used to actually committing serious crimes and getting away with them, and here I am getting hassle for a crime I had fuck all to do with. Maybe this is indeed karma, I think to myself.

Anna looks up at me, her face reddened and eyes puffy with free-flowing tears. 'I'm sorry. Although he was a shit to me, it didn't start like that, just the drugs really. He didn't deserve to die like that.'

'What happened to him? I thought it was the fall but the police interviewed me again yesterday and told me that he had other…injuries.'

Her mum passes the window inside and looks at me for a moment with a blank and quite unfriendly expression, which suggests that Anna may have mentioned me to her before.

'He had been battered and stabbed. They think he may have died from that even if someone hadn't finished it by chucking him off the cliff.' She sobs deeply and I probably should give her some space, so I ask if she wants me to leave her.

She stands up, reaches out and hugs me. I feel the tears seeping warmly through my t-shirt and I hold her for a while, her sobs making her head jerk every few moments until gradually they subside and I offer her my handkerchief when she steps back, not looking at me.

'I might come over later. Thanks, Adam.' She turns and goes inside, leaving me to my thoughts and wondering exactly how high up the list of Police suspects I now am. I walk back to my cottage and drive down to get Niall, see if he's heard anything else on the village grapevine.

He's in the tiny back garden alone, drinking tea and eating from a small plate of chocolate biscuits. He tells me that Liz will be back soon for what she called a serious talk and is still pissed off at him, so we take a walk to let her arrive home and perhaps calm down during Niall's absence. I tell him about the situation after making him promise not to tell anyone else and, waster though he is, Niall is one of the few people I would actually trust with my confidence.

He starts to process the information. 'Right, from what Anna says, this guy, Robert, probably got the sack from the rigs for failing a drugs test, yeah?'

I agree and let my personal Holmes carry on.

'He's made an arse of his relationship with Anna and wants to get away from his wee junkie pals in Aberdeen. He gets a job over here and stalks Anna, but she finds out, batters fuck out of him and throws him off the cliff. Mystery solved.'

'Fucking hell Niall, you're a genius. I don't know why we even bother having a police force when you can figure stuff like that out in two minutes.'

'I know. My talents are wasted here.'

We walk along the side of the burn that loops back to the main road and take a path back to the village centre.

He goes on. 'What was he doing here though? I mean, if he wanted to speak to Anna, she's not that hard to find. Just ask any roaming native and he'd have been at her door in ten minutes.'

Niall is spot on, plus Anna has umpteen relatives in the area too so her extended family probably takes up ten per cent of the local phone directory. Her late father wasn't a Mharisaig guy though, if I remember correctly she once told me that he was originally from the Dumfries area.

'Maybe this guy Robert was caught up in something.' Niall offers. 'If he hadn't paid his bills for gear, maybe that's how he ended up getting a doing.' I think carefully about this, as it's something of a specialist subject for me.

'It's possible but he'd need to have done something more than run up a bill with his dealer. These guys won't get their money back by offing every user who defaults. He would have got a kicking, definitely, but killed like that, no way.'

Niall looks at me with an unusually serious expression. 'You know an awful lot about the rules of the jungle mate.'

I laugh and tell him that I read a lot of books.

'Aye, fucking sure you do.' I wonder if Niall has his reservations about my situation and realise that my stratospheric rise from skint university student to wealthy property magnate may not be entirely above suspicion.

'Anyway, Anna was pretty upset about it.'

'Yeah, I bet she was. Something cheered her up the other night though, her and Liz were hee-hawing like loons on the phone, even told me to go to the pub, which means she didn't want me to hear something spicy.'

Oh great, Liz now knows about me and Anna, which probably means that everyone in the village will soon hear too. This makes it difficult for me to bring Gillian here. In fact, it makes the whole Mharisaig thing impossible if I want to keep seeing her, which right now I really do.

'So, do the cops think you had something to do with this guy?' He asks softly, glancing around.

'Not sure. I mean, who knows if they will cunningly piece together the clues of me coming back to town the day he died, then finding the body and that fact I'm sleeping with the deceased man's ex-girlfriend.'

He hoots. 'I fucking knew it, that's what they were being all secretive about! You are a shocker mate. I've got to hand it to you. Every time you come back it always makes the place more interesting.' Niall spends the next few minutes speculating on what the Police will make of me and what I should do, much of which is utter bollocks.

Eventually, I close him down. 'Niall, give it a break. I didn't touch him, so there's not going to be evidence for them to implicate me, they will look elsewhere and I'll drop off their radar, simple as that.'

'I get that, but the fact remains, someone did top him and it was only a couple of miles away. If it wasn't something obvious like getting in debt, what was he killed for?'

I sigh. 'God knows, but I wish I had been far away when he was. I came back here for a break but instead, I've ended up dismantling that shitty cottage and becoming a suspect in a drug-related murder investigation.' I pause for a moment and realise that I still have contacts in that particular industry but I certainly don't want to call them, not from any traceable line anyway. I'd closed down the whole narcotics operation for the Allantons before I came here, so maybe the Edinburgh guys would have left too, their pay-off enabling a life in the sun or whatever they decided.

'I'd better get back.' Niall broke my concentration. 'Liz will either have calmed down or I will be in for another hairdryer conversation. Alex Ferguson had nothing on this lassie.'

Poor bugger, I thought to myself. Although I have my troubles, I'm deeply glad I'm not Niall.

Robert the Adam

Robert McBride knew that had entered a phase in his young life which transcended all that had come before. He'd endured some turbulent phases, like the early death of his parents, being in care of his uncle and going off the rails, the drug thing, losing his job on the rigs and lastly, losing Anna. In her, he had lost the best person he'd ever known and now the toil of the last couple of months work had reached its culmination, the repayment of stolen money to Anna and a last chance to speak to her, persuade her that he had taken the hard road to get there.

He had the packet of cash hidden safely in his inside pocket now, unnoticed when he left the Post Office and with a mission to find where Anna lived. He hoped dearly that she was still in Mharisaig, that his journey had not been wasted and that she missed him, even just enough to speak with him and let him tell his story. Not the stuff where he robbed the pensioner and had to leave Aberdeen in case that mental bastard Quinn got to him for shagging his wife, but the bits after that. He'd tell of his remorse, his desire for a new life, his work on the forestry, his new-found passion for climate change action and environmentalism *per* his two colleagues from Fort William, but this would just be the preamble to telling Anna that he loved her, would never let her down again, would adore and worship her eternally if she let him, but said in a less needy way than he realised that might sound.

Robert wished that he had cleaned himself up a little. He felt that he may smell less than pleasant and be muddied from the trek to Mharisaig, but there was no possibility of that improving unless he could get a B&B

and clean up there. He wandered around the village and eventually got directions and a description of Anna's mum's house, on the upper outskirts of the village. After gauging the reaction of the lady who gave him these directions, Robert decided that a clean-up would definitely help to avoid further crinkled noses and disapproving gazes. He'd had the beard for a while and back then, Anna preferred it neatly trimmed, but he wanted a new start, a clean start, so that was the final factor in his actions. Robert returned to the shop to buy scissors, razors and deodorant, along with a toothbrush and toothpaste. He also bought some wine to take with him, just to have something to give her mum when he dropped in.

The moronic shop assistant was actually of some help in finding a B&B, apparently the pub nearby had rooms above which could be used for a reasonable rate. A short walk took him there, round the back to where a sign guided him to an upstairs office. There wasn't anyone at the small reception desk and he wondered if he'd be better checking down at the bar, but Robert McBride wasn't sure how these things worked, so just reached into the booth and took the keys to a room, assuming that he would check in or whatever before he went to find Anna's house. Opening Room 4, Robert left his stuff on the bed and showered, got rid of his beard and cleaned to a standard he hadn't achieved since well before Anna left him. He stretched out on the lumpy bed and unintentionally fell into a deep sleep until he wakened with the realisation that darkness was falling and that time was short to see Anna that day. He put on his cleanest jeans and black Levis hoodie, sprayed himself liberally with deodorant to help the overall effect before leaving and taking all his belongings with him. Maybe he'd actually check in later, he thought, but it was their fault for not having someone on the desk.

It took a couple of wrong turns but eventually, Robert reached the higher point of the village where the description from the directions matched his surroundings. A quaintly-ivied cottage stood to his right and if he was on the right road, Anna's should be farther around the corner and in the next gate. He rested for a moment at the gate of the cottage, turning to see a black-clad figure with a balaclava standing across the single track road from him, not looking friendly at all. He almost evacuated his bowels on the spot, but managed to find the nerve to shout 'what the fuck do you want?' at the figure, who took that as a signal to approach him, drawing what looked like a small switchblade from somewhere as he did. Robert dropped the wine and his bag on the grass and, since his assailant was positioned between him and the village, he ran for his life up the hill, taking a left instead of a right in his terror and on into the woods.

Robert McBride had been a decent, quick footballer when he was at school and not all of his natural fitness had yet left him. The noise of his heart and lungs exerting themselves soon deafened him, but he determined to run as fast and as far uphill as he could until he had no more energy in him. Then he would turn and if no-one followed, he'd hide in the dense forest until this bastard passed by and then wait until morning to wind his way downhill and back to safety. This was a superb plan right up until he sensed the ground dropping away, and stopped sharply at what would have been a potentially fatal drop into a gorge. This abrupt end to his escape forcing him to turn a lot earlier than he would have liked, and realise that his pursuer was not too far behind him. Moments later his pursuer stopped running and stood just a few metres away from him.

'Look, I've got some money here. Take it and let me go – tell whoever sent you that I'm sorry, please.' No reaction from the masked figure at first, almost like he was deciding what to do, then he walked towards Robert, who took a weak swing at him, before the air was knocked from him by a punch in the stomach. He tried to wrestle him, but all that did was set in motion a sequence of punches and kicks, expertly given and painfully received. Robert tried to keep telling him that he was sorry and offering him the package of money. He then tried his best to convince him that he'd got the wrong man, but this confused to-and-fro just enraged his attacker further. A last pleading ended in the knife penetrating Robert's stomach, the screaming pain almost making him faint as he tried to fend the attacker off with one hand while stemming the blood with his other. Despite the agony, he had enough left in him to totter back from his assailant, turn and run along the edge of the crags. He tried his injured best to get away, but the path was narrow and too slippery, and a few steps later as consciousness left him, Robert McBride fell head first, silently to his death.

His murderer watched the scene, looking down angry and frustrated at the sight of his victim, the last vestiges of life ended by the rocks on which he landed. Picking up the blood-stained envelope of money, he looked inside it and shoved it into his pocket. That done, he strode quickly back along the route where he had chased his quarry, picking up the discarded wine and bag at the cottage gate, and retracing his steps downhill, keeping to the shadows and onwards to his accommodation, away from prying eyes.

Whatever happened to Robert?

After we visit my parents' place for a look at the progress, I drop Niall off home, get back to the rental and make myself dinner. Given that I still can't cook properly, anything I make has to be both simple and low-risk so mainly microwaveable stuff or fruit are my mainstays when restaurants are not available. This evening I have the worst Bolognese I have ever tasted, most of which ends up in the bin despite my hunger. This thing with the dead guy is bugging the hell out of me, but when I see Anna approaching the house, I know that I must be an active listener this evening, maybe while helping her, find out something which would help me.

'Hi'

She glides into the kitchen and sits down, accepting a glass of wine which I bought earlier from the shop, so of poor quality. She makes a face but that doesn't stop her taking another glug.

'How are you doing?

'OK, I guess. I just got a shock really, still can't believe it was him.'

'What did they say he was doing up here?'

She rests her elbows on the table and shakes her head. 'Working for a contractor, they said. Maybe trying to meet me, I mean he could have gone anywhere, so there's no way it's a coincidence he was at Mharisaig. I'm driving myself crazy wondering why he never contacted me.'

'When was the last time you saw him?'

Anna gives a snort of derision. 'The last time I saw Robert, he was heading out for what I assume was an alcohol and drug bender with his wee scumbag mates, having stolen all our money from the account along with the cash my mum had given me for my birthday. I left before he came back and stayed with Ruaridh until I got a career break organised, a week or so after that. Robert didn't even try to contact me, although that might have been because Ruaridh thumped him and scared the crap out of him.' She drains the last of her worryingly yellow Chardonnay and holds the glass out for more, which I accommodate.

'So, was he always like that? I mean, what the fuck were you doing with a clown like that?'

She takes the full glass from me. 'I seem to have a difficulty finding decent boyfriends. The one before that was also into drugs, although not in that way.' I wish she wouldn't keep bringing this shit up, but I preserve my patience.

'Robert was fine when we met. I bumped into him when we were out in Aberdeen with my friends from Abertay. He worked on the rigs and was a genuinely nice guy. The problem started when he got in with that crowd of brain-deads and went into a sort of a spiral. We hardly spoke for the last few weeks. He just came back from work and went on bender after bender. His eyes were like piss holes in the snow back then, whatever he was taking. He got into trouble and was suspended so must have got the sack I guess, must have wanted to see me so took a job in the area and the next thing I know about him, is the police are at my door to interview me.'

'So, did he have relatives who identified the body?'

'Yeah, his uncle Hector lives in Aberdeen, the cops told me that they found out about me from him. Nice old guy, no family but he was always kind to Robert, took him in and did his best to bring him up. His mum and dad were useless alkies apparently, both died when he was at secondary school. No wonder he was fucked up.'

'Did the cops say if they had any idea who did it?'

'Other than you?' She says with a sniff. 'No, I was too taken aback to ask much. They just wanted to know if I'd seen him, knew he was in the area, where I was around the day he died, that kind of stuff. They did ask if I knew of anyone else who might have a grudge against him, but that would most likely be an Aberdeen thing and I didn't know those people.'

I watch her take sips of the wine and wonder to myself what would have merited a termination for Robert. If he'd owed money and done a runner, it's possible that they went to give him a beating and it went too far. God knows I've been there. It's also possible that he stole something from a dealer, in which case they would also be within their rights to kill him. If the cops dig about in Aberdeen, they might find someone to grass up the guilty party, but I'd doubt it, especially if it was a major player. Those guys aren't daft, that's for sure.

Anyway, Anna needs my sympathy and from what I can see, more wine.

'Did you see Niall today?' She enquires. I respond in the positive and it looks like she has something to tell me.

'Why, is he under suspicion too?'

'No, he is driving Liz mental though.'

From what I've seen of Liz, it's a short drive.

Just at that, the door opens and a loud hello comes from the hallway. Niall enters the room, carrying a huge ex-army green rucksack with a sleeping bag tied at the top.

'No.' I tell him. 'No fucking way.'

'Just till tomorrow Adam, promise. Liz went radge at me again, threw an ornament at me and everything. I'll sort something out but I need a bed for tonight and I'm skint.'

I smile at Niall and walk over to the cupboard, get the keys to the summerhouse and fetch a four-pack of lager from the fridge. Handing them both to Niall, I shepherd him out of the back door and direct him to his overnight residence, despite protestations and close the door by way of finalising the arrangement.

'Wasn't that a bit harsh? Poor Niall gets chucked out by Liz and you won't even let him use the spare room.'

'Yeah, that's one way of looking at it. Another way is that I was good enough to give him a bed for the night in a lovely summerhouse, albeit he will get wakened up by cows, sheep and various other noises right beside him at 5 am. I gave him four beers to help him sleep, so it all balances out, I think you will find.'

'I need to go soon. Mum doesn't seem to have taken to you and gave me a bit of a warning before I came over.'

'Did you tell her that you are attracted to bad men?'

She thought for a moment. 'I think she has probably arrived at her own conclusions on that front. My track record speaks for itself.' She downs the wine and walks into the hallway, stopping at the bottom step of the stairs, looking back at me as I wonder where she is going.

'Well, come on, or are you turning me down?'

For all my many faults, especially now that I am a better person, I never want to be accused of turning Anna down.

Niall flies the Nest

I awake to the sun beaming through open curtains, sheep baa-ing and no sign of Anna, who must have left me sleeping, as often happens. A check on my watch shows that the livestock, despite their best efforts, have failed to deprive me of a long-lie and it is just after eight am, although I am not sure what time I got to sleep. Remembering Niall is in the summerhouse, I smile to myself at the thought of him being even closer to the sheep noise and hope that he's cursing me. Going downstairs, I put the kettle on and shove bread in the toaster when I see him emerging from the wooden house like an unfolding blossom of Highland male splendour. My imagery is wasted as he starts to take a piss at the side of the summerhouse and I now regret giving him four beers just before bedtime.

Opening the door, I shout a loud 'Oy!' at him, which makes him panic and try to get his still-spraying knob back in his trousers. I'm metaphorically pissing myself while he, well, is.

'You bastard, I thought that was the Police!' He yells at me as I walk over, he's raging and with a very wet look to his light grey tracksuit bottoms.

'Well, you shouldn't go around pissing on people's summer houses. There is a perfectly good toilet inside the cottage.'

'Aye, which you wouldn't let me stay in, so that you had a place to yourself to get your evil way with poor Anna, you rotten big bastard.'

He lurches back into the summerhouse and then emerges wearing a pair of non-pissy trousers, brushes past me and into the cottage, presumably to the indoor toilet. This is a better start to a day than I've had in a while, I think to myself.

I make two coffees and wait for him to emerge a better and cleaner man. When he does, he sits where Anna was last night and says thanks for the coffee, before spooning three heaped sugars into it. No wonder he's three stone heavier than his school weight.

'Sleep OK though?' I ask, as genuinely as I can.

'Aye, it was fine, the wee sofa wasn't long enough but I got to sleep after the beer, no problem.'

'What are you going to do? Back to Liz or ask your mum and dad to take you back?'

He scratched his head ferociously. 'Nah, my dad made it abundantly clear that once I'd moved out I wasn't getting back in. I think they like the peace and quiet to be honest, although I'm sure if I was really stuck they'd let me. It's me that doesn't want to go back. It would make me feel a right failure.'

I smile at him. 'As opposed to the success I see before me?'

He laughs, a good one and he knows it. 'Aye, a right mess mate. Might be better in the long run, Liz is just pissed off at me, no matter what I do, so we're better apart anyway. I'll sort something out - just need a few quid to start me off. Once the roofers are away, me and the lads will get back to helping with your place, I'll be happier to have something to do as well.'

This reminds me that I haven't spoken to Allan Douglas for a while, so we get ourselves sorted and drive down to see how his builders are getting on and find out when he'll be back. They are just arriving and there's a scaffold up to let them access the new roof, which I'm fairly sure that Allan didn't mention to me as a cost. We walk inside and see the structure frame, really well-built and about a foot higher than what was there before, to let us have more ceiling space upstairs. One of the disadvantages of being tall is that homely cottages take their toll on one's napper and our place was absolutely in that category, so we decided to make some discreet alterations without troubling the Council for their approval.

One of the builders comes in and tells me that Allan is expected back down the next day, so he shows me what has been done and what the next phase of work will be. Niall takes a back seat as he probably feels like a bit of an amateur compared to these actually qualified and time-served blokes. My interest in the minutiae of building works is minimal however, so ten minutes is enough for me, and then I thank the fellow and leave him to it. As my cottage was in pretty awful condition beforehand, there's no actual worrying about damage being caused, so the only way is up. We stand in the garden and look around. The garage is gone and the now vacant space is covered with roofing tiles and bits of scaffold.

'Are you getting a new garage?' Niall asks.

'No, I thought I'd get a summerhouse built for homeless pals and other unwanted lodgers.'

'Fuck off.'

We wander back to the car and drive to Liz's house. Niall cautiously unlocks the door and peeks inside. Her car isn't outside and he thinks she has a shift at the hotel, so wants to pick up the rest of his stuff before she gets back. I sit in the living room and watch TV while he fills black plastic bags with clothes, shoes and a few bits from various rooms. Not a great haul, I observe and tell him.

'Aye well, we're not all loaded pal, no millionaire jobs ready to walk into up here.'

'Well, you've got the building thing going, haven't you. A bit more experience and that could work out all right.'

He stopped for a moment. 'Aye, it could. The truck isn't ours, it's Euan's dads, as is the tools we had on it. We thought it would give the impression that we were, you know, capable.'

I smile. 'It did, right up till the four of you got out and looked fucking clueless.' He laughs at this, but is more ironic than heart-felt.

'Aye, we need a bit more skills before that one takes off. There's not much money up here, that's the reality, probably less than there was when we were at school. Have you noticed that almost everyone who went to university has stayed away? All the clever ones, basically; Tess, Derek, Michelle, Stewart, Ruaridh, Tommy, Alex, wee Ronny and even my arsehole brother is away in England making plenty dough. I'm left here with the fucking simpletons. Even Jim Broon has a decent job in the forestry and he's as thick as pig shit.'

I nod. The last time I saw Jim, I had broken his nose and he was apologising for calling me a cunt, which caused the fracas leading to the fracture. Niall has indeed found himself in something of a rut. I hope he isn't suggesting that I help him get out of it, as my life is still at something of a crossroads and the nature of my previous employment means that I still want to be a loner in some respects. Still, he looks like he needs cheering up.

'OK, get finished here and crash out in the summerhouse for another couple of nights. When the roof is finished down at the cottage, you can stay there and get on with things. I'm going to take up the option of renting this place for another fortnight to let you get the garden cleared and the inside painted or whatever.' Almost as I finish speaking, I have a feeling of regret for mistakes I'm yet to make.

'Thanks Adam, that's brilliant. We'll get the plastering and painting done, no problem.'

'Em...let's keep it to just the painting mate, Allan has already arranged the plasterer, you know, the new ceilings and all that are tricky.' He agrees and I can only imagine what kind of total arse of the plastering him and the rest of the Mharisaig cowboys would have made.

We get him and his bags of detritus up to the cottage and installed into the summerhouse, which I make him promise to tidy up before he leaves and on no account to piss anywhere near. He accepts my rules graciously however I have the lingering impression that he would much prefer to have a room inside the cottage, which is not going to happen. I have become accustomed to privacy, first as a largely neglected only child, then as an introverted student in Glasgow, and more recently in Knightsbridge and travelling alone to the cities, going about my former business. That's not to say I don't enjoy company, I do, but I much prefer it on my own terms and certainly not in this cottage, unless of course, it's Anna.

I leave Niall to his nesting in the summerhouse and drive down to the other side of the village to get a phone signal and do some catching up. Firstly, I call the Portfolio office and talk to my guys there for the best part of an hour, arranging for information on the latest property deal to be accessed online to let me read the conditions and sign electronically, then pass to John for his presumably equally disinterested signature of final

107

approval. We've just finished with a really major project in Singapore and are starting another, larger venture in London, so this is the next in line to receive our investment and keep the profits thundering into our accounts. I call John, but there's no answer so I leave a message and tell him I'll email him.

Fetching my laptop from the boot, I click on the link my wee team of efficient chaps have already sent me. I check through them cursively, electronically sign and send the documents onwards to John Allanton. I wonder how he is faring. I hope his early retirement from the narcotics trade is suiting John better than it is me.

I take a moment and call the office at Inverannan and Niamh answers, passing me to Gillian who transfers the call to another office for some privacy. A couple of clicks later, she is alone and we can talk.

'Hey, how are you?' I ask.

'Oh, Ok I suppose. My aunt Mairead in Portree had a big operation and they let her out too early, she couldn't really look after herself so me and mum went there for a fortnight. My uncle is a waste of space. He wouldn't make a cup of tea if his life depended on it, so, we went over and did all that while she got some peace to recover. She's much better now and mum gave my uncle a right talking to, showed him how to cook a bit and generally scared him into helping Mairead. We'll see though, he's the old school tin-god type.'

I smile at the thought and ask Gillian to tell her mum that was brilliant and well done.

'Yes, I thought you'd appreciate mum being good at turning up and frightening people into doing what she wanted.'

'Oh haha, very funny.' I can hear her sniggering at me and it gets me going too.

'All behind me, you know that.'

'Better be. When are you coming back?'

'I'll be another two or three weeks. The cottage was worse than I thought and it needed a new roof. The guys are working on it just now but I need to stay till they finish, keep an eye on the progress and do my bit.'

'Is it your mates doing the work?'

'It turned out they weren't as qualified as I was lead to believe so no, it's a proper company doing the work. Got them at short notice too which was ideal, but there's a ton of work still to do.'

'Are you still staying there while it's all going on?

I pause momentarily for my prepared line. 'No, I'm staying with Niall and his girlfriend, not ideal but it will do until the cottage is ready.'

Fuck me, a white lie I didn't want to tell, but neither do I want Gillian to come down here for a visit and find out about my rented cottage with direct access to my ex-partner Anna. This is a problem of my own making and I need more time to navigate my way through it. We chat for a few minutes more, agreeing that I'll come back up as soon as I can, then close the call. Right now, a big part of me just wants to leave Mharisaig and go to her. Although I could leave the cottage to someone, even Niall to keep an eye on, I feel that I should really spend more time here. Am I still here because of the cottage, or Anna Berkmann, I ask myself, and I don't have the answer. I seem to have fallen for Gillian and then for Anna, again and at the same time. What a mess I make.

Gunning the car in annoyance at myself and my never-ending catalogue of interpersonal fuck-ups, I drive out of the village and south for a while, the open roads giving me the chance to drive like a maniac. Eventually, I calm down, turn round and drive back, more steadily this time and finally up to the rental cottage via the shop. I look for Niall when I get in. Perhaps he is sleeping in the summerhouse. Sure enough, he emerges bleary and wearing only a worn-looking pair of shorts, comes over and sits in the kitchen, yawning and scratching himself. Mharisaig's Odd Couple are soon joined by Anna, who knows that Liz has chucked Niall out and spends the next hour doing a counselling session which I avoid by sitting in the garden with a coffee and revelling in the thought that at least his life is still much shittier than mine.

Anna eventually leaves, telling me that we are all going down to the pub later since it is Friday and Niall needs cheering up, which although true, I'd much prefer if someone other than me had the job.

Life in a Northern Pub

We walk down to the bar just after seven, the evening warm but clouds covering the sky and the humidity bringing swarms of midges at intervals as we head downhill to the village centre. It takes longer than it should to get there as we meet a couple of Mharisaig dog walkers on the way and have to give those repetitive but brief updates on our developing lives. Anna omits her disastrous relationships, Niall his too, and I don't mention that I'm rich as fuck after working in illegal narcotics for a couple of years. It would be funny to reply honestly to their questions but perhaps unwise and certainly less pleasant conversation for the old biddies. While Anna is doing the talking I imagine the conversations. 'Oh Adam, I hear you've finished up with those drugs fellas. That's nice! You've not even murdered anyone for a wee while either, oh that is just lovely, well done you!'

As it is, we eventually get into the half-filled bar and take the last available table before the evening rush gets going full flow. I surreptitiously leave a hundred quid with Scottie behind the bar and tell him our order, to keep our glasses filled and give him a tenner for the trouble. Being wealthy and lazy must have some advantages after all. I take the first round over and we toast absent friends, Anna's words and neither Niall nor I say anything for a moment until she composes herself.

We're a couple of rounds in when more fellow Mharisaig youngsters come in, looking well gone and no doubt having indulged somewhere else before heading here. It's all good-natured and how-are-you-getting-on, so not bad and they stand not far away but we can still talk between us. Anna is still troubled, and rightly so about her ex-boyfriend. The cops have called on her twice with questions and although she couldn't offer much help, she tells us that their working theory is that Robert may have been in the crosshairs of a minor Aberdeen gangster who may have connections to serious criminal activities. The police had asked her if she knew this gangsters name and Anna pressed them to explain who he was, which they then revealed, inappropriately, perhaps.

We're on this subject when Jim Brown turns from his position near us. I hadn't noticed him as he stood with a cluster of lads who I think are a couple of years younger than us.

'Are you talking about Robert McBride? I worked wi' him up at the planting so I did. We thought he'd done a runner but there it was, few days later the Polis turn up and tell us he's deid. Bloody shame, he was a right nice laddie.'

Anna and I exchange glances and she gestures for Jim to sit beside her, which I am unsure is wise but would also like to hear what he has to say.

She asks him about when Robert, when he started with them at the forestry.

'Aye, it was maybe two or three months ago. The other guy who worked with us got in a fight with big Gregor. We all had to jump in because he was getting a bit of a doing. Gregor is a big mental bastard and he shouldn't have started anything with him. Anyway, a while after he left, Robert started with us and that was fine. The other guy was a prick anyway and Robert was all right, he was.' Jim is well pished and letting information flow freely, Anna picks up on this and keeps going. He's enjoying the limelight and her attention I think, so I and Niall just listen ardently through the hubbub of the bar.

'So, did he say anything about why here was here, in Mharisaig?'

Jim gives her a leery grin. 'He did that hen, and your name was mentioned. He thought I wouldnae know what he was doing, but I'm not daft. Said he knew an Anna from a wee chance meeting in Aberdeen and that he might come down and look you up one day. He couldnae do that till he had saved up and paid some debt, so he never spent a damn penny the whole time he was up there.'

Anna looks like she's going to well up with tears, so I take over and ask. 'Jim, what was he doing up at the crags? Did he say anything before he left?'

He shrugs and says 'I don't think he did Adam. To be honest I didn't even see him leave, we just got up in the morning and he was away, which was queer.'

'What do you mean?'

'Well, Robert liked the compound. It's where we keep the equipment, all the stuff and where we sleep up there, in a Portakabin. He stayed all the time, weekends on his own. He locked himself in and all that. Robert even liked mental Gregor being there, that one sleeps in a container on his own at the front gate like a big manky watchdog.' Jim sank about a quarter of his pint, thirsty from all the talking, but not finished yet.

'So, he told me that he felt secure in there, didn't want to come down here for a drink, even though I told him he could bide with me for the night.' I don't blame Robert for turning that invitation down, the Brown family were not known for clean habits and their house would be a midden, not that I could talk.

Anna has composed herself enough to join back in, after dabbing her eyes with a hankie.

'So he never said anything about where he was going?'

'Nope, not a thing did he say to me. The polis asked me all this, asked all of us. We got interviewed one after another in the boss's office but I dinnae think we helped them much. Gregor is half-daft, so even if he seen the laddie leave he might not remember. Lives in his own wee world does that one.' One of his groups shouts to Jim that it's his round and he tells us that he has to go.

He stands and walks away, then turns and comes back, leaning on the table and moving his face down so that he can talk softly.

'I did hear one thing though, big Geoff the boss, he told the cops that Robert had asked if his month's pay was in. Maybe he had enough to pay his debts and was going to get his money out the bank. Anyway, I hope they catch the bastard that did it.' With that and another glance at Anna, Jim was off to join his increasingly loud and inebriated chums.

We sit in silence, interrupted by the gracious barman bringing yet another round. I hand him two twenties and tell him to sort Jim and his group out with a drink.

Niall is first to speak. 'So, he was probably robbed then. You'd better stop flashing the cash big man. You'll be back up the suspect list again.' I give him a look intended to suppress further comments of that nature.

Anna leans in towards us. 'He would have been coming down to Mharisaig for money, that's for sure. Robert had one account that he thought I didn't know about, an old Post Office savings book. If he had enough to pay me what he had taken from our building society, he could have been coming down to arrange to get it, maybe already had done.'

Niall might have missed some of the build-up to this and the details of their break-up, so Anna fills him in while I think through this.

'That's why the cops were going into the shop then. Wonder if the wee guy that works there would help us out.' Niall ponders.

'Why don't I ask him?' replies Anna, nodding towards a table diagonally across from us where the lad himself sits, at a small beer-laden table, with a cluster of pimpled under-age drinkers, tolerated by Scottie the barman as they are almost eighteen and accompanied by his own son. She walks over and, ignoring the goggle-eyed admiration of the adolescent group, has a kneeling whispered conversation with the boy while we sit and wait. A few minutes later she is back with us and confirms that Robert McBride had phoned in a request for a cash withdrawal and picked it up the day he died. The police had been in to talk to him and he was just pleased that he'd done nothing wrong, which his boss had assured him of later. Another round of drinks arrives and Jim Brown's small group shout over thanks for the free drinks, which I acknowledge with a raised glass.

'So, Robert gets the money from the post office and what? He heads away from the village up to somewhere he doesn't know, maybe looking for Anna? He gets a kicking and is robbed, thrown off the crags? This doesn't sound likely at all, not here in Mharisaig.' Niall is befuddled, possibly more by the booze than the complexities of the end of Robert McBride.

Other than offering theories to Anna, I can't help much and the drink is starting to go to my head too. I glance at Niall and his eyelids are drooping slightly, so I suggest we call an end to the evening. We walk back up the hill, meeting no-one this time and Niall lurches off to his summerhouse, leaving Anna and I alone again.

Broony the Hero

Broony had left the pub with his mates after a great night. The bar was jumping and everyone was there, first time in a while and what a laugh they had. A few cans at Callum's place first, then in for some real pints and plenty shooters, ideal. It was a funny start to the pub though, sitting with Anna Berkmann, fat Niall and that big bastard Darnow, but they were bang on, just curious about poor Robert McBride and Broony helped them, because Robert had been his mate and these people knew him, well Anna did and she was a lovely lassie.

They had even bought him and mates a round, not for anything but just to be nice. When they three left the pub, one of his pals said something crude about Anna but Broony told him to shut the fuck up, she's a lady. This didn't spoil the vibe though and the drink was flowing, the shooters were getting fired down their necks and then they got chucked out, despite asking for a lock-in, just because they were all pished.

Jim Brown still lived with his parents in a row of estate workers houses on the north-west edge of the village. All the others lived on the other side of the village, so he staggered one way while they whooped and lurched away the other. He had forgotten to take a piss before leaving the pub and although it was hardly five minutes to his house, he needed one very badly indeed. There was no-one about, so he went behind a broad tree and let it go. He'd just finished this impressively long beer evacuation when he sensed someone walking, nearby but on the other side of the road. Jim was well drunk, but he could see a shadowy figure, dark-clad with a hoodie up and heading uphill towards the north end of the village. He looked like a burglar, so Jim was having fuck all of that, not in Mharisaig. Not in his wee village.

He followed at a distance, knowing every bend in the road and tree which helped him stay out of sight. Sobering up slightly, he became a little nervous, but he'd always told people that he was a battler, a wee tough guy and here was a chance to do something for real instead of just made-up stuff. He'd chase the guy away before he could break in or whatever he was up to. They passed his parent's house, kept going to where the properties were well apart and nothing but darkness between them.

A few minutes later, at the bend in the road, Jim watched the guy as he entered the gate of that house that was rented out, a cracking wee place that he had always liked. The garden was always smashing with flowers and stuff and Jim watched as the guy sneaked about, ready to break in, the bastard. Jim picked up a half-brick from beside the gate and wondered if he should chuck it at the burglar and then start shouting, see if someone would come and help. This approach, he thought, wasn't brave. He needed to confront the guy, face to face like a hard man would. Watch him run away and then hurl the brick, knock him out with it and raise the alarm, keep him there till the police came for him. Get in the local paper, maybe even.

He crept through the gate, his heart thumping for all it was worth. He found himself looking at the burglar's back as he tried the front door handle. Then the bastard heard him and turned around and Jim raised the brick, waiting for him to run, but he didn't. He came towards him and Jim threw the brick, missing his target narrowly. This seemed to antagonise the burglar, so Jim matched him step for step, reversing through the gate but the guy ran forward and jumped the fence, flanking him and blocking the route back downhill to safety.

118

Broony turned and took off away from the village, pursued by the fleet-footed burglar, uphill towards the forest. Even in his drunken state, that wasn't where he fancied ending up, so after a minute, he veered left onto the old church track and what would eventually lead to a path back to the south side of the village. Jim was no slouch at the running, but got a stitch and had to stop after five minutes, his pursuer unfortunately not far behind him.

'All right pal, sorry. You head back down and break in, I'll no stop you. Batter on, honestly, my mistake.'

The man had slowed to a walk but was no more than 15 metres behind him and closing.

'C'mon get yourself to fuck, I've been in the pub all night and I just want ma bed now.'

Still nothing and Jim was absolutely shaking now.

'Fuck you, ya prick!' he shouted and set off again a decent sprint around the corner and into the derelict churchyard. Hiding behind one of the few still-vertical headstones, Broony watched as the dark figure followed his steps, checking behind each stone as he went until he was almost upon him. There was a clear space for him to run into, as long as the ominous figure stayed on the row he was searching.

Knowing this might be his best chance to get away downhill, Broony made a dash to get back past the burglar, but the dark figure had noticed the movement and got him well. As he tried to run past, the short crowbar struck Broony viciously on his forehead, making a distinctly metallic clang as it fractured the frontal bone of his cranium. His inert body was then dragged into a sitting position on the same headstone he'd hidden behind just moments earlier.

Although the killer wanted away, back to his real quarry, he had to force himself to accept that he was not going to fulfil his mission that night. It was disappointing, but he realised that he wanted to use the opportunity to take some pleasure from this one, still alive as he was.

Standing above the crumpled and unconscious Jim Brown, he lowered his backpack and extracted what he needed for this project. Firstly, he taped the mouth closed, then slashed his knife along his victim's middle, opening a cut from side to side and pulling the escaping intestines out onto the moss of the graveyard. After the first few appalling moments of the gutting, Jim Brown, thankfully not having regained consciousness, started to shake in cardiac arrest. After another deeper, incisive and exacting slice of the knife into his exposed organs, Broony died after trying, his very best, to be a hero.

The figure stood over his disembowelled body and with just another push and a slash to finish his work, he felt an overpowering sense of release, exultation, an almost perfect moment of long-restrained ecstasy. The perfect isolation meant that he had time to savour it, letting his gratification fade and return, until gradually feeling it ebb for the last time as he looked down in complete ownership of Jim Brown, this accidental death of an unimportant man, given some lasting infamy by his own hands, his ritual and his power. He took out a paper note and placed it under a rock beside the body, just away from the worst of the blood spill.

Knowing that the last vestiges of pleasure were leaving him, he looked around and considered his retreat. He was covered in the Jim Brown's blood and had to get back, get himself cleaned up and just wait for another chance.

After just missing tonight, he knew that the luck of Adam Darnow couldn't last forever.

Police Squad

This time, I wake up and Anna is still there. We kiss and the day starts wonderfully well. Later, I make us coffee and contemplate whether I should just buy this place and stay here, but these are mere musings and I dismiss them from my mind as the coffee machine burbles to completion. She joins me in the sunlit kitchen and we drink cappuccino while we watch the livestock milling around the next door field. No doubt Niall in the summerhouse is oblivious to any noise after last night. He can usually drink more than me, but not last night, he was staggering and could hardly talk on the way home. Maybe it was the fresh air, Anna tells me.

We hear a shrill voice from somewhere and its Anna's mum, rightly assuming that she spent the night with me and waving at her to come over. I leave her to it and wash the coffee mugs before getting a shower and considering waking Niall. Rather than this, I drive down to the village hotspot and get a signal, so phone and arrange another week at the cottage, after which time another group have booked it, so I've now got a date when Niall and the lads have to finish and get the fuck out of my house, or I'll either have to go up to Inverannan or find somewhere else near here.

I drive back up, wake Niall and tell him the plan and that we should go and get whatever paint he will need. We swing past my parent's cottage and the roof tiling looks finished, Allan Douglas is inside with several tradesmen, all busy and checking his list to see what needs to be done next.

'It's looking great Allan, guys are doing some job.' I tell him, shaking his hand.

His lilting voice is a little shaky and he looks like he has a cold. 'Aye, that they are Adam. Not long to go now, just cracking on with the electrics and plastering and then you can get back in to paint.'

I tell him that Niall is going to do the painting and he tells us a place in Fort William where we can use his trade discount, so we thank him and drive there for some shopping. I'm no interior designer and Niall is a Neanderthal so we take advice from the staff and leave with umpteen tins of Farrow & Ball paint which seems nearly as pricey as the stuff I used to deal in. I also furnish Niall with brushes, rollers and a load of other stuff which might enable him to do a half-decent job. After my car is weighed down with a boot full of expensive decorators' paraphernalia, we pick up some major supplies at the supermarket, which go in the back seat, and drive back to Mharisaig where Anna sees me arriving and joins me in the garden of the cottage.

'Hi, are you OK?'

'Yeah, but I've had the police back for another interview. They were searching in the forestry tracks and found Robert's phone. It had my number, his old uncle's and one other which they wanted to ask me about.'

'Whose?'

'It was my cousin Ruaridh's mobile, though god knows why he had that. Ruaridh couldn't stand the sight of him. The police are going to get their counterparts over there to question him in Stonehaven, but I told them that he wouldn't have anything to do with Robert.' She tells me that Ruaridh is a straight guy, nothing but a great help to her and I believe it, he was never anything but good company when we were young, he liked a drink but was a clever guy with a good personality and was usually found holding forth at nights out, a great storyteller.

I don't elaborate to Anna, but there is the possibility that Ruaridh was keeping an eye out for Robert McBride, maybe making sure that he stayed away from his cousin and ran across him when he came down to Mharisaig. It would take a chance meeting I suppose, but the cops will have him down for an interview, that's for sure. For me, it's no bad thing as it keeps them from sniffing around me, but Anna looks upset at this situation so I sympathise.

'They are away up there again, seeing if their dogs can turn anything else up. I just wish Robert had stayed away. There was no need for him to come anywhere near here and look what happened, he's dead and there's no point.' She turns away from me and I'm not sure what to say. Their family will be distraught if it's Ruaridh, so probably better if it's just some passing junkie saw their chance and robbed him but it went too far, maybe.

She goes back to her house after a shout from her mum for lunch and I drop the paint down to the cottage, devoid of workers but looking like most of the hard graft on the structure is complete. I need to order furniture and maybe carpets but have no talent in that direction, so need to find some help and it definitely can't be Niall. I return and change into a running kit and find that my trainers are wearing thin so I need to replace them too. Detesting the mundane aspects of life like buying clothes, I prefer to pay for someone professional in London to send me whatever people wear, and this works far better than me choosing.

I decide to run in the opposite direction of the crags, better to avoid the police presence. Downhill I sprint, through the edge of the village and out towards the ruined bothy where me, Niall and the others misspent our youth, drinking cheap booze and trying to negotiate adolescence in Mharisaig. We thought back then that it was the armpit of the world, boring and frustrating, offering little for teenagers looking for experiences and excitement, albeit I never had any money to pay for them even if they were on offer. Perhaps it has its qualities if you are looking for sanctuary from the wider world, albeit I have inadvertently entangled myself in a murder investigation, which isn't ideal and sure wasn't part of the overall plan to stay away from trouble.

Running has always been an excellent enabler for me to gain perspective on any nagging issues and today it is no different. I figure that surely I'm not a serious suspect in this murder thing and it's positive that Allan Douglas has my parent's cottage reconstruction well in hand. Perhaps I can start to see light at the end of the tunnel and get ready to leave when all that is over. Niall, even though he is not exactly competent, can handle the rest of the work. He will stay at the cottage to give me some space before I leave, but even though I've booked the rental for a week, I decide that I'm going back to Inverannan to see Gillian and let this Robert McBride thing blow over without me. I really love Anna, I know, but we were doomed from the start and given that I love Gillian more, I need her first and foremost. I'm going to pack up tomorrow morning and leave Mharisaig to rumble on without me. I'll come back in a couple of weeks and see how my pals have done with their painting and desecrating, if that is how it goes.

As I turn a few miles later, the sun goes behind the deepening cloud cover and the rain starts in earnest. I splash back along the puddles on the tracks and I'm blinded by the downpour, just looking downwards to make sure I don't trip. I stop when it becomes even more torrential, sheltering in the lee of a broad ash tree, in part of an old estate which over the years lost its focal point, a mansion which was built of materials which could not sustain the severity of Scottish weather, finally being demolished after the second world war after its last use as a hospital for the recuperation of injured soldiers. When I was a young boy, my school class went there one day and the teacher told us the story and showed the overgrown foundations of the once-impressive building. I suppose it wasn't that different from Inverannan House, another of those bastions of wealth set in isolation, shielded from the poverty of the ordinary people of 19th century Scotland. Their owners, if you dig back far enough, all became rich from sheep, slaves, tobacco or sugar, in no particular order. Perhaps I'm just the most recent personification of this model, making my money off the back of others' suffering and afterwards my capital is clean too. Property and secondary investments were ever the best way to launder our dirty money.

The downpour eases off and I'm soaking anyway, so I pelt forward and along to the village, arriving at the shop. A crowd, including Liz, are blethering outside, maybe after sheltering within from the downpour. She sees me, so I feel obliged to stop and ask how she is.

'Better now your pal is gone. I hear he's cadging off you instead of me now. Good luck with that one. He thinks the world owes him a living.' She definitely has fallen out of love with Niall, I reckon.

She moves towards me and moves into hushed gossip mode. 'Did you hear what happened? They found another body deid this morning and you'll never guess who it is.'

Indeed I won't unless this fucking harpy tells me. She pauses for effect, clearly relishing the fact that something terrible has happened and she knows about it.

'Jim Brown, wee Broony. Up near where they found that other one, at the Auld Church.'

Oh shit.

'The police are up in force, been ambulances and all sorts flying past here for the past half an hour. They seem to think it's a murder by the number of cops up there.'

Oh shit.

Just at that an unmarked car with two official-looking types inside wheechs past and I have a sinking feeling about this. I also have a notion that my plan to flee to Inverannan has just been well and truly shafted.

'He was in the pub last night. We were talking to him, he was with his pals.' I tell her, by way of partly repaying the gossip favour.

She already knows this, however, and resumes her bulletin, telling me that the other laddies last saw him, drunk and incapable, heading to his parent's house after midnight. One of Liz's friends is best friends with his mum, so the information network in Mharisaig made its connections with impressive speed. Who needs superfast broadband when you have this lot, I think to myself.

I jog away before Liz has time to reload her gossip cannon, and sprint up to the cottage as quickly as possible before another sharp rainfall descends. Showering, I try and figure out if it is in any way possible that I can leave Mharisaig without appearing guilty but I know in my heart that I'm not getting away, not yet. There's plenty of ready-made food in my rental cottage after our trip to Fort William, so I get dinner sorted and

127

wonder where Niall has got to, not that I'm missing him. There's a six-pack of lager absent from the fridge, so I work on the assumption that they are with him in the summerhouse.

I had come in through the side door to let me leave my wet gear in the utility room, so I'd missed a note lying inside the front door. It's a printed card from Police Scotland, asking me to contact Constable McGarry at my earliest convenience. Given that the cottage doesn't have a phone, I am knackered from the run and can't be arsed driving back down to the village, PC McGarry can go and take a running fuck to himself.

This does me no good, as my considerations on what the hell will happen next are broken by the sound of more emergency vehicles and a helicopter engulfing the area with noise and urgency. It doesn't take long for my doorbell to go and then the chaps in blue thump the front door of the cottage like a fucking battering ram on repeat. There stands PCs McGarry and Wallace, identifying themselves again very formally and asking permission to enter and search my premises. I don't hesitate to agree, as I have nothing inside which could land me in any trouble. On the contrary, whatever they think I've done will probably be appeased by my co-operation, or so I suppose.

As they step inside with little comment, I let them batter on with their search while I make a cuppa for us. Knowing why they are here, I guess that the death of the lad Broony has brought me back to the fore of their investigation. Given my innocence, I hope that this visit will let them get on with their enquiries elsewhere and I can live in peace. They check all the rooms, the washing machine and tumble dryer, the utility room, the bins, every drawer in the house and must be within a hair's breadth of getting a forensic team in.

Ten minutes later they sit down, deigning to have their tea and biscuits and giving me some brief information on the fate of Jim Brown, whose short and insignificant existence had come to an abrupt end just under a mile from my rented cottage. I get more or less the same question set as before, where was I and did I know the deceased blah blah blah. I tell the truth, they can check with Anna that she was with me, and still they look at me with detached suspicion. I'm getting the impression that someone more senior is eagerly waiting to hear the outcome of this interview.

After a time, the duo run out of questions, so I decide to take advantage of the gap to try and be their pal.

'Look guys, I only knew Broony from school and the only time I have met him since was in the pub. I'd nothing against him and I've no reason to harm him. He was just a wee guy from Mharisaig, and I'm sorry he's dead.' I look at them in turn, straight eye to eye, but no response comes, not that I expected any.

'Thanks for your co-operation Mr Darnow. We will be back in touch once the investigation moves forward.' Well enough trained after all, I'm not detecting any chance of hearing how Broony met his maker, so I just follow the cops to the door and close it after they go.

The next day or so brought an eerie, almost surreal atmosphere to Mharisaig. The clouds rolled over and a drizzle of rain laid a pall of mist and dampness over the village. Anna dropped over, but she was quiet, distant even, and didn't stay long, she was taking her mum to Fort William for some shopping and staying for an overnight at another cousin's house there. Niall went down to the renovated cottage with his crew and started on clearing up the garden, so other than giving him a few hundred quid for refuse skips and gear, I spent the time alone, thinking and wondering. Niall moved into my parents' old place too, taking his rucksack of clothes and sleeping bag with him, even tidying the summerhouse before he left.

Police Scotland kept a high-profile presence in the village and it all channelled past my rented cottage, along with media punters to get their journos filmed up at the graveyard where Broony's life ended. I found out more from the TV in those two solitary days than I did from anyone else. After the initial blurb about a fatality, it turned into a *shocking discovery*, then the next day it was linked to a *Murder in Edinburgh* the year before and finally, the grisly details seeped from the crime scene into the public domain. Jim Brown had been ritually disembowelled whilst still alive, his entrails left decorating the graveyard around him and lastly, his face cut, in a manner as yet undisclosed. Whatever had been done to poor Jim was reported to be a near copy of the Edinburgh murder and by fuck, the words *Serial Killer* then slid into the media reports as the darkness, rain and gloom seeped over Mharisaig.

Ruaridh

The police had knocked on Ruaridh's door earlier that day, before even he went to work and stayed for the best part of an hour, making him late. Quite a grilling, making him feel that they were putting more pressure on him than he deserved, but he kept his manners and showed them that he was no criminal. He told them that he hadn't been out of Stonehaven in the past week, just working in his role at the Chartered Accountancy, which is what he wanted to be; a partner once he'd navigated the years and the work needed to take him there.

They asked about his recent activities, when he'd last seen Robert McBride, how he already knew about his death, and when exactly did this information reach him. Anna had indeed phoned him not long after she found out herself, still upset and wanting to talk to Ruaridh, her confidante, about what had transpired. She had called him again when she learned that Robert hadn't died accidentally, and those were the last times they had spoken. The police probed him on his business life, whether he knew anyone in Aberdeen and dropped a couple of names in to see how he reacted, no doubt. Ruaridh never flinched once, their questions answered in a measured and concise way, even if they were asked more crudely than he thought necessary.

The police pressed him especially about why his mobile number was only one of three on Robert McBride's mobile phone, but he could shed no light. It was as much of a surprise to Ruaridh Nolan as anything else they told him. They let slip that a check on the phone records proved that no call had been made between the two numbers, so his denial of any contact was both plausible and evidential. They left him not long after, and he watched from behind the curtains as they strolled to their liveried car, sitting for a few minutes before driving off sharply from his flat.

He'd rented the apartment because it was a stone's throw from the old harbour and he had been quite taken with the idea of the coastal walks and afternoon drinking with friends in the pubs there. In reality, he worked long hours, studied when he wasn't working and hadn't yet made any friends to drink with, so he wished he could go back to Mharisaig and live with all his friends and cousins again. There, he had been a pal to many, a raconteur who had a rapt audience any time he started one of his stories. Here, he was just an accountant guy who wasn't really from Stonehaven. It seemed to Ruaridh that it was just different here, even down to the sense of humour. He couldn't make people on the east coast laugh like he could back home. They seemed dour and found things funny which he did not. Still, he'd had a couple of girlfriends, briefly, and that helped ease the loneliness for a time.

His involvement with Anna back then, after she moved into her riverside flat in Aberdeen, had been sporadic and brief. There had been just a few trips up to see her rented flat and then meet her boyfriend Robert. Ruaridh wasn't taken with him at all. He seemed, well, shifty. A bit of a wide boy, handsome enough and they made a good-looking couple but Ruaridh was a good judge of character and this guy was setting off his alarm bells. They went out for a meal the second time he went up and still he felt a degree of antipathy towards Robert, but couldn't quite put his finger on what it was. He didn't wear a belt with his jeans but that wasn't enough for the dislike that he felt. There was a telephone conversation after that when he called and Anna wasn't in and Robert was trying to be blokey and funny but to

Ruaridh he was just being a dick. Maybe it was the east coast humour thing again but he thought not. After thinking about him for a time, Ruaridh did indeed put his finger on it. Robert McBride physically reminded him of Adam Darnow, that fucking bastard who had broken lovely Anna's heart and sent her back home to lick her wounds and stay with him in Stonehaven for a while till she could face the world again. She had finished uni, they were close then, before this Robert came on the scene and Ruaridh was once again abandoned.

After the phone call with McBride, Ruaridh had looked at Anna's recent social media photos of the couple. He wanted to compare Robert McBride with Adam Darnow to see how similar they were. Unusually for someone of his age, Darnow had no online presence whatsoever, other than a listing as Director of a couple of companies. The diaspora of Mharisaig tended to stick together tightly online and Adam was the only one he could identify who was not on any social media platform, not even with a fake or funny name as some had adopted. Darnow was either a Luddite or he wanted to remain low-profile beyond the norm. He had to search others media to find a group photo with Adam Darnow from their teen years. Ruaridh then remembered that the guy went to university a year early and left another of his distant cousins, Michelle Nolan, distraught and cast aside too. Ruaridh also knew that he had dated another friend of his, Tess, and that hadn't ended well either, but he wasn't sure if that was Darnows fault or not. Still, he was clearly a bit of a scummy love rat and bore more than a slight physical resemblance to this new boyfriend, Robert McBride.

Ruaridh moved two photos together, the bearded McBride and the younger Darnow and there it was; a striking similarity except for the facial hair. The shape of the head, the nose line and even the eyes were about the same, both men with brown thick hair and if he didn't know better, he'd have guessed they were brothers, and not with many years separating them. He printed photos of both to let him check the resemblance in more detail and sat with a bottle of beer to ponder the importance of these parallel boyfriends.

It certainly looked, on the face of it so to speak, that Anna had latched on to the new bloke as a throwback to her lost love. Robert McBride certainly did not have the intellectual or cultural capacity to match the witty and artistic Anna. Neither did he have any particular charm or conversational skill which most people would value in a partner. He didn't even seem to have been blessed with a great deal of manners or social skills, which would help if Anna brought him to meet their friends or relatives. He was also, despite having started working recently on the oil rigs, a bit of a loser financially.

All that Robert McBride appeared to have going for him, Anna-wise, was a similarity to Adam Darnow, the secretive figure from Mharisaig who had coldly abandoned her for some unknown lifestyle in London. This anonymity was in itself intriguing to Ruaridh, who knew that businesses and businessmen thrived on their online presence, that ambitious people promoted themselves and threw online tendrils far and wide to increase contacts and opportunities. Adam Darnow, well he just didn't exist online.

Back then, after she had started living with Robert McBride, it wasn't too many weeks until the problems started for Anna and she began confiding in Ruaridh again, a great sadness for her and a delight for her cousin. The situation with Robert wasn't just a spiral. It was a predictably idiotic disintegration of a foolish man,

134

an act of utter self-harm which was at the same time awful and fascinating to observe from afar. The calls from Anna became more frequent. She didn't have that many friends in Aberdeen, none which she could open her heart to, and started to come down to Stonehaven to visit again when Robert was on the rigs or driving her mad. Ruaridh took her on walks and to the pub and hid his feelings as he always had needed to. What he couldn't stand was the impact that the moronic Aberdonian was having on her. She was losing weight from the stress and she seemed near to tears every time they met. Perhaps this was the relief of talking to a friend and a cousin, after having to live with an increasingly coarse and distant addict. Anna was perfect, to Ruaridh, and this useless fucker wasn't going to harm her, not on his watch.

He decided that he would take a long-overdue spell of days off, to coincide with Robert McBride coming back from the rigs. Ruaridh would find out what he was really up to, maybe enough to end the relationship. He followed Robert when he met the group of scumbags he seemed to have got in tow with. Ruaridh took surreptitious photos on his phone, of him with a woman, cuddling and snogging, but he knew that to show these to Anna would be a harm he could not bear to inflict on her. Ruaridh spoke with some guys, men in the pub who looked at Robert's pals with obvious distaste, and they didn't hold back telling Ruaridh who they were and what they were like. A shower of nasty junkies, football hooligans who caused bother wherever they went and found their own odious behaviour a lot funnier than anyone else. This fascinating surveillance took him another couple of trips north, until Robert McBride went on a bender worse than before and Anna left him anyway, coming to stay in Stonehaven before moving back to Mharisaig after her dad passed away.

Ruaridh had helped her clear the Aberdeen flat and used his car to help transport some of her stuff to Stonehaven, then on to Mharisaig. McBride had come back to the flat when he was picking up the last of the boxes and even tried to give him a hard time, so Ruaridh allowed himself a few moments of rare enjoyment, punching the shit out of McBride until he lay bleeding and flat out on the ground beside his car. He had wanted to stamp on him then, to leave him a bloody mess, but there were people watching and that was not the time to do it properly, best not to get himself into trouble for that rodent.

This situation, however, left Ruaridh with something of a quandary. He'd achieved a pyrrhic ending. Anna had cut herself free from the shit McBride, but when she moved away to Mharisaig she was no longer in Ruaridh's life. He was in a state of despair at this outcome and determined to do something to Robert McBride to make him pay. His last trip to Aberdeen was speculative, Ruaridh even toyed with beating up the bastard again, giving him a real doing this time, but he was a fundamentally more complex man than one who would settle for that paltry revenge. He was also fearful of being caught and generally unwilling to sink to the level of McBride with such an unsophisticated confrontation.

He went to the riverside flat, but there was no sign of life at all, the rooms were empty and he supposed that Robert McBride had been evicted or perhaps had moved out to avoid paying rent arrears. Ruaridh was on the verge of driving back home, but decided instead to visit the rancid city centre pub which his quarry frequented. He had two soft drinks there, watching the bar busy up and there he was, the smiling bastard, buying drinks and then sitting with a different woman, rough-looking with a ton of make-up and an overtly friendly approach to

McBride. Ruaridh moved so that he couldn't be seen and started talking to a couple of older regulars whom he'd cultivated previously for information. He bought them a drink and himself a pint, although he didn't drink it beyond a sip. He told them that he recognised the lassie sitting over there but couldn't place her, and the older guy with the shaved head told him that she was the infamous wife of a one-time local gangster, now more or less straight and working on the rigs. He typed the names into his phone as if he was sending a text message and clicked a rapid selection of photos of the couple before he left, glancing over his shoulder to see the amorous couple preparing to leave. Ruaridh snapped another few photos of them entering a taxi before leaving for home, his job for the evening completed to a most satisfactory conclusion.

It took very little online research to identify this Granite City power-couple and where they lived. They had a wide circle of friends and their social media was accessible, full of photos of nights out, parties at home and, a year or two before, a host of photos and congratulations for their lovely new home and for a part-time business listed there, the address of the woman and her cuckolded husband.

Ruaridh wondered if they had an open marriage and all this would be in vain, but he hoped not and carried on regardless. He printed the photos, along with an enjoyably embellished letter naming Robert McBride, and recounting all the things that he had fictitiously boasted of doing to this man's wife. Enough to enrage the husband beyond control, he trusted. From what the men in the bar told him before he left, the man was, despite being in his forties, something of a past legend in the city for his temper and his pugilistic skills, which was exactly what Ruaridh wanted to hear.

So it was that this official-looking envelope was posted and hopefully opened by Ally Quinn after he returned from his shift on the rigs. Ruaridh was unsure what the exact consequences of this intervention would be, although he deeply enjoyed the prospect of exacting remote control revenge on Robert McBride. He would surely come to regret stealing Anna's money and making her miserable, but mainly his offence was driving her from the east coast, away from the cousin who loved her more than anything.

Ally Quinn, Cuckold

The shifts were taking a toll on Ally Quinn, a damn sight more than they used to. He had always been an individual who prided himself on his resilience, his strength and the fact that he was absolutely a man's man. A guy who could provide for his family, his wife and kids, you know. Nice houses, cars for them all, pocket money and weddings paid for generously, open-handed at the bar and a group of pals who his kids called aunts and uncles, as well as the wider group of actual relatives he felt patriarch to.

When he was young it was easy. The boundless energy of his early adult years carried him through, but he hit 45 like a fucking stone wall, that was his *annus horribilis*. The heart attack had diminished him, like someone just took 20% of his power away in a day, along with his libido and then soon afterwards his hairline, lost in the next two short years. Even through all that, he kept plugging along, dropped some of his side-lines onto his younger pals and relatives and trying to manage working on the rigs and a social life when he was back. The problem for Ally was that it just all changed, no matter how much he didn't want it to. His two daughters both had kids, both marriages failed at that time and they went from success to burden at the same time as his hair was swirling down the shower plughole in clumps each day. His wife felt the pressure of this and started drinking and partying without him, no longer waiting for his time off the rigs to go out, but making her own company. She lost interest in Ally then, apart from keeping up appearances at gatherings, of course, and spending the money he earned, that was the only value she drew from him after then.

Later, the gloom of those dark months weighed him down more than he could bear, but he came to understand that he had to fight back, had to regain his mojo, as he thought of it. He worked his way through various ministrations that fucking disinterested quack of a GP tried on him, and eventually started to see a pathway out of his malaise. A combination of diet changes, legal and illegal substances and rigorous gym workouts got him at least physically back on track, albeit he was still totally fucked after two weeks working on the rigs and that was the last thing he needed, with his wife the way she was. That damned Friday, he got back in from a stormier, wetter journey home than usual, and needed nothing but a shower and sleep.

'What's all this Rhonda?' He interrupted his wife's trip to the fridge for what looked like a pre-mixed cocktail before she went out with pals.

'Letters. What does it look like?' This was the type of shite Ally had to put up with, having to open fucking bills every time he got back while she did damn all to help. He inhaled and exhaled fully and calmed himself, not wanting to respond in temper and kick off another fight, this soon into the weekend.

Ally went into the conservatory and dumped the letters beside his chair for later. He headed upstairs, showered, changed into lounging clothes and poured himself a malt, sitting down to watch TV and hearing the front door close as his beloved wife left for the evening without a word of goodbye. Ally muttered a swear word under his breath and started to open the post, knowing that he could at least slightly relax after that chore was complete. The third letter, official as it seemed, was locally posted. It was definitely unlike the usual crap from Swindon or Northampton which just told him how

140

much his credit card bill or some other bloody expense would cost him, and was of a personal nature.

Inside were home-printed photos, of his wife and a young scally in a pub, close up and kissing. A letter accompanied them, telling Ally that he was a mug, a fool and that everyone was laughing at him and at the bottom of the page, a close-up of his wife's lover with his name and address on the back. Proof positive right enough and at first, Ally felt the deepest wretchedness of his life, his tears cascading onto the photos until the paper of the worst one was damp. Then as he drank more malt whisky through the evening, his old, oft-subdued temper started to flicker back into life. He knew that his wife, at least at the start of the evening, would be out in town, so better leave a trip to this young fellow's house address as Plan B. No, he wanted to catch them out together, see this with his own eyes.

Their house was well outside the city centre, so Ally prepared what he needed, and then took a taxi into the main drag to try and find his wife. She would ignore any of his calls or messages he knew from experience, so he called his oldest daughter and asked her to find out, surreptitiously, where her mother was, without letting her know it was for him. Ally told her it was important and not to ask and used that near-forgotten stern voice that she still recognised. This was not the time to question him. Five minutes later, a pub name arrived by text and Ally Quinn set out with purpose towards his errant wife.

Rhonda Quinn was in party mode that night, as she often was. She liked the young men of Aberdeen very much, and had found a new beau a couple of days before, to replace Robert McBride, who had disappeared without even calling her. Depending on how she was feeling, Rhonda liked to stay until closing time in the pub or if her needs were urgent, go to the flat of whoever she was with or to take them to her family home, if her husband was away. Her other option was to book into a hotel for a couple of hours and tonight was one of those nights. She would be back home by 2 am, a credible time for her cover story of having left a late bar, blethered with pals and then a long wait for a taxi. Her drowsy cuckold couldn't challenge her without an indignant rebuttal and a fiery response which she knew from experience, he would shie away from.

She knocked back her cocktail and whispered in the ear of Josh, or Shiner or whatever the other laddies called him. He was quite handsome in a rough way, not as good looking as Robert McBride but the same type she liked, maybe like her husband had been, when he was in his early twenties. At the start, Rhonda was always dead keen on them and so it was with Josh. She was unarguably in her early, besotted phase. She leaned over close to him, pushing into his shoulder, whispering to him and Rhonda knew that few young men would say no to what she said.

Josh followed her from the bar and out into the chilly evening, across the road and along the side street into the hotel which she had booked from her phone earlier, once she was sure that he had turned up and was staying. She emerged less than two hours later, makeup re-applied and showing no signs of anything but a night out with the girls, into a waiting taxi and ignorant of the eyes of her husband upon her.

Ally Quinn had watched their evening unfold, the last drink, the whispered invite and the arm-in-arm walk to the budget hotel not five minutes away. He was fermenting with fury but the couple were walking through a busy street, passing witnesses as they went, so no approach could be made, not then, even though he almost did before making his choice. Ally had watched them walk inside, hurrying, desperate for each other, but still he forced himself to wait. He wasn't sure if her boyfriend would spend all night in the hotel, making Ally wait longer for vengeance. However, a short time after Rhonda left, there he was, emerging into the now empty street and lighting a cigarette before striding west towards the main road.

Ally had already spent his time checking the street for CCTV and knew that none covered the last 40 metres of the route until it intersected with the main road. He wore a hooded jacket and had all-dark unmarked clothing on anyway, but didn't want any video evidence to betray him. His trainers made no noise as he emerged from the doorway just after the laddie passed and he struck him with all the force that the frustration had built in Ally, the metal socket extension bar vibrating his powerful forearm as it made contact. Still, the young guy wasn't knocked out completely and got up swinging his arms. Ally stepped back to let his untrained blows fall on empty space before stepping in towards him and cracking the metal bar on his forehead. As the young man sat dazed before Quinn, he took his wallet, stood on, then kicked away his phone and pounded him with a long, sickening series of blows which made little sound but did great damage. Quinn took off his gloves and, placed them in a plastic bag along with the metal bar, and then the bag went inside the rucksack. He pulled out a baseball cap to cover his face, and with his jacket reversed to its light coloured side to complete the transformation, he ambled back along the other end of the side street, crossing the road and onto a route he had known since he was a boy in the city, a way that would take him away from his crime undetected and unfollowed, home to his wife.

It was almost morning when he neared the estate where they lived, the light playing on the upper fringes of the pallid skyline and showing him the way. Past a light industrial compound and along a path dissecting the overgrown site of an old manufacturing works, Quinn ignored his exhaustion and made good time. The contents of his rucksack were emptied in five separate locations along the route, in bulk bins and the last, the metal bar, thrown into an open, deep drain. From where the path took him, he had access to his house through a gate in the back fence, one he used years before, when they had a dog, long ago when he was happy and young. The house was silent, no alarm on, and he showered thoroughly, before putting his clothes in the hottest wash in the machine and crashing out on the sofa.

Mid-morning, Rhonda came down and he could hear the kettle wheezing into life for her coffee. Unmoving, Quinn listened to her clattering for a mug, noisily pulling up the kitchen blinds, then scraping one of the tacky-looking stool out to sit at the raised breakfast bar. He knew that she would, as was her habit, check her social media, her messages and knew who in particular she would be waiting to hear from, but Ally Quinn knew that revelations on that front would find her soon enough. The rest of the morning and afternoon he ignored Rhonda, keeping his temper in check and waiting to see when she would find out. He was watching the football on TV when he heard the wail come from upstairs and a smirk momentarily crossed his face before he assumed an expression of blank indifference and climbed the stairs. In their bedroom, his wife sat in tears at the edge of the bed, her phone shaking in her hands. Quinn took the phone from her and turned it off, placing it in his back pocket and sitting beside her.

She would not turn to him, even in her anguish. She shrank away to the top of the bed and began to shiver, uncontrollably, fearful and cowed. Earlier, Ally wondered if she would realise straight away that it had been him and this pretty much told him, let him know which one of his options would be most suitable. He also knew that his wife would have a decision to make and that much in their life would change based on this. Whatever she picked, Ally Quinn wasn't going to be walked over again, no fucking way. He'd got his mojo back after all.

The next morning, Ally Quinn put on his coat and stepped out into the sideways driving rain coming off the North Sea, and locked the door of his house behind him. He had messaged his daughters to let them know that he and Rhonda had got a late deal for a fortnight in Spain, were already at the airport and that mum had only gone and left her phone in the house. The girls were surprised, but pleased that their parents were getting on well enough again to take an impromptu holiday. Rhonda's bruises will have gone away by then and, if she knew what was good for her, she wouldn't be back in the City Centre scene again, nor be telling her daughters about Josh, or the treatment she just got from her loving husband.

Ruaridh Visits Mharisaig

Ruaridh Nolan could bear no longer to sit on the sidelines, in Stonehaven, far from Anna and all that was Mharisaig. Every night, for as long as he could remember, he dreamed of living there with Anna. He had his house there, well it was his parents place technically, but they lived in a Retirement Complex in Fort William now, cared for and settled in their warm apartment. The house in Mharisaig was a beauty, one of the largest in the village and once filled with the Nolan family, who were now scattered throughout Scotland and farther. His parents discussed their Will with them collectively, in that very house just before they left for their new flat. Ruaridh, as the oldest son, felt that he by rights should inherit the property plus a share of the money, and was irritated when he found out that his siblings had an equal claim on the estate. His wee brother, Tavish, was a complete waste of space and didn't seem to care about Mharisaig, and the others were not much better. Only Anna Berkmann, his lovely cousin, seemed fond of the place when they spoke of it, which made Ruaridh's dreams all the more vivid.

So, he took even more annual leave from work, using it earlier in the year than he'd hoped to, and packed the car for another trip back to Mharisaig. Much like Adam Darnow, he didn't want his presence to be known in the village when he arrived, which was easy as his empty property is set well back from the access road to the village. It is private, gated and locked against intruders. The drive home from Stonehaven took almost four hours, east coast to west coast after gathering supplies at the supermarket to avoid having to use the shop in Mharisaig. The route to his house does not require him to go into the village, so he met not a soul when he arrived. The property, a traditional Georgian villa originally built by a local doctor, sat in as isolated a plot as any in the area. It is only a ten-minute walk to the village centre, but with nothing but forest on the south and westward sides and no paths or thoroughfares to overlook Ruaridh's idyll.

He unlocked the metal gates and drove around to the back of the house, the tradesman's entrance as his dad used to call it. Back out and locking the gates again, Ruaridh checked for prying eyes, but there were none. It took him ten minutes to unload his car and get everything away in cupboards and the fridge, after which he looked around the cold property, the ageing furniture covered with dustsheets and the air filled with the cloying odour of abandonment. Still, he loved the place, no sadness there for Ruaridh Nolan, just a burning desire to be the father here, the patriarch who fills the house with a wife, children, dogs and he would, he must, achieve his dream.

Leaving the front window shutters in place lest the light signify his presence, Ruaridh set himself up in his old bedroom. He would stay there, at the back of the house, keeping to the kitchen below and bedroom upstairs lest his presence be noticed. Resting for the evening, he worked through the files he had brought with him, before his supper, then into a deep sleep borne of familial dreams and fantasies.

The morning brought rain, light but constant, dousing the verdant shades of Highland springtime. Trees which were once under control, now loomed higher and closer to the villa, blocking the infrequent sunlight. Ruaridh liked to spend his first day of each visit uncovering the furniture, vacuuming the flooring as best he could. Heating the rooms with the expensive LPG-fuelled system was the only option for the location, installed back in his father's time. By the afternoon, the house that he remembered, that he visualised every day of his life, was back to the way it should be. Ruaridh walked from room to room, ensuring that all things were the way they should be. After this ritual was complete, he felt an inner peace, a calmness which gave him control over not only the house, but his plans for the future. The last part would be to go for a run, but considering his desire for anonymity, this could only be done with his face covered. He had brought his running beanie hat, a neck gaiter which would make him too hot but would be worth it and sports sunglasses, again not required but helpful to avoid identification. Ruaridh had run here many times and knew that, after a mile on the road, he could take a path which only a few dog-walkers use, one which the infrequent long-distance ramblers use to reach the coast after a westwards journey which does not pass through Mharisaig village.

He set out at a decent pace, the rain cooling him as he extended his stride and soon the road was well behind him as he kept a steady, regulated speed until he reached a high point and the view of two lochans to the north and the last row of hills between him and the sea. Turning, he removed his neck gaiter and ran more quickly, taking advantage of the downhill stretch and the need to breathe in the pure air of the north-west, filling his lungs with the cleansing Highland air. Back at the road, he resumed his regular pace and finally back to his house, through the ivy-fringed wooden side door which he always thought looked like the entrance to his own secret garden.

Ruaridh watched television that night, hearing all about his village from the STV news and watching as the interviewer spoke in front of police tape, outside a churchyard, not two miles from where he sat. He had of course known Jim Brown, been in his company many times without really engaging with him. Broony was part of the village underclass, a tier or three below his own, but in a small community those barriers did not prevent them socialising when the larger age group convened, usually for a drink. Ruaridh sat and thought about who else was, like Broony, poor and of the same category. He had a few names and wondered about Adam Darnow, who wore thin and unfashionable second-hand clothes but somehow seemed to be the eternal epicentre of all the Mharisaig youth. Ruaridh himself, he knew for a fact, had the best talent for storytelling, for jokes even, and was the raconteur of any party, but Adam Darnow was always something higher, even with odd socks and t-shirts two sizes too small. Why did his poverty not keep him in this underclass, with Broony and Ronny Thomson and the others?

So his thoughts progressed on this theme, as it had oft before. Ruaridh could not understand why Adam Darnow, a boy with no money, tatty clothes and an air of discarded negligence had been the pinnacle of youthful manhood in Mharisaig. He was quietly spoken, unlike the young Ruaridh. Darnow was clever, but not as clever at school as Ruaridh. He was probably quite handsome, but people thought that he, Ruaridh was good-looking too. So what on earth made Adam Darnow the person who could charm Anna, and had attracted Tess, and Michelle and probably others, all beautiful and all intelligent, what made this bastard better than Ruaridh Nolan? Ruaridh did not have the answer, but he would find out, one day, because he fucking hated Adam Darnow.

Ruaridh lay back on his bed upstairs and remembered the time that he, Adam Darnow and a few others from Mharisaig had their trials for the Inverloch school football team. The side was difficult to get into, the standard being high and always competitive. For this reason, Ruaridh had trained hard, running every day and honing his football skills with friends or just in the garden, kicking the ball against the stone wall in his garden for hours. He imagined each touch was part of a competitive match, imagined sending his marker the wrong way and blasting a goal, only interrupted occasionally by his mother for the noise his ball made, repetitively scudding off the wall.

The trials were after school, at the start of third year, as the first two years pupils were deemed too physically small for the team. Ruaridh knew that he himself was one of the best players from Mharisaig. He'd captained the wee Mharisaig Primary School team and been so proud, his father watching their games every Saturday morning. The school teachers who took the Inverloch team were highly vocal here though, quite off-putting he thought. They put them through drills, races and then some short seven-a-side games until they were all pretty knackered and keen to see who was getting picked. They sat in bib colour groups, drinking water and trying not to stare too obviously at the cabal of coaches while they debated and gestured. In the end, they shouted over six candidates to join the older boys in the school squad and Ruaridh was not one of them. He watched in envious horror as only one boy from Mharisaig, Adam Darnow, was picked. Ruaridh could feel tears of disappointment and anger rising and strode off at the front of the others to get changed and return home to the sanctuary of his room.

Like the rest of his pals, he watched the school team a couple of times in tournaments and the first game featured Adam Darnow, who did absolutely fuck all during the game but scored twice. The next time,

Darnow came on as a substitute and scored the winner, never even celebrated, the shit. That was the last time Ruaridh seen him play and he heard later that the coach had dropped him as he generally didn't turn up for training and when he did, he failed to exhibit the requisite effort levels. Even that failure turned out well for Darnow, who many said was the best footballer in Inverloch School, but couldn't be bothered trying. Ruaridh had to watch helplessly as Darnow's inadequacies turned into some kind of cool cachet and he didn't even have to kick a ball or train to be branded the best.

The memory of this caused Ruaridh to get agitated again, which he tried not to let turn into a full-blown panic attack. He knew that this meant that he wouldn't sleep for another hour at least, until he'd calmed down and gone down another train of thought. Even in his bed, at home in Mharisaig, he couldn't relax because of this years-old antipathy towards someone who probably doesn't even remember him. Ruaridh really fucking hated Adam Darnow.

The Usual Suspect

It is the third day after the death of Jim Brown when the cops arrive for another Q&A with me. This time, my visitors are proper detectives instead of the underlings and have a much more intelligent interview technique, all in the name of ensnaring me deeper into their investigation, of course. Anna had kindly given me an alibi for the time of Broony's death, although I reckon that these guys are heavily focused on dissecting the timeframe to see if I merit a return to their suspect's gallery.

We're sitting in the kitchen and these two are across from me, Forbes and McVeigh from Inverness station and me, the innocent man. I guess we've finished with the formal part and they have some chat which they want to finish with.

'So what was Mr Brown like at school, when you knew him?'

I look across at him. He's a hard cop to read.

'Broony was just one of a group of lads that went to the school, not a close pal. I didn't know him well enough to say what he was like.'

'But you must have had some impression of him.'

I exhale slightly. 'He was just a standard wee guy, not the brightest spark and, well, I honestly didn't have many dealings with him.'

The cop, Forbes, checks his notebook. 'You knew him well enough to break his nose at a party.'

Here we go. Fucking Mharisaig, where no piece of gossip will lie unturned for long. I'd hit Broony for insulting me once, years ago, when we were not much

152

more than boys and now some arsehole had told the cops on me.

'That was just a dumb thing, years ago, at a party.'

The other one, McVeigh, chips in. 'You have a reputation around here, did you know?'

I ignore him.

'Apparently you've come back here with plenty money and are something of an enigma to the locals. Left with nothing and came back with plenty. How did that happen?'

This is exactly what I expected, and my cover is both verifiable and bullet-proof, if a little rags-to-riches.

'I left to become a journalist, but there was no money in it. I got a job with a Property business, done well, got promoted quickly and they made me a partner based because of my business development achievements. I'm still doing this, and hope to be for the foreseeable future.'

'Well done Mr Darnow, it's nice to hear a success story. You did all that in what, two, going on three years or so?'

'Yep, in London it's all about results. I made them plenty money and they rewarded me, simple as that.'

'Good for you.' I get the impression that they don't believe this for a minute but my business situation is clean, visible and thank fuck, all the illegal parts have been disposed of effectively by me and the Allantons.

Forbes peers myopically at his notebook and then McVeigh, which really irks me.

He goes on. 'We are examining the link between at least one of these murders with another, last year, in

Edinburgh. Can you tell me where you were on the 26th and 27th April of last year?'

I look at him blankly. I'm trying to remember when we did a deal to bring in a huge consignment of gear from the Middle East, but I think that was May. I smile and fetch my laptop. Opening my offline Outlook Calendar, Legitimate Business Version*, I turn it to the cops for their perusal.

'I was in Singapore from the 20th until the 22nd, then Melbourne from the 23rd until 26th and flew back via UAE, got to London on the 28th.' They jot down my details, no doubt for a later check with the Passport people. Forbes nods at me and spends a moment scrolling up and down my partially fictitious timeline, although this foreign trip was thankfully genuine and thus verifiable. He takes a mobile shot of my screen.

The two of them stand up at the same time and start for the door. McVeigh turns and looks at me.

'What made you break Jim Brown's nose?'

I meet his gaze. 'If I remember correctly, there was jealousy on his part that I had previously been going out with someone he liked.'

He nodded. 'We hear that you have a reputation in that respect too Mr Darnow. Please contact us if you are planning on going anywhere.' Not waiting for an answer, they leave without as much as a goodbye.

I hear their car drive past the cottage and see it speeding towards the village. I sit and wonder what else today will bring when I look out at the now brightening skies and see Anna walking towards me, back from her trip and no doubt wondering what the state of play is with me and Police Scotland. Opening the side door, she hugs me and after a couple of days of solitude, the feeling of long-missed human warmth and company washes over me.

Starting the coffee machine and shoving the laptop away, I tidy up as Anna sits and watches me intently.

'So, what did they say?' I pass the mug to her and she touches my hand with her fingertips.

'Probably just what you'd expect them to, if you've been following the news. Asked where I was last year when that guy in Edinburgh was murdered, what I thought of Jim Brown and a few other things.'

'And?'

'Well I was abroad on business on the dates they asked about, so I guess that's me back off the serial killer roster.' I take a sip of the hot coffee and wish I'd put more sugar in it.

'I couldn't tell them much about Jim, but someone had helpfully told them that I'd broken his nose when we were kids.'

Anna hoots with laughter, which makes me scratch my head in frustration and curse Mharisaig.

'You know what this place is like Adam. An interesting visitor like you can't keep anything under wraps in a wee village!'

Never a truer word was spoken.

'Did you tell them that Broony was besotted with Michelle and she was in love with you, but you managed to break her heart?'

I sigh at how everyone here knows about the never-ending litany of interpersonal mistakes that, despite never intending to, I always make.

'Not anything specific. Just had the distinct impression that persons local had been giving information to help the police with their enquiries.' She nods agreement and appears to be just about holding in her laughter. I go on.

'I barely remember Broony. He was just a minor guy in our big group, liked a drink and wasn't smart enough to have a conversation with, so I guess we didn't talk much together.' I tell her, unable to remember more about our late departed school friend.

'Do you remember when he tried to go on that rope swing? It was the high one over the back road?'

Thinking back, I do remember that someone had fallen and hit their head on a tree stump, but not that it was Jim Brown.

'He had wanted to do join the Air Training Corps or something, but he couldn't fly after bursting his eardrum in the accident. Really unlucky.'

I nod, but maybe that happened when I was at university or something, there's nothing else coming back to me. We finish our coffee and I ask if she wants to come down and see how Niall and the team are getting on at my parents' cottage.

Ten minutes later, we're looking at what my front garden which looks like the third day at a Music Festival after heavy rain and ten thousand welly dances.

'Fuck sake' I say under my breath as we follow the sounds of carnage towards the back garden. There, three morons are watching two other morons with rotavators, mushing the land into an unholy brew of grass, weeds and mud. Their objective is unclear, as are their clothes. We stand until they see us and Niall comes over, white teeth visible under a dense layer of Highland crap.

156

'What do you think? Fucking magic these things. We tried to dig it up, but it was taking ages so we hired these bad boys. Another hour and we are done, the topsoil is coming tomorrow and then the turf – you'll be sitting in paradise by the weekend mate!'

Niall has clearly gone insane.

'You've certainly been busy Niall.' Anna tells him, while I wonder whether Niall has a chromosome in the wrong place or over-indulgence in alcohol has eventually taken its toll.

'Aye, we filled three skips with all the bits of garage and weeds and everything, hard work but we're getting there.' He looks at me for my opinion and I'm trying to find one. On the plus side, the garden looks three times larger, although about a hundred times muddier. When I told Niall to tidy up the garden I honestly expected neither this degree of upheaval nor the resultant no-man's land of mud and twigs.

'Aye, well done mate. Some job.' I manage to respond, although probably not sounding as enthusiastic as he may have wished. Gesturing for Anna to join me inside, I hear Niall telling the others to keep going while he gets cleaned up.

The inside of the cottage, except for the mess in the kitchen, is looking great. The walls are all freshly plastered and nearly dry. Once it is painted in my extortionate Farrow & Ball, it will be better than it ever was. Not that it was ever a show home, but there it is. We do the tour of the upstairs and Anna is more than impressed.

'The ceilings are higher aren't they?' I nod.

'Yeah, the builder, Allan, was brilliant, lucky to get him at short notice. I guess all this isn't complicated for them I suppose, but it makes quite a difference.' A look over the new bathroom and we're done, downstairs to find a relatively clean Niall waiting in the kitchen, dressed in shorts and t-shirt.

He grins. 'I got a shower from the new outside tap. Very bracing.'

'It's looking fine in here too Niall. You painting after the garden is done?'

'Yeah, two of us are going to paint after tomorrow, three finishing the turfing and we'll all get stuck into the inside after the weekend. Be ready for the furniture by the end of next week.'

I must admit, I'm impressed by their work ethic and it's possible that I might not regret paying them for this work. Niall looks like he's keen to find out what's been happening with the Police for the last couple of days, Anna intuits that I can't be bothered explaining, so does it on my behalf.

Niall crows when he hears that someone has been speaking to the cops about me.

'Ahahahaha! I fucking knew it!'

Anna looks at me, puzzled.

He smirks at both of us. 'I heard that the police were asking to interview anyone who might have information, and that a few of our public-spirited fellow residents were more than keen to get involved.' He tells us the culprits' names and I'm not surprised at any of them.

'Well it's nice to know that people are prepared to drop me right in the shit, it sure is.' I snarl.

'Come on Adam, fuck all happens up here unless you are here. You turn up, people get murdered and there are cops and TV cameras everywhere. They don't know if you're just a laddie from Mharisaig or Satan himself.'

Neither do I, sometimes.

'Well, can you tell anyone who might listen that I was abroad when the Edinburgh guy was killed and tucked up with Anna when Broony got done. That should keep them away from me.'

Anna is looking at me with a mix of amusement and pissed-offedness. 'You are happy to besmirch my reputation to help your own?'

'OK, don't tell them about Anna.' I give her a big cheesy grin and she shakes her head and moves on, very magnanimously I think.

I start to chuck some rubbish in a bin to tidy the kitchen a bit and Anna asks Niall how he's doing.

'All right thanks, Anna. I tried to speak to Liz but she is still not keen. I'll stay here until the painting is done, after that I'll see if my mum and dad will take me back for a bit.'

He glances at me to see if I interject but I don't want to move back here until it's sorted, even though I need to be out of the rented cottage in less than a week. It all depends on this police investigation I suppose, and what I decide to do next.

'Has Allan Douglas been round? I've not paid him the last fee for the work.' I ask Niall.

'Aye, he was in yesterday to see how the plasterers got on.'

'What is Allan like? I've never met him.' Anna says, while trying the kitchen drawers for some reason.

'He's spot on is Allan, a bit serious, but a lot of islanders are like that, hard life out there in the wilds. Got his dad's whole business handed to him after he passed away right enough, the lucky bastard.' Niall tells her.

The sound of idiots with heavy machinery interrupts us, so we leave Niall and set out through the new front door, then pick our steps along the short but now-muddy path to the gate and on to the car. Anna looks at me and smiles, possibly still amused by the thought of all the bloody locals telling the cops about me, or some version thereof. It shouldn't be a surprise, but is somehow deeply annoying to hear that people talk about me behind my back. If only they knew.

I realise that the past couple of hours have all been about me and ask how Anna is doing, and how her trip was.

'All right, it was a really good catch up with the family and all the kids, my mum so enjoyed getting away. Did I tell you that Ruaridh was on the phone to me? I hadn't told him that we were going away and he got all panicky and thought something had happened to me.'

I'm not sure what to say to that. Ruaridh sounds a bit overprotective towards Anna, but I guess that's just his nature. He was a good laugh with a drink in him, in company, but always a bit OCD with schoolwork and stuff, a bit highly strung might be the right description. I tell Anna that it's natural that relatives are concerned, with all that's gone on, and drop her off at her mum's with promises to catch up later.

I take a drive back to the village, catch up with some emails and make the call to Gillian, the one which I have been putting off for days. My prescient dread of the unavoidable conversation was all too accurate and not

160

for the first time, I find myself getting a right telling off from a person much smarter and better than me. Gillian had read the papers, the gossip and all the lurid shit and let me have a severe dose of her opinions on the matter, which I try to explain and then apologise for. Half an hour later, I wearily start the car and drive up to the rented cottage probably still in a relationship, more or less.

Whodunnit?

The next morning, a perfectly clear spring day, I am again awakened by the repeated baa-ing and moo-ing of the farmer's appalling animals. Despite my vocal protestations, they ignore me and continue to cluster to the part of the field nearest my bedroom window. Never have I wished more to be back in the city, in London, in my river view apartment with double glazing and noise-reducing insulation, and no fucking livestock within earshot at 5 am. I pull the pillow over my ears and finally get back to sleep, awakened much later by a knock at the front door. It's Niall and he's much less muddy than the last time we met.

'What is it?'

'Fine way to greet your best friend and hard-working garden landscaper, that.' He surges past me and puts the kettle on, so I let him.

'Again, what is it?'

'I have some spare time as the gardening chaps are over-staffed, and the plaster is not quite fully dry according to Allan. He was there to check on it first thing this morning, and I told him that you had money for him.' He pours us both a poorly constructed coffee, which I stand and repair with additional coffee, sugar and milk.

'So, at the risk of sounding repetitive, what do you want?'

'Apart from passing the message on that Allan Douglas will meet you tomorrow at noon at the cottage, I am here because I am fed up working in shite and have nowhere else to inhabit, as I seem to be persona non grata with anyone else who has a house.'

162

We look at each other and burst out laughing, Niall is still the man who makes me laugh most, especially when it is at his own expense.

'Well mate, we losers have got to stick together.'

He looks dubious. 'Aye, how are you a loser?'

Nor for the first time in his life, Niall looks confused. I put him out of his misery. 'Well, my girlfriend has unavoidably heard all about the mental shite here, and no doubt her parents have too.'

'What are you talking about? Of course Anna knows.' He looks at me like I've gone mad.

'Not Anna, Gillian, my actual partner from Inverannan.'

Niall just about implodes with laughter at me, which takes a while to ebb.

'How do you manage to do this to yourself?' More sniggers.

I put my head in my hands and through my hair, which I realise is too long and greasier than it should be.

'I wish I knew. Gillian is beautiful, clever, good-hearted and loves me. Still, I come here and Anna walks back in, and I just let it all happen like an idiot.'

Niall looks at me. 'I think you have a powerfully self-destructive instinct which causes you to fuck up relationships before they can become serious, as a result of parental abandonment.'

This is not only profound but also miles out of character, and far too intuitive for Niall to have come up with himself, so I look at him for an explanation.

He looks sheepishly at me. 'I was in the pub last year for a bit of a school reunion with a crowd of them, and

Anna, Tess and Michelle were talking about you. I tried to defend you on the basis of immaturity but they had some fixed views about the subject which they told me, and that bit stuck in my mind.'

I groan at the thought of everyone openly dissecting my psyche over drinks in Mharisaig, and the fact that I wasn't invited to a school reunion. I dismiss this as I was in something of an anonymity drive while working for the Allantons. Niall looks at me with concern now that he's finished laughing at me.

'It wasn't all bad. They all seem to think you are handsome, and had some lewd comments to make about other stuff...which is where I left them to talk about you in private.'

This is just grim, and for the first time since god knows when, I feel my face redden.

'Niall, I need to get back away from here and back to London, these Scottish villages are killing me.'

At that, we look at each other and something akin to a penny dropping occurs to him.

'Fuck sake. Adam. What if the murderer is after you, and McBride and Broony just got in the way? Oh fuck.'

Oh fuck indeed. We sit in silence while we percolate this suggestion and it could be that Niall, idiot savant, has something here. Something else then clicks with me, and we need to get online, so I tell Niall to come on and we drive down to the village hotspot and open the laptop. A quick search and there's the images of Robert McBride, grainy and poor quality, but we both know that there is a facial likeness to me. I check the Edinburgh murder victim even the younger photos, no resemblance to me, but still, back to the McBride photos and there it is. If I had a beard, we'd be like brothers. We look at each other and I start the car, driving up to the rental cottage while Niall jabbers at me that Anna must know that I and Robert were lookalikes.

'Well I don't look like Jim Brown though, do I?' I challenge him, as we walk into the house.

He thinks for a moment.

'Right, what about this. Someone's husband, who wants you dead, comes up here and mistakes the Aberdonian for you, chases him and kills him. Realises from the papers it's not you, comes back up but Broony sees him and the same thing happens. The wee guy dies trying to save you.' He holds his hands open and waits for my opinions on his theory.

'Nah. I get the mistaken identity as a possibility, but Jim Brown never owed me anything, and the last time before we met at that party I had thumped him for calling me a cunt. Not likely that he was defending me with his life.'

Niall nods. What he doesn't know is that I have more to consider than non-existent angry husbands, but I'll leave that be for the moment and listen to his theories.

'OK, what if it is a serial killer and you are the target, just these two clowns got in the way? Maybe Broony was just practice for him or something. Is that not how they work?'

'How the fuck should I know? Look Niall, the police think it's definitely the same guy as this Edinburgh murder, all the guts taken out and whatever the lunatic does. That's not an angry husband or someone I've casually pissed off, it's fucking Jack the Ripper.'

While it was initially exciting that we'd struck on something, I'm now realising that I'm in the Highlands with no more weapons than a kitchen knife and quite possibly there's a savage psychopath out there waiting to kill me. From Niall's expression, it's likely that he's figured out the perilous situation at the same time.

'We need police protection Adam, this is not right. What if the guy is coming back, or still here?' The colour has drained from his face and I'm not surprised. Even in my old line of work, being told that a serial killer is looking for me is not ideal.

'Look, the cops are driving up and down here every half hour. There's nothing to worry about unless they go, in which case we can tell them what we think.' I say this to comfort Niall, but in reality I'm not going anywhere near the cops. I've covered my tracks as well as anyone could with my past dealings, but a determined police investigation could still quite possibly uncover someone who would talk, maybe even had evidence or corroboration, and that would be me in jail, so no, there would be no police called in by me.

Niall tries to persuade me to call them, but I ignore him until his persistence, borne quite rightly of fear, wears me down.

I turn to him.

'Niall, I'm not in a position to have police involvement in my life.' There it is, simple as that. Let's see how he takes it.

After a long moment, he shakes his head. 'Fucking knew it.' He says, looking at me and for once completely serious.

I give him a brief and necessarily redacted version of my recently-terminated criminal career, then leave him to his thoughts and walk out into the garden for some much needed fresh air. When I get back in, Niall says that he needs to get back to see how the guys are doing and refuses a lift. To check if he's still more or less OK, I ask him to meet me in the pub at seven and he nods, slight wan smile too.

I guess he's pissed off at me, but there's nothing I can do, maybe I shouldn't have told him even the small amount that I did. The rest of the afternoon I spend figuring out what my options are, given that the cops will have to be told if I leave the area. I could go to Inverannan, but if someone is after me, I couldn't cope with another fucking rammy at that place and the anonymity of London, plus the access to weaponry is getting more attractive by the minute. Even an overnight there and then a flight to Australia or somewhere might be good, put some distance between me and whatever might be hunting me. I mull over this and a few alternatives, wondering what my old mentor, Sir Mathieson Allanton would do, with his military skills and the experience of running a criminal organisation for fifty years or so behind him. I fall asleep and am wakened by Anna, knocking on the door and waving. I remember what Niall told me about the school reunion and groan inwardly, before letting her in and following her upstairs.

We walk down to the pub about seven and Niall is already there, alone, but there's a few in the bar at the other side. He holds out his hand and says 'Niall McRae'. I shake his hand and tell him my name, so I guess despite my history, we're still pals. Smiling at Anna's puzzled stare, I walk to the bar, leaving her to enquire of Niall what the hell just happened.

Handing five twenty-pound notes to Scottie at the bar, I get a round in and give him the usual instructions plus a twenty tip for waiter service. I'm detecting stares and a little antipathy from a group of younger laddies but I ignore them, which is easy as we're sat in what is more or less an alcove to the left-hand side of the bar. Anna asks what's up and Niall spends five minutes filling her in with our theories before he gets to the Robert McBride issue and stops to permit me to elaborate, which I'm thinking might be tricky.

'OK, what is then? If you are the target, why are two other men dead?' She's whispering, but in a slightly hissy manner which suggests that I need to word things sensitively, as much as I am able to.

'It's possible that Broony was somehow intervening – maybe. He could have seen the murderer and tried to stop him, god knows.' Anna seems about to say something, but stops.

'There's another thing.' Niall thankfully chips back in.

'We've had a look at the press photos of Robert McBride. We think the killer may have mistaken him for Adam. Without the beard, there's a bit of a resemblance.'

Anna looks at Niall, then me.

'You two can just fuck off.' With that, she leaves and we have a moment where neither of us knows what to do, but we leave our drinks and follow her.

She's sitting, head looking down, at the bench beside the beech tree and ignoring our approach. We sit on either side of her, waiting to see if she's willing to talk to us or just rightly pissed off.

After a few long awkward moments, Anna starts but doesn't look up.

'I lied to you about how I met Robert. The first time I looked at him, I thought it was you, I really did. Went up to him and everything, just that when I got close, I realised it wasn't. He was smaller than you, different hair

168

and that. I backed off and went to sit with my friends, but one of his pals had noticed what I'd done, so Robert came over and asked if I was OK.'

Now she looks at me and there are tears and I feel like I've caused this, because I almost certainly have. Tears are dripping down her face and intermittently falling onto the concrete plinth of the bench, but she can talk without cracking.

'So, we talked and drank and he was, nice, and genuine and seemed a bit like you, only without the fucking baggage or whatever you always have. He asked me out, called the next day and it went from there, right until he showed me that he was even worse than you, if there is such a thing.'

Niall correctly intuits that this is very much a personal matter and walks back into the bar. Anna and I spend the next twenty minutes talking, well, me explaining and apologising and her trying to find out what was the matter with me. We agree to talk again the next day, and are interrupted by her mum, stopping in her ancient diesel Volvo after seeing us and offering Anna a lift. As usual all I get is an icy stare from Mrs Berkmann, but at least Anna has a safe trip home and I can get back inside and get on with getting drunk.

I watch the car rumble off, burning oil as it smokes itself up the hill. There's noise from inside, so I guess the football has started on TV but when I open the door, it looks like the end of my hopes for a peaceful evening. The group of lads are now standing at our table, giving loud and heart-felt abuse to Niall, who is standing nose to nose with one of them and in the process of telling them to join him outside. When they see me, they back off a little, but Broony's pal, Nero or something is his nickname, appears to be full of liquid courage and tells us and rest of his crew to get ourselves into the back car park.

Niall, the Mharisaig young team and I leave the pub and walk collectively round the back of the pub into the gravelled parking area, where traditionally there is freedom for us locals to batter each other to inbred pulps, unseen.

This Nero guy, a stocky red-haired specimen of Highland youth, is clearly full of lager and testosterone, so bunches his fists and comes straight at me.

He misses with his first haymaker, turns a drunken full circle and comes in again, nearly getting me with a left. I move backwards and away from each, but it looks like he's going to rush me so I jab with my left and crunch him with a direct right, too fast for him to see it coming, straight into the side of his mouth. It feels like I break his jaw and maybe some teeth. He goes straight down like a sack of tatties and I turn to see Niall grappling with two of them, and two others are standing jiggling nervously and probably wishing that they hadn't followed Nero. They both back away but don't leave, so I help Niall by shifting his two assailants with carefully-aimed short punches. Neither is badly hurt, so they get up and try to have a go at me, but a few moments later they are lying beside Nero. Niall runs at the other two and boots their arses as they run away, so well done him.

We head back inside and Niall goes to the bathroom to wash his face. I watch as Davie McDonald and auld Chick accept what looks like ten-pound notes from the barman, who then brings us over two fresh pints. The old boys raise a glass to me from their seated position at the bar and I raise mine back to them, no doubt as betting men this was not their first pugilistic gamble. I watch as Scottie and his two pals rewind the CCTV for a re-run of the action, no doubt there will be time for them to see it again before the football starts.

Ally Quinn, Gangster

Ally Quinn hadn't felt this good in years, not since his kids were wee. He had chucked the rigs and went back into business with his brother, Simmy and their pals, who welcomed back the prodigal with open arms and said it was exactly what they needed. It had been an easy reunion, the lost brother returning, bringing all the families together again too. Ally's daughters were delighted that their dad could again fund their lifestyle, flats and cars. Parties started up again, Ally and Simmy and the others with grandkids now but they were still hard men, just some were balder, fatter, and all were a fair bit older than their first surge into the criminal underbelly in the northeast of Scotland. Rhonda came along to all the parties too, the other wives and girlfriends knew that she'd had a *bit of a breakdown* but not the details and that she was on tablets for depression and anxiety, which they all knew lots about. They chatted to her and she sat with them, glazed and quieter, much less the centre of attention than the role she once used to relish. Still, her daughters and their children kept her busy and they stayed closer now too, in houses that Ally and Simmy had sorted out for them.

Ally kept busy too, he was away almost as much as when he was on the rigs, often for two or three days, which Rhonda didn't mind at all. She watched the grandkids, watched the TV, watched from the window onto the cul-de-sac to the outside world which she had withdrawn from since her husband had damn near killed her. She had flashbacks, panic attacks about Josh and what Ally did to him, then what he did to her. The meds helped but Rhonda knew she wasn't right, she was sad and scared inside and it didn't seem like it would end. She knew that Ally now went with other women, drank and took drugs and battered people and knew that she'd get worse, if she told the cops or her daughters what had happened. Often, before that night, she had wished that the old Ally would return, but be careful what you wish for, Rhonda thought to herself. He was the old Ally, but crueller now, reactive and dominant, his behaviour unpredictable. He could go into these monstrous rages if he was contradicted or disobeyed, so she didn't, not any more.

Ally, on the other hand, was having the gangster equivalent of an Indian summer. Having sorted out his domestic problems, he focused on his career and did so with a combination of experience, ambition and drug-fuelled excessive violence. Now with their business HQ in a unit outside the city, Ally was personally spearheading a new initiative, one that would make damn sure that no lesser mortals fucked with them.

Simmy, a man of girth, baldness, tattoos and heavy muscle was in the business unit, watching his older brother speak to three of their local distributors to determine which of them was responsible for the unsanctioned cutting of their product. He had a bad feeling about Ally, as his intake of cocaine was increasing at a worrying pace, and him with that heart thing.

'So, lads, how are you doing?' Ally smiled and clapped them on the back, all pals together.

'Aye fine boss, no bad.' They chimed, almost as one. Ally ushered them towards the corner of the room, him facing inwards and them trapped.

'So, is business good? You making a decent score, eh?' Again, positive responses were forthcoming.

Ally took out a small chromed hatchet from his inside pocket and leant with it on the wall, causing the three young men to try and sidle away from it.

173

'So, which of you have been cutting my gear? If you tell me, you're fine. If you don't, it means that I can't trust any of you, so I will fucking tear into the three of you, right now. Talk.'

He looked closely at each in turn and they all seemed about to piss themselves with fear. One of them stared at the skinniest specimen and looked like he was urging him to confess, which he did.

'I did it, just a wee bit. I'm sorry boss. It'll not happen again, promise. I'll get you money, make up for it, honest.' The lad, about 25 years old he guessed, reminded Ally of his youngest daughter's ex-husband, whom he especially disliked.

'It's OK lad, we all make mistakes, we just need to be honest when we do, and then I know that you are someone that I can trust.' Ally smiled at them again and ruffled the skinny fellow's hair, gesturing for them to go.

'Now, get back out there and make me some money – and you need to get extra to make up for this, remember.' As the lad turned and nodded to give his agreement, Ally leapt at him and sank the hatchet deeply into his forehead, spraying blood over himself and the entire area.

'Fuck sake Ally!' Simmy yelled at him.

The two others tried to get out through the locked door, but when Ally heaved the hatchet out, he started taking swings at them too. Their screams filled the room as Simmy considered standing in his brother's way, but felt that he was not quite man enough to risk that approach. A few minutes later, two badly cut dealers and one dealer who cut badly were dying on the floor.

Ally stood, crimson from fingertip to face with the blood of his employees. Simmy prised the hatchet from his fingers, and unlocked the door to the shocked faces of the rest of the crew.

'You two - get Ally cleaned up, then take him to the flat, now!' He instructed. 'The rest of you, get in here and give me a hand, for fuck sake.'

It took them all of three hours to figure what to do, then carry out their cleaning work. The one with the forehead wound was dead. Nothing could be done about that, so he was bagged and taken to be buried in waste ground about an hour west of the city. The two others were left outside the Royal Infirmary after a bit of elementary first aid from Simmy. He couldn't be sure that, if they lived, they wouldn't inform on them, but he did wonder that if they weren't shit scared of Ally by now, he was a poor judge of men.

That story became an urban horror story for all time in the city, the survivors keeping quiet to the cops for the sake of their lives, but telling pals why they were off to England and a new life with less pyschos. The following days were pivotal for the Quinn gang, off the back of Ally's hatchet event. Two groups of minor competitors caved in and the main suppliers allowed the Quinn's to take their territory, although Simmy worried that too much was happening too quickly, and that it was based on the abilities of his unstable, coke-fuelled older sibling. Still, the money was awesome and two leagues up from where they had been, before Ally waded back in.

Simmy had held a couple of long talks with his brother, man to man, and that seemed to help with his drug intake. The others in their team were less sure but calmed down as the days and weeks rolled past with no further major incidents, and just the positive increase in business and money to concentrate on. One of them, Sal

175

McCormick, chucked it completely and went off to stay in Blackpool, saying that he'd never sleep right again after the hatchet thing, and they let him go. This was not a business for men that worry about blood. He was replaced by a new guy, Tam Houghton, recommended by a pal of Simmy's and he was a gem, a great organiser and a hard worker who knew how to make the money come in.

During this time, as the Quinn gang were rising, the oldest brother had a side agenda which the others were aware of, but chose to ignore. Ally was fixated on Robert McBride, unable to forget or forgive, and hiring men to look for him. After two weeks solid searching, they reported back to Ally that they'd tracked McBride through his old oil industry employer, and that he had definitely left his apartment, owing rent but the landlord didn't know where he'd gone. From their contacts in the area, they figured that McBride may also be the figure on police-circulated photos mugging a pensioner, although there was no shortage of suspects who roughly fitted the bill for that one.

It was another week, during which Ally persevered with the limitations on his cocaine consumption, before he heard anything positive back from the two investigators. They had gained access to a guy in the Housing service who gave them the lead they needed, that McBride had stayed in a scatter flat in the city. That contact helped them, for a significant recompense, by calling friends in a few other local authorities, and eventually, Robert McBride was traced to a short stay in Homeless accommodation in Inverness, not long after the mugging. They concluded that he'd been tipped off about the potential threat to him from Ally Quinn, maybe even knew who had sent the photos and letter. There, the trail went cold for a time, until they visited the Homeless flats in Inverness and made contact with another council officer there, who enticed by a thick envelope of used twenty-pound notes, gave them the assistance they needed.

An unopened letter was found in the back office of the Homeless unit, one which offered Robert McBride a job with a forestry contractor, complete with contact details for their base near a place called Mharisaig. Robert must have accepted the job and left before the letter arrived, so the practice in the office was to retain mail for one year before shredding it and thus, the investigators started to close in on Rab the Tab.

After Nero

My first reaction on waking up is that I have little memory of the latter part of the evening and a dull ache in both sets of knuckles. It takes a few minutes to piece together my movements and I run through it as best I can, with a few scenes missing due to the whisky, reminded to me by the residual taste in my charred mouth. The talk with Anna, the car park rammy, the football, the pub mobbed with people later and the old guys sitting with us and telling tales, the lock-in, the vague image of the barman giving us a lift here and quite possibly Niall might be on the downstairs sofa. I go into the bathroom and I'm sick, first time in ages and wish I'd never left the cottage yesterday at all. A glance over the stairs shows me Niall's sock-covered feet protruding from the lounge sofa, so I pad past the lounge, closing the door on him as I go. Fifteen minutes later I'm empty but feeling much better after the purge, a large glass of Irn Bru and the duo of painkillers, Ibuprofen and Paracetamol, that proud Scottish weekend morning tradition.

The sight of two police vehicles zipping past my kitchen window tells me that the investigation is ongoing and I wish that they, the entire situation, and indeed the whole world, would just fuck off and leave me alone. I sit with my coffee and check the time, 10.30 am and I haven't heard a sheep, cow, alpaca or whatever other ungodly beasts bleats usually break my sleep. I finish my coffee and get a shower, put on my shorts and head out for a restorative run, five miles I reckon but it takes me more than ninety minutes so probably double that before I pound back uphill to arrive back at my rented cottage. I look in the lounge and Niall's feet haven't budged but I can hear his light snoring so he's still with us. Brunch next, toast and eggs and I feel great, the sweating got rid of the booze and I cast my mind back to the old guys' patter last night.

Auld Chick and Davie McDonald had been joined by three others, their regular drinking gang for the past fifty years and god knows how, they all look hale and hearty for it. They came over for a blether, as when the bar gets busy they have to migrate from their favourite stools to let the orders flow, so Niall asked them to sit with us and give us their patter. You'd never think it when you are young, but the old guys are the funniest. A lifetime of slagging each other, heard everything before so they know what is good and what is not, it was one of the best nights ever. We bought them drinks, well I did, and they told stories. One stood out, as my dad was part of it.

These guys were all way too young to have fought in the Second War, but they did national service all over, Hong Kong, Germany, up north near here and a few others. Scrapes were told, near-deaths like when McDonald fell off the walkway to his ship and nearly drowned between the harbour wall and hull, fished out by pals just in time or he'd not be in and apparently neither would I. Chick told me about what McDonald did to save my dad from choking when he was a wee boy. McDonald did the thumping and squashing that they didn't know then was the Heimlich Manoeuvre, but it was. My dad never forgot this and dropped a bottle of malt in for him every New Year, which by god nearly made me cry, and I don't cry easily. In that moment, full of drink, I missed my parents more than I could bear, and was glad when Chick told us another story and distracted me.

He told us about the time when they were teenagers and there was a newspaper frenzy about the Loch Ness Monster, over at Drumnadrochit the locals were making a fortune from tourists and Nessie hunters. These bold Mharisaig lads wanted to come up with a plan to attract tourists here too, would make their fortunes selling crap to visitors, along with supplies and accommodation. Chick's parents at that time owned a motel, long-gone now, at the main road beside the village.

I had asked Chick what they came up with and in the gap, the whole pub fell silent. When he said *"Mharisaig Mhorag"*, the whole place erupted in laughter and I thought Niall was going to die laughing. For some reason, this old tale had never made it to us before, so Chick kept it going, telling us how they tried to take photos with his old Box Brownie of Davie's childhood rocking horse draped in green curtains, up at the wee lochan above the village and how they nearly froze in the icy water and the poor wooden horse sank forever in the peaty water, along with Eric's shoes and Davie's half-hunter pocket watch. We collapsed when Chick told us about trying to persuade The Oban Times editor to run the story by getting him roaring drunk in Fort William, but he was so pissed he forgot completely the first time, so they had to get him less drunk the second time.

Eventually, the story was run and picked up by a slice of the national media, but didn't last and only a few gullible souls fell for it, so Chick was left with boxes of ceramic Morags and tartan memorabilia which still gather dust in his garage. The barman brings over his own *Mharisaig Mhorag* from the collection of guff on shelves behind him and it's passed around the pub like a precious idol, causing more laughter to all who see it. Fucking brilliant, we thought.

After that and more, the barman kept the place open until people left, or were carried out and then he very helpfully drove a number of us home in his clapped out people carrier. I think Niall was sick outside in the garden and we may have sat out there, and a quick look shows me that we did. An almost empty bottle of wine sits on the garden table and a pat of vomit decorates the flower border area. I find the garden hose and rinse the area and water the untended flowers, then cut the grass which I had a vague memory of being asked to do by the lady from St Andrews when she extended my let. Anna comes over and we make lunch, then Niall is resurrected when he smells food, although his pallor suggests that today might not be a good day for him.

'So, did you have a good night?' She smiles at Niall.

He belches loudly and Anna makes a face. No wonder Liz chucked him out.

'Liz phoned this morning, apparently you two were fighting with the young lads behind the pub.' She gives me and Niall a quick check, Niall is unmarked apart from a graze on his cheek and my only traces are my swollen knuckles. Anna snorts.

'So what happened?'

Niall finishes chewing some toast.

'Well, while you two were blethering outside the pub, they started to give me some shit about Jim Brown, that we were talking to him that night and then he gets killed, like we were the fucking murderers, so I told them to get a grip. Yon Nero twat starts on with something else and I told him to get to fuck, and then Adam came back in. We end up in the car park and your man knocks Nero out and I've got two of them trying to get me to the ground. Adam skelps them too and the others ran away.

Not much else to tell. Heard from someone in the pub later that Nero is away getting his jaw wired up.'

'So what was it that made him start the fight?' Anna asks.

'Fuck knows. He's got a temper and he had a drink in him, so maybe it was just that.'

I'm starting to wonder about this. At the time I just assumed that they were drunken Mharisaig laddies looking for a scrap about their pal, but maybe there's more. If Nero had a grudge, or something else, something relevant, I need to talk to him.

'Did he say anything else before I got into the pub? It doesn't seem enough to get him in that rage. He was dead set for taking us on, even when I told him to settle down.'

Niall shakes his head. 'Honestly, I don't know. The five of them were talking all at once, so I didn't catch everything. It was definitely about Jim Brown though, I just thought whatever they were on about, they thought you were to blame.'

I definitely need to talk about this Nero, or one of the others, so Niall gets dressed and Anna goes back to her mum's. They are going to visit another relative in Mharisaig in the afternoon. I drive us down to where, according to Niall, Nero lives, but there's no-one home or he's hiding, so we move onto the next on the list. Two houses later, a scared-as-shit Callum McAndrew peers at us from behind his security-chained door and two puffy, bruised eyes.

'Callum, we want to talk to you. Let us in.'

'Fuck off, you put Nero in hospital ya bastard'

Niall is trying to persuade Callum to unchain the door when I boot it in, taking the chain off its wee catch and propelling the reluctant youth inside and onto the hall floor. I enter, Niall looks around in amazement and checking in case anyone is watching. Callum is rather dazed, so I pick him up by his hair and lead him into the kitchen.

'Niall, can you check if anyone else is in the house, please.'

My pal, looking almost as dazed as Callum, closes the damaged door and trots upstairs for the aforementioned check.

I sit across from Callum in the manky kitchen and sigh. He's fighting back tears and looks fit to shit. Taking advantage of Niall's absence, I slip neatly back into my old persona.

'What the fuck was that about last night son? Tell me what you know now and I'll be on my way. Give me any shite, and I will break every one of your teeth, right now.' I'm leaning right into him, and like always, I can smell the fear. He starts as if to lie and I shake my head before even a sentence can be uttered. He stops any attempt at talking nonsense and recommences, the truth this time, I think.

'It was Nero. His uncle is in the polis. Heard him talking to his da about wee Broony, said he'd been gutted like a fucking fish and everything.' Callum is crying freely now and we are joined by Niall, who shakes his head to confirm that we are alone in the hovel.

'What else did he say Callum?'

'He said that they were looking at a serial killer, like it says in the news. Says that they are you ken, following lines of enquiry.'

I lean back.

'That's all fine Callum, but you don't start fights for what everyone knows already. Keep going. I've not got all day.'

'He said that you'd been interviewed twice and had an alibi, but they didn't believe you, think you are involved.' He sniffs in the dripping blood from his nose, which caught part of the force of the door when I opened it.

'Nero told us that his uncle reckons it was you, and your alibis are false, or it was someone else.'

I turn to Niall. 'Solid police work that. It was me, or someone else. These guys are fucking genius. Have you got anything to add before I decide on your teeth, Callum?'

'Aye. Nero's uncle says that you had, ye ken, motives. McBride was trying to get back with your girlfriend and Broony, well you never liked him, broke his fucking nose for nothing. They are trying to see if you're connected to the guy that got killed last year too, the one in Embra.'

I sigh at the idiocy around me. At least Callum has given me something of an insight on the state of play with Police Scotland, and possibly why they haven't offered me protection against serial killers. I need to get out of here.

'Look, Callum, even though I couldn't give a fuck what you or your shit-for-brains pals think, here it is. I didn't kill McBride, Broony, or the guy in Edinburgh. I'm not going to break your teeth, but neither am I going to put up with anyone fucking with me or Niall in our pub.'

I take his hand softly, turn it over and feel it shaking. A quick snap and I've broken his index finger, covering his mouth with my other hand to suppress the squeal.

'Now remember this the next time you decide to talk about me behind my back. And, if you tell anyone how this happened, I will be back for your teeth. OK?'

He nods, tears running down his face and mixing with the blood from his nose. I stand and head for the door. Niall looks at me as I pass and turns to Callum.

'And clear this place up, it's a fucking midden.'

The Watcher

He had been observing Adam Darnow, on and off for days and weeks, from close and from afar.

At first, when he started this project, there had been excellent cover for him outside the cottage where Darnow stayed, and none could overlook him. Each night, he'd watched from the undergrowth, tempting himself to go inside the house, to kill Darnow the way he so badly wanted to. Often, Anna Berkmann would be there and sometimes Niall McRae, hardly anyone else. Each night, when it looked like his prey was tucked up in bed sleeping, he left off his surveillance and made for his accommodation.

His surveillance, the long nights, the discomfort and the delays were all salved by the memory of the killing in Edinburgh, how it was perfection itself. The grotesque scene which had awaited the police was a masterpiece to him, the impeccable creation of his genius. He reminded himself that planning was an integral part of the operation, working day after day to eradicate chance and then to take action, the mechanism moving perfectly, ticking along with silent efficiency. The other killing, down south, it was worthwhile but hollow, and the one in Glasgow was hardly any better. Still, he remembered both fondly and was glad he'd done them, but there was no feeling of satisfaction, he needed time and his knife for that. At least it had made him understand what worked for him, and what did not. What he did to Jim Brown, now that was closer to what he needed.

He was confused though, about the first one here in Mharisaig and did not know if it had happened in a dream, for he was confused at times, more so when he missed a dose of his medication. Nonetheless, it didn't change anything, he still had to kill Adam Darnow for what he'd done and it had to be done at the point of his knife, ideally with his particular method.

This venture here in Mharisaig could perhaps not, as yet, be considered successful. His target was a lucky man indeed, this Adam Darnow. He supposed that some of us are luckier than others, just an inherent trait, perhaps. Sometimes though, he surmised, one's luck might appear life-long but all too sudden run out, struck perhaps by disease, a serious illness, or in this case, his razor-sharp twelve-inch stainless steel blade. He could feel the tension rising in him when he thought of his mistakes.

Jim Brown had got in his way, and he blundered by killing him by ritual. He had carved Brown out with his knife, giving him exquisite yet temporary satiety for his urge to kill Darnow, but still, he regretted it afterwards as it showed the police that it was him, here in Mharisaig. Even the thought that he'd failed on that front made him tense, another failure in his life sneering at him, goading him to make sure that he didn't get caught, didn't fail before he could leave this place and take a break, rest for a month perhaps. After that time, he'd decide whether or not to continue with the next phase of this vengeful segment of his life or to move on, perhaps.

After Brown, his monitoring of the rented holiday cottage had to be intermittent, until the police had completed their searching of the area, and they were indeed thorough. Eventually though, the place was left with just police tape and notices, so he could get back on track and complete his mission to kill Adam Darnow. On the night that he had killed Brown, he had watched the target, with Niall and Anna, all going together to the village pub. He followed them there, waited until they had left and followed them back uphill, by which time

187

the anticipation made him fit to burst. He knew that Adam Darnow was not alone inside, but had to get into the cottage, even if just to tease himself, smell the place, the scent of his quarry. He was about to try and pick the lock when he became aware that he was not alone, and that Jim Brown of Mharisaig thought himself man enough to stand before him.

He thought about just chasing the foolish boy away, for his identity was well covered and he had not yet left any evidence for the police to follow. Then the voice came, pleading and pathetic, whining and terrified. Then his bloodlust for this pointless individual could not be stopped, even if it meant a pursuit into the moonlit forest towards where Robert McBride had died. So he ran, easily following the inebriated youth uphill, through the moss-covered and heavy-tyre-pitted route along the woodland path until his victim stopped, the breath coming hard through his lungs, maybe harder than it should for one his age.

He'd found him in the churchyard, that was the best thing, a wonderfully macabre place to kill, which he'd bear in mind for other projects. Brown had tried to run past him, but being drunk, he was easy to catch. The same controlled fury came on him then, same as Edinburgh, and his artistry with a sharp knife was perhaps even more beautiful than then, although the satisfaction at an accidental kill was nowhere near so great.

After that day, he backed away again from the project, knowing that the police would be back and that even they would quickly connect his handiwork with that of Edinburgh. He stayed away from watching the cottage for a time, just listening to media responses and monitoring police band radio, to give him some feeling of the live action as the cars came and went.

He enjoyed his stays in Mharisaig, it became almost like a time-limited game with live murders and police, and he was controlling the participants. The objective now was to complete the mission and get away with it, ideally leaving no clues, just like he managed to do in Edinburgh. He felt a deep glow of satisfaction every time he heard in the news about that, about how the police were trying hard but even now, had no leads. He was definitely up one-nil there, actually five-nil counting the others and the two in Mharisaig, and would soon be up another, when Adam Darnow finally succumbed to his blades.

The rented cottage where Darnow stayed was constantly passed by the police, their forensics, the TV people, the newspaper people and some ghouls who attend such a spectacle, but he was good at waiting. Life had taught him that there was a time to be patient and a time to take action. There were too many risks in being out and about with his knife and with his other tools, but the game continued. He decided that Adam Darnow may be worth toying with in the meantime, so he composed a message to a roving reporter whom he recognised on TV. He knew well how to use a disposable email account and hide his IP, so off it went, a tiny particle of mischief to make up for the ennui of delay.

Pay the Man

The day after our chat with young Callum, I drive to Fort William to collect the payment for Allan Douglas and his builders. Before I leave, I check the date and note that I have two more days left at the rental house, so back home to my newly refurbished home I must go, albeit reluctantly.

The roads are quiet, so I let my speed go way faster than the limit, almost losing control and skidding off the road on a bend ten miles outside Mharisaig. I slow down after that, coincidentally passing a couple of speed cameras which would have got me if I hadn't cooled the driving down. When I arrive, the town, its season getting into full flow, is a mix of brightly clad walkers and the less prominently-dressed locals going about their business in the spring drizzle. It seems a lifetime ago when I and my pals would visit here, some Friday nights, the lure of some social event overcoming the fear of getting into a fight, coming to the hub for a drink and some excitement, such as it was. Back then, it all depended on getting a lift home, of course, so often we were packed into some crappy Corsa or something, four in the back seat and maybe even one in the boot if there was space.

Right now though, I'm wearing the only coat I have with me to protect me from the rain, and the rest of what I have in Mharisaig is winter clothing, so I decide to use the luxury of actual shops to sort out my interim wardrobe for spring. After a brief and half-hearted clothes shop, I then manage to persuade the guy in a furniture charity shop to prioritise me a few items for the cottage, to tide me over until I can order something new. I pick an eclectic selection of the available furniture, pay him £800 for the lot and, my cash reserves needing to be replenished, set off for the bank.

After I get the cheque for Allan Douglas and a load of pre-ordered cash, I realise that time has passed quickly and that I need to get back. A quick stop at the supermarket and then off I go back to my own private hell that is Mharisaig. When I get to the cottage, Allan Douglas is standing in the front garden pointing out something on the roof to Niall, who is nodding like he knows what he's being told, although I bet he doesn't.

'Afternoon gents'. I shake their hands and Allan repeats his pointing at the roof gesture.

'That took a bit of work to get right, double dormers are always a bit fiddly. The lads did a neat job with the lead work though - look at how straight the finish is?'

Allan is clearly a man who takes pride in his work, and we are taken inside for the extended highlights of the refurbishment. This is fine for ten minutes but after an explanation of the benefits of this particular type of combi boiler, I just want Allan to take the payment and go away.

'I'd better sort you out, Allan.' I tell him, reaching inside my jacket and handing him the cheque and five grand in cash. He takes it and looks up at me, puzzled. I tell him that it's a bonus for doing the work quickly and at short notice.

'No problem. Suited us too, we needed a gap filled, and this was perfect. Thanks.' He's a strange lad right enough, not a smiler and seems a bit intense. Still, top builder and job done here. After another five minutes of herding him towards the door, we say cheerio and Allan zips off in a battered works van. Niall turns to me.

'I had him for an hour before you arrived, by the way. Explained in fucking great detail how the cottage roof structure works, which was brilliant, honestly.'

'Was it as good as the boiler story?'

He shakes his head. 'No, that was the best bit, a tale we can recount at the pub if everyone needs cheering up.' I pat him on the back and we go inside to see what else needs to be done. The paintwork is almost complete, so Niall will focus the Mharisaig building squad on this for the rest of the day and tomorrow.

'I need to get out of the rental Niall, two days left mate. This means that I will need to get back in here, unfortunately'.

He looks at me with a resigned expression, possibly waiting for me to make him an offer to continue to crash here. I leave him wondering, although if he was stuck he could stay but I'm not inviting that.

Niall wanders outside to ask the guys to finish up the last of the gardening and come inside for a minute. I have a quick chat with them and tell them that I will be buying the drinks tomorrow night, after they finish their project, so god help me I've arranged another drinking session. I drive back up to the rental and fall asleep on the sofa until awakened by a knocking right beside me and Anna, looking in from the gloomy evening shower. I unlock the door and she joins me inside, shaking her hair to dry it and sprinkle me.

'My mother just gave me a lecture about you.' She informs me, matter of fact.

'Is she protective of your reputation?'

She looks distrustfully at me. 'Probably, but I think the recent events are also causing her more than a little concern. She thinks that you may well be responsible for mass murder, ritual and/or serial killing and that I am insane for even speaking to you, let alone having, as she called it, *relationships* with you.' I nod and don't know what to say.

'She has also threatened to chuck me out if I keep seeing you, but I think it may just have been said in the heat of the moment. She used to threaten that all the time when I was younger, although sometimes that was about you as well.'

Anna sits beside me at the same moment as the clouds, for the first time in a while, part to let a heavenly glance of spring sunlight shine onto her face. Her hair, dark and still wet from her short walk here, plays on her shoulder and not for the first time, I think I love her.

It's night time when we leave the cottage, I can't hack the pub today after all the hassle with that moron Nero and the rest of them, so we drive the fifteen miles or so to a restaurant at the coast, which is brilliant, then we stay the night. It's like a release from the suffocation of Mharisaig. Now, we are just the normal couple eating, drinking and taking an overnight in the Highlands, keeping to darker corners of the low-ceilinged bar in case someone recognises me. They don't, so we talk like it hadn't all happened, before me in London and McBride and the Mharisaig murders. We spend time reminding ourselves of all the things that happened at school, then Anna gives me more updates on where everyone is now and I even remember people I'd not given a thought to in years. In a moment when she's all talked out and having a drink, I ask her about the school reunion where Niall told me that I was the focus of conversation.

She looks at me and smiles, that beatific one she seems to have cultivated to get away with something, or seeking forgiveness.

'Yeah, I remember that evening distinctly. Tess was there, a few others, the boys had shuffled off to the bar to do shooters and talk pish about football or something. Michelle started it all. She and Tess seemed to have joined forces to get over you quite successfully. They gave us all the dirt too, your Glasgow Uni stuff and all the rumours. I was able to fill in some blanks for them, probably made it worse for you. Sorry and all that.' That smile.

'What happened at Inverannan?'

She stops me in my tracks with this one. How the fuck does anyone outside the Portfolio know anything about that? Does she mean me, the narcotics or what? Maybe Gillian, is it that?

'What do you mean?' I try to look puzzled but she laughs at me.

'It was one of the chats at the reunion. You ended up chucking the journalism after that piece up at Inverannan, you remember you told me about it before you went? Well, we both know that you changed after that. So, I guess when I told the others, we just wondered what went on.'

She leaves it there and I am starting to wonder if she is wearing a wire, then I remember that I had inadvertently but comprehensively checked that in the bedroom before we came down for dinner. How much to tell, I wonder.

'So, what were the conspiracy theories at the reunion? I'll tell you if you are hot or cold.'

She laughs, 'OK, I think the girls whittled it down to three options.' A big slurp of her pint of lager goes down. 'First, that you stole money or a painting from Inverannan, which you then sold in London and that set you up there.'

I look at her, straight in her beautiful, pallid blue eyes. 'Cold.'

'OK. The other one was that you met someone up there, a woman, who took you on as what, an escort, you know, a male prostitute for herself and that all the London stuff and money came from her.' Now it's my turn to laugh.

'Cold, very cold.' I tell her.

'Fair enough, I thought that was unlikely too, you're not that good.' Aye right, I think.

'The last one was that you got mixed up with some unsavoury characters up there and ended up working with them, got a job as a hitman for them.' She tells me this in a more serious voice than the other two and looks at me with a more direct gaze, which I meet.

'Cold as fuck.' I tell her, and she collapses in drunken laughter, and I join with her the tiniest moment later.

West End Woman

We miss breakfast and drive back from the hotel, via a sunny walk at the loch just two miles north of Mharisaig. We'd been there as kids, but not often, as it was dangerous for swimming and, despite the stunning views, held little of interest for bored Highland teenagers. Its main claim to fame was the fishing, which my father took me to occasionally without much success or indeed enjoyment. Anna tells me that her dad had fished there too, took their wee boat up on a trailer some Saturdays when he wasn't working. She goes quiet and I remind myself that she is still hurting from all that, and perhaps all this shit in Mharisaig wasn't helping. It is probably surprising that she hasn't run away already.

I hold her tight as we stand looking at the mountains to the west, the snow still visible on some parts and it is picture perfect, like we are right in this moment. We kiss, standing on a chilly spring morning under Scottish skies, feeling the cold northerly wind whip around us but it doesn't matter. I could love Anna forever, stay like this for a hundred years. Inevitably, the sun goes behind a cloud and we take shelter from the start of a shower back in the car, and reluctantly set off for the final leg to Mharisaig. I drop her off at her mum's and swing the car back around and down to the village to get some signal and see what's occurring in the rest of the world. I have a few documents to sign, which I do without even reading them, and glance through a couple of emails which I reply to. Not for the first time, I think about pointing my car towards the south road and leaving this shit-show behind me, but I know the cops would take that badly, and with a profound sense of resignation, go back to the rental cottage.

My packing for the imminent return home doesn't take too long, I bin a couple of things that I don't need and look out everything else that needs to be laundered, as my parents' cottage does not yet have those facilities. The rest of my time is spent loafing around, shifting things between washing machine and drier until evening comes around and I have enough clean clothes to last me a while. I get sorted out and head out to meet Niall and the chaps in the pub, taking care to make sure no-one is watching or following and steering clear of the dense, overgrown bushes which border the other side of the single track road. I'm feeling jumpy, not my usual condition, and this is worsened as an unusually noisy car belts towards me and screeches to a halt.

A woman, clad in what might be considered bohemian dress and headgear emerges and approaches, hand out in welcome, which I ignore.

'I recognise you from the media.' She appraises me and I say nothing. 'Catherine Aston.'

She reaches inside her skirt pocket and offers me her card, which I take and it tells me that Ms Aston is an employee of a well-known and little-respected news outlet. I drop the card to the ground and walk away from her. I can hear her beseeching something in the background, but she is best ignored, so I do. A few minutes later, her car passes, stops a bit ahead and she gets out to try and collar me again.

'Mr Darnow, I can be of *great* assistance to you.'

'No, you can't.' I tell her and resume my walk by circumventing the rumbling vehicle which she gets back into and repeats her overtake, stop and get out tactic. I feel like breaking the car windows and threatening her, but remind myself that good behaviour and a low media profile is in my interest, as ever it was. She's persistent though, I'll give her that.

'So, what can you help me with, Ms Aston?'

'We would like to do a piece on this whole serial killer thing from your perspective, how it has disrupted your life, how it felt to discover the first body, all that. We'll pay well, especially if you can give us something juicy.' She's standing in my way and I get a better look at her and I now recognise her from my days in Glasgow University, she was a rising star of two years above me and I guess that since there, she'd shed her journalistic purity and took the cash offered to work for this fucking rag. I smile at her and her back at me.

'Well, I'm busy just now, but you could walk with me if you like?' She leaves her car, skewed and all but blocking the road and joins me for the downhill stroll to the pub, during which she tells me about how she'd like to interview me, write up the story from someone central to it.

'Am I central to this, Ms Aston?'

'We think so. Find the first body, pals with the second, interviewed by Police Scotland how many times? Lots of locals think you are involved and it looks like the authorities do too.'

I stop and look at her. 'I'm caught up in this, but there's no story, it's nothing to do with me. What you've just said, that's all there is, no real involvement other than living in the village and being the subject of gossip, which I can assure you is nothing but bullshit. You are wasting your time and money as I've no story to tell. So the answer is, respectfully, no thanks.' She stares at me, and gives me a little sideways knowing look, which is slightly unnerving.

I'm trying to read her, but she had a reputation as a damn sharp mind and these journos can be fickle and untrustworthy. I know that I would be, in her place.

'I remember you from Glasgow Uni, Mr Darnow. You were a bit of a minor celebrity for ten minutes when you got arrested for dealing. I'm sure we don't need to include that in our piece here though.

So it's her turn to be on the offensive as she sends out her little threat, but the incident is ancient history, and there wasn't even a formal charge never mind a conviction. I'm about to tell her to get to fuck when she senses this and starts again.

'It doesn't need to be a one-way street Mr Darnow. I have some information which you might find enlightening too, if you are curious about the wider situation. We have got details which I'll bet the police haven't shared with you, and I would be glad to do.'

I think about what young Callum told me about the Police view on my involvement and reckon it's worth finding out any other information, so tell her OK. I know that any involvement with rats like her is unlikely to end well, but I'm well used to acting innocent and don't think that she will present much of a challenge.

She starts back off uphill to car and turns. 'Tomorrow at 10 a.m., at your place up there?' I nod agreement and she stops again to look at me.

'I also remember that one of my pals fancied you. I can quite see why now.' With a tinkling laugh, off she goes, the multi-layered loon.

By the time I get to the pub, the lads have got fed up waiting for me and actually bought their first or possibly second drinks themselves. I'm in the mood now and after shoving a significant wedge of cash behind the bar, set out to catch up with them as best I can.

An hour later and Niall has resumed his smoking habit, which he gives up intermittently. We are outside the front of the bar and he's showing signs of relaxation after two large whiskies and three pints.

'Fucking Liz mate, mental.' Ah, bollocks, it's that time already, I think.

'What's she done now mate? Suing you for half of your estate and wealth?'

'She's welcome to that Adam, or twenty quid, whichever is highest. Nah, she's been on the phone wanting to talk.'

'About what? Last vibe that I got was not one of reconciliation.' He snorts.

'Her plan is to understand what went wrong in our relationship, and, as she says, learn from it in a mature and progressive manner.' A long pull on his cigarette ends in a coughing fit.

'That sounds like a worthwhile exercise mate. Every day is a learning day, after all.'

His spluttering isn't helped by the expletives which he's trying to answer me with, so it takes a drink of his beer to wash down the impotent rage and nicotine. Eventually, he composes himself and is all better after a loud burp.

'Aye, it's hard to argue with, but there's no way I'm doing it. We'll just talk about my fucking deficiencies, I will feel bad, she will feel better and at the end of the *process*, I will still be shite at relationships and Liz will have vindication that she can do better than me. Fuck that. I'm Scottish, I'm useless and I'm not fucking discussing it any further.' Each point is vehemently put, and hard to disagree with.

'Never mind mate. You just need to find someone with lower standards.'

'Fucking right.' He replies, missing the irony which matters not, and I pat his back reassuringly as we walk back into the bar.

I join in with lads drinking until I reach the point where I remember that a serial killer might be after me, then miss a few rounds unnoticed while the others escalate their intake. By eleven they are all long gone and I say my goodbyes, reassuring them that the money behind the bar is still there when I am gone. I take a moment to thank them for doing the work on the cottage and our camaraderie reaches its pinnacle. Before I leave, I ask Scottie for something and he meets me outside the back after I leave, handing me a two-pound hammer. I hand him a fifty to thank him, which he takes and tells me to watch myself.

The wind has dropped now and the stars illuminate my way back up, so my solitude apart, I'm not too nervous. If whoever is after me tries to jump me, I am moderately armed, sober enough to see him coming and not inherently an easy target for most. That said, I'm glad to get inside and lock up, checking every room and drawing the blinds and curtains before jamming chairs under the door handles back and front. I take the precaution of sleeping in the spare room, which in the reflection of the morning I consider alcohol-related as any intruder is unlikely to know where I usually sleep. Ten am comes round and my doorbell goes, Ms Catherine Aston standing there, a confection of purple and black journalistic unconventionality which manages to be at the same time alternative and horribly predictable.

I usher her inside and make coffee, as she prepares her phone to record us, sets out her notebook and most interestingly, extracts a yellow file with what looks like typed sheets and glossy photos inside.

'So, to begin, we can pay you an initial two thousand pounds for the piece, a little more if it catches on a bit or gives us something juicy. I will form the article and you just have to answer my questions, simple as that. If you think of anything else though, feel free to talk and I will just jog along with whatever you tell me. Is that OK?'

I agree, but it's absolutely not OK, and I have no intention of playing anything but the innocent pawn here, so I spent forty minutes doing exactly that. Catherine, as she tells me to call her, gradually becomes more disinterested as the pointlessness of her article becomes more apparent with every bland answer and insistence of unawareness. Eventually, we are done and I ask about the information she has for me.

She livens up again and gives me a wolfish smile before handing over the file. I open it and it's either from a police source or someone has been doing a grandly similar piece of work. A summary of the murder in Edinburgh, complete with some appalling photos, then the same for McBride and lastly poor Jim Brown. The pages on his life and times are short and uninspiring, but his death is a sight to behold. As with the Edinburgh victim, the face is cut in the shape of a cross, straight down through the forehead to below the chin and horizontally through the mouth, ear to ear.

I remember to look like this all should bother me, so I feign disgust and go to the toilet afterwards, as if to recover. Catherine is kindly making coffee when I get back.

'So, what do you think? Gruesome, eh.'

'Aye, it is. Who the fuck would do this?'

'Well, the cops think that it might be you.'

I glance at her. 'Do you agree with them?'

'Not for a moment. You've got an alibi, you don't fit the profile although your background is hazy at best, and I think you're only the principal because there's no-one else.' I should be glad of this, I suppose.

'Yeah, well I can assure the cops, you, and anyone who asks that it was indeed nothing to do with me.'

I pick up the file and lift out the summary page on the Edinburgh victim.

'What's the story on this guy?'

Catherine sniffs. 'He was a businessman, investor, well respected, pillar of the community and a perfect family man.'

'Yeah, those don't exist. What is the real story?'

She flounces her hair back. 'There was more to him than he seemed. A bit of a dodgy character, businesses all over and plenty glad he was dead. We don't have the resources to spend on unravelling guys like that, but he wasn't even remotely legal.'

'In what way?' I lean in closer and try to urge her to talk.

'Some of his business contacts were jailed for fraud, white collar stuff, but he was a smart guy, didn't leave a trail home and watched from the sidelines as the angry customers reported his cronies to the law.' She leans back and I guess that means that I'm not getting any more information on Edinburgh.

'My turn Adam, what do you really know about McBride?

'I never met the guy. The only time I clapped eyes on him, and I didn't know it was him, was when I saw his body at the bottom of the crags.'

'Just a coincidence then, that he was the partner of your past and current girlfriend?' She's a right persistent digger this one, I think to myself.

'Anna has nothing to do with this either. Whatever McBride was involved in must have been in Aberdeen. He's run here because he knew where Anna was from, and the only coincidence was that I found his body. Given that I'm one of the very few who go running about the countryside here for exercise, that's probably not much of a stretch either.

She doesn't look super-convinced so I spend the next five minutes disassociating myself from any similarities or meaningful links to him, playing dumb and denying everything with short answers. After I finish, Catherine gives me a thanks-for-fuck-all-talk and looks like she is going to ask for her two grand back. She packs up snappily and leaves another card for me, taking the file with her. It's time for me to go too, so after I tidy and finish packing, I lock up the rental cottage for the last time and return home, to my parents' cottage in Mharisaig.

Ally Quinn and the Hunt

The life of Ally Quinn was just getting better and better with each passing day. In a relatively short but intense space of time, he had been resurrected from beaten-down family man to one of the most feared and important men in the dark, criminal scene within the city. Ally now lived, most of the time, in a new flat in the city centre, where he resumed the narcotic-fuelled excesses of his youth, and that was just great to him. Simmy made him slow down a wee bit after he had a few episodes, as you might call them, but in general, Ally was the man.

It was around the latter part of this time, after Ally slowed down his intake, that two things happened.

The first, unexpected event was that one of the previously pre-eminent dealers had, for whatever reason, fucked off sharpish, and left a massive gap in the market for the Quinn gang. There was a brief period where the supply of narcotics required for the city had dried up, but Simmy knew some European wholesalers so that was sorted, and with a bit of muscle, they persuaded both their friends and rivals that Simmy Quinn was here to stay at the apex of the narcotics supply for the Granite City. Key to the growing solidarity of his firm was his older brother, rejoining the business after a period of actual paid employment, which nobody understood anyway.

The second piece of great news, for Ally anyway, was that one of the top names on his hit list had been found by his investigators. Robert McBride was in hiding, or so he thought, working at a forestry place on the other side of Scotland. The investigators had done a grand job, for which they were generously rewarded and given an emphatic explanation of the need for client confidentiality, as Ally had plans for McBride.

The next opportunity he had, after their daily chat with Simmy's crew, Ally took his brother aside as a courtesy to let him know that he needed a bit of time off.

'Whit the fuck fur?' Simmy uttered in disbelief, they had a lot on their plate now, and Ally was needed as part of their exponential expansion.

'It's a wee problem fae a while back. Guy fucked with me, big time, then done a runner. I'll just be up and down maybe once, maybe a couple of times till he's sorted.'

'Aye, I get that, but can it no' wait for fuck's sake? We've got mair work than we've got bodies tae dae it, ken.'

Simmy was feeling the pressure, no doubt about that, thought his big brother. For all Simmy looked the tougher of the two, it was always Ally who had a different spark about him, when they were young and again now, a fear which he inspired, which Simmy just did not.

'Look, I'll attend to my stuff today, but get Houghton to stand in, he's the boy you need the noo, a right good laddie.' Simmy shook his head, but after watching his brother embed an axe in that guy's napper a few weeks ago, even he didn't like to contradict his psychotic sibling too far.

'You're some chiel Ally. We're fucking in the middle o'mental and you're on a fucking revenge trip. Fuck sake.' He sighed, knowing that Ally would do whatever he wanted anyway. 'Just keep the heid doon, if ye can, and you're on your own, cannae give you any lads tae drive or anything.'

Ally grinned, that dark one that had about as little humour as a smile could ever give.

'Nah brother, I'm fine on my own for this. Be back afore ye know it.'

With that, Simmy had to cover his brother's activities with the new man, and Ally left to make his arrangements.

They had a couple of cars which they had recently taken as part-payment of debts, still registered to the owners, thus couldn't readily be traced to them. Ally took the least prominent of them, a Vauxhall, leaving the Range Rover and the Audi for the others to use in the city. He had a pencil-written list of tasks from Simmy, and underneath he'd jotted down more, covering his very specific requirements for dealing with Robert McBride. Ally Quinn was looking forward to being alone with McBride, spending an hour exorcising the anguished memories of what the fucker did to his wife, and by extension, to his reputation and manhood.

Robert McBride, in truth, had become more than just the sum of his actions. Of course, Rhonda had been at fault, along with whoever sent Ally the envelope with photos and the note, untraceable unfortunately. Notwithstanding, McBride now represented the epitome of his lost years, the post-cardiac arrest humiliation with which he had too long been burdened. His resurgence, borne of anger, had made him look at this phase as if from above, with disbelief that he tolerated the absurd life in which he had found himself, back then. Grafting like a fucking idiot, coming back to his lush of a wife, putting up with sons-in-law who messed his girls about, why in god's name did Ally Quinn do nothing, all that time? Only in this last while did he snap out of it. Before Rhonda made her big mistake, Ally had made a few flickering signs that he was able to take his frustrations out on others again, but only in secrecy and not enough to break his then-habitual life of routine and humiliation.

At the time, after he wasn't well with his heart, he just wanted to avoid jail. That was the primary fear which re-routed his middle-aged life. Back then, he wanted to be a better role model for his family, which meant that his illegal income went west. He tried to deal with family issues with patience and understanding, which meant that everything went to shit, no-one was scared of him, no-one respected him, not one little bit.

Rhonda watched him withdrawing, losing interest and then losing the love for him which he knew wouldn't come back, especially after he murdered that laddie. No, fear would do. Even hate is better than disgust, thought Ally, if that's what she had for him. If it wouldn't have meant the jail, he'd have killed Rhonda too, back that day. He let her go with just a kicking, a proper one like he'd thought about. She might go to the cops, he knew, but what evidence was there now to connect him with the boy, or to say that he'd leathered his wife even. None, so Ally had well and truly got away with it. He knew that all you needed was to stay unrecognised, leave no evidence and even if the cops knew it was you, they were onto plums for a trial.

So it was, after completing a few brief but harsh tasks on behalf of the firm, that Ally set out in another man's car towards the west coast to find his quarry and bestow retribution on this scally, this rodent whose face he knew from those photos, the last representation of his fallow years. All enemies must fall and so would it be for McBride, under the blades and fists of the renewed Ally

Quinn. The journey was long and the car was slow, but he didn't mind at all. He'd only been that far a couple of time before and used to find it boring, the scenery was fine and dandy, but when the kids were young there seemed little entertainment to be had in the far west of Scotland. Older now, Ally quite liked the wide open space, the new spring colours and especially the anticipation of his mission.

It took him five hours, including dinner in a village pub near Aviemore, busy enough with tourists to make a lone traveller merge unseen. At the end, he had no daylight left and sought refuge in a cheap hotel, the staff seeming less than keen to admit a customer at that late hour, but they did with no good grace even for pre-payment in cash. Ally lay in his bed, contemplating the next morning's work and using his phone to review the roads and maps included in the file provided by his investigators. In the morning, he rose at seven, ate a full breakfast and left by eight am, false name given and barely a trace for any to follow. He did a line of coke before leaving, just to sharpen up a little before he got to this forestry compound.

It took a fair bit of finding, but Quinn eventually located the track to the compound about 10 am. He drove up to near the gate, got out and checked for CCTV, but it was OK as far as he could see, nobody about either so he guessed they were out working, it being a Tuesday. The location scoped, there was nothing else to do but wait, so he passed the time by driving around the area on his map, little to see here he thought, so a few miles on to a village, Mharisaig, where he bought sandwiches at a little village shop, not wanting to go into the only hotel there in case his face would be remembered. It was there, sitting in his Vauxhall, eating a cheese and pickle sandwich, that Ally Quinn became confused. In front of him, getting out of an expensive vehicle was the man he quested for. The photos did not do him justice, Ally thought, as the broad-shouldered young man emerged from the same shop and drove off along the right turn after the shop. No beard, but it was definitely him, or a close relative. Nope, it was him all right and Ally Quinn started the car to follow, his pursuit now focused on a harder target.

Media Spotlight

Back down at my parents' cottage, I am pleasantly surprised at the sight of the furniture van from the charity shop in Fort William, ahead of schedule and already disembarking its contents. Niall comes out the cottage and we stand as the sofa is hefted by two wiry youngsters down from the vehicle and through the new front door, a narrow fit but they somehow manage it. We head inside and all is looking much more homely, I now have white goods in the kitchen and two older chaps come downstairs, telling me that that the beds and wardrobes are in place. Ten minutes later, I tip the guys generously and I'm left with Niall to admire the interim household they brought to me. Nothing at all matches, but it's comfortable and seems to be all there. Even Niall's painting and decorating looks to have been done fairly well so for once my parents' old cottage is respectably presented and free from the dusty lack of care which always typified it.

There's some finishing outside which still needs completion, specifically the fence panels to go up at the bottom of the garden so, despite my lack of natural affinity with manual labour, I join Niall to get it done. By 4 pm we are finished and I will never, ever do that stuff again. Niall wanders off upstairs for a shower and I heat up some pasta, which is shit, so we go to the pub again for something cooked and less rank than my basic fare. Despite my underlying desire to be alone, I agree to let him stay in the other bedroom, partly to help him out but mainly so that I'm not alone if a serial killer rocks up.

After a relatively sensible evening, we get back and crash out, the familiarity of my surroundings soothing me to sleep, along with all the food and lager.

I wake to the sound of Niall shouting my name from downstairs and momentarily I don't know where I am, or what the fuck is going on. By the time I react, he's in my bedroom and thrusting a copy of a newspaper in my face. It's about page five or something and my face is emblazoned above a defamatory headline which tells me that *Local Man is Prime Suspect* in the murders here in Mharisaig and goes on to more than suggest that the cops think I'm the fellow for the Edinburgh slaughter too. That gutter bastard Catherine Aston must have decided that my version of events wasn't juicy enough and that the prurient rumours were the best-selling option for her. Niall is looking at me incredulously but I don't know what to say so I roll over and pretend it's not happening. I hear his footsteps clumping down the stairs and about an hour later, I rouse myself and seek him for more information. He's watching the crappy TV I bought and eating toast, he nods at me and mutes the channel when I sit beside him.

'Well, what the fuck are you going to do about this? It says that you deny any involvement, but the rest of the fucking thing points straight at you – listen. *"Police sources say that they have no other suspects at this time."* It goes on. *"Locals stay inside for fear of their lives."*

'You need to phone a lawyer or something, get an apology printed or something, this is shite!'

I look at him and take a piece of toast from his plate.

'Nope, that's pointless. Even if I get one, retractions are done in small print, lost in a side column and nobody cares by then anyway. They've got lawyers too and are defensive unless they feel it easier to chuck a few quid

212

away for peace and quiet, but almost always they just ignore the damage, not their problem.'

He looks deflated, so I go on.

'The best thing to do is to have a strategy. I worked with some guys who taught me how to react to situations, what buttons to press and how to get on top and now, my old son, that's what I'm going to do.' I pat his shoulder as I leave the room and go for a shower, to try and figure out what that admirable yet vague intention might look like in the real world.

By the time I get back down, Niall has found some Post-Its and is writing something on a series of them. I look over his shoulder and he grins.

'It's the main players' mate, getting a board up'. He points to the wall beside the TV, which has the old cork pinboard from the kitchen on it, with a piece of paper with my name, bang in the middle.

'Why is my name the only one up there?' I ask.

'I'm doing more! Give me time for fuck's sake.'

He starts to pin all the names up in a random manner until I stop him. I put all the Mharisaig ones to the left, the victims in the middle and any others to the right.

'Just the way my mind works mate, geography and all that.' He nods agreement and I start to think out loud.

'So, let's assume Broony was an accident. He's unimportant, a wee guy who got in someone's way, OK. McBride, we don't know, he could have been a target himself or as you helpfully pointed out, mistaken for yours truly. This Edinburgh guy, what do we know?'

Niall opens the newspaper, no doubt to jog his limited memory.

'He was, you know, a businessman. He had investments or something, a posh twat with loads of money.'

'I know a little more than that mate, he was a chancer who pissed off lots and lots of people, unfortunately none of whom are the suspects for this board. What I will do is put up this.' I write the name down on the Post-It and pop it close to the victims.

'Who the hell is that?' he asks, peering at the name.

'*Biasd Bheulach* mate. Old ghost story from the islands, my dad told me it one night when we were doing that scare-each-other story thing. Bheulach is the guy who turns up in the night. Nobody knows his real name or what he looks like. Just slices and kills for some unknown revenge, not one soul ever finds out why, he just does.' I sit back and admire my creativity. Niall was looking rather fascinated in my account of dad's story, but is now staring at me with a mixture of horror and incredulity.

'Your dad told you stories like that? No wonder your head is fucked.'

I grin. 'Yeah, I don't think textbook parenting was strong in my family.'

'So, this Bheulach guy, how do we catch him? We don't have anything - neither do the cops if they still think it's you.'

I stand and use the board to make my point. 'No mate, we know a fair bit. We know he's been to Mharisaig, at least twice but probably much more. He must have stayed somewhere, or drove here each time. He may have direct knowledge of the area, or maybe been able to check it out online. If he's after me, he must have picked me out or knows me somehow. If he was just after McBride, why come back for me? Unless of course, we were both targets for him.'

'But, this doesn't get us a name or anything. How do we find out any more than the cops?'

I smile at him, but to be honest, better that I don't say anything, yet.

Rhonda's Revenge

After the last of his trips to the Mharisaig area, Ally Quinn was feeling that the whole situation was so high-risk that even he was baulking from remaining involved. This, however, was about to become a relatively safe space compared to that he was about to be thrown into in Aberdeen.

It started with Rhonda, as many of his problems traditionally did. From the hitherto chemically castrated depths of her psyche one day emerged a newer, more volatile woman. Inspired by daytime TV to face down her demons, she stopped taking the tablets and, finding a significant stash of her husband's narcotics in a cache beneath the floorboards of the study, embarked on a week-long solo house party. So extreme were her one-woman revels that the police were called at their peak, and finding a middle-aged woman in some distress, with both nostrils coated in cocaine, they had no option but to pop the music off and take Ms Quinn into custodial care for a time. Rhonda provided the police with an initial honesty splurge, and even the day after, when the reality of the withdrawal of prescription and non-prescription drugs was taking its toll, she kept on with a stream-of-consciousness admission around her own morality and the resultant actions of her husband, a man now well to the fore of local police minds.

Rhonda told of how boring her life had been with Ally, how she went out just to feel alive, to enjoy things again. Then she told them of Josh, her paramour who was unlucky enough to be around when the music stopped. She talked them through the beating from Ally and that he had all but admitted killing poor Josh, so that re-opened the murder enquiry right there. She told them about why Ally had battered her, for the photos of her and poor Rab the Tab, and that moved things up a level or two.

Senior Police figures were notified and eyes were now well and truly fixed on Ally Quinn, but then Rhonda opened up about the drugs firm, Simmy and Ally and the others and them taking over from the old dealers, new suppliers from the continent and the lads back on the rise. She gave the cops all their names and showed that while she sat dormant in the corner at their parties, Rhonda Quinn had missed not a damn thing. For behind her valium-frazzled façade, she knew that Ally would be fucked when she set the cops on him, Simmy too. She had enough in the bank and a good four-bedroom house in her own name, so she needed no men to pay for her, or to dominate her, or to scare her. Rhonda was playing her hand, and playing it well enough that the cops wondered if it had been all an act to attract them in the first place, then to mug them in with all the admissions. In truth, her machinations didn't matter one bit. Rhonda was shafting the Quinn gang, naming them all, giving the cops their secrets and locations, all that she knew already and had heard since the revival of the firm.

Ally Quinn learned of the situation from his youngest daughter, who had been contacted by Police Scotland after calling them previously in search of her missing mother. His daughter told Ally that mum was in custody and he knew, intuitively, that Rhonda would be talking.

He'd just got back from Mharisaig, now a bastard of a shambles, back into their burgeoning business here, and all that was required from him. The call was taken in a storage facility in the west of the city, where most of the crew were present for a group discussion. Simmy was in the middle of recounting how he dealt out a beating to someone who reneged on a loan payment, trying to pull a fast one while the business was too busy to keep tracks on that side of things. Ally stopped the laughter by taking his brother to one side.

'We might have a problem.' Ally confessed softly. Simmy looked at him and shrugged.

'Rhonda is with the cops. She's been a bit mental the last while. Think she had a bit of a party to herself and got lifted.'

'No kidding, we thought she was a zombie.' Simmy turned to make sure the others weren't able to hear.

'You think she'll tell them anything? Fuck sake Ally, its Rhonda! She's been with us for nearly thirty years. Same school and everything, she'll no blab.' Ally looked less certain.

'What are you no telling me, Ally? Come on, if the cops are onto us, I need to know what the script is.' His deeply inset brown eyes, which Ally always thought made him look pig-like, were staring in worry at him now.

'I had a wee problem with Rhonda a while back. Some arsehole sent me pictures of her and this laddie, you know, drinking and all that, while I was on the rigs. After I seen these pictures, I went out after them, but it was a different guy, same patter though. The guy, well I couldnae stop, so he's deid. The other guy from the photos, that's who I was chasing, ye ken. Rhonda, at the time I just gave her a black eye and that, put the fear into her and she's been like that since. Tablets from the doctor, ye ken, helps one thing and disnae help another.'

Simmy could not believe what he was hearing, however the sound of approaching police sirens told him that now was not the time to question his brother's shortcomings in marital matters. They were in a facility

218

with supplier-level quantities of narcotics and an urgent need to run like fuck, which they did. One shout from Simmy and every one of them scattered to their cars, taking flight on every connecting road in the industrial estate and hoping that the cops weren't smart enough to barricade the two road exits, which they weren't. The cops got four of them though, Houghton included, who knew more than anyone about the current state of their empire and may not have the requisite loyalty when faced with a long-term jail sentence. Simmy and Ally escaped unchallenged in their blacked-out Range Rover, heading for Ally's flat for his passport until they reached the corner of that street and were faced with three police cars. They backed off, and at the sound of an approaching helicopter, made good their immediate escape on foot through the busy city centre and to Simmy's apartment.

Either Rhonda hadn't told the cops about this flat, or she didn't know where it was, but they had enough time to get Simmy's passport, two pistols and enough money to get them away, if such an opportunity could be found. On a coast with many ports, there may be someone willing to take risks for the right price, so that was their plan until the reality of their predicament sank in.

'We're fucked Simon, that's it. I'm sorry.' Ally told him as he finished zipping his bag shut. Ally only used his proper forename when he was in a situation which merited sombre behaviour, and this was most certainly one.

Simmy paused and his hefty shoulders drooped.

'What'll happen?' He asked his brother in the softest voice he'd used in a long time.

'Ten, fifteen years. Out in less, maybe, but maybe not. They'll have all the stuff they need to prove we're the big dogs in the city and the others will not be long dropping us in it to get shorter sentences.' Simmy looked momentarily like he was going to blurt out an intention of threats, but he didn't have the energy.

'Can we run?'

Ally smiled at him.

'I can run, and you – and the others - can tell them that I was the capo.'

'The fucking what?'

'The boss, you fucking twat. I'm going to head to meet a pal at the ports, see if I can get abroad. You hand yourself in and stick to that. You'd been a wee dealer until I rocked up, took over and there it is. Just get the same message to the rest of them and you're looking at five to seven years instead of the rest of your life, which is what fifteen is for guys our age.'

Simmy looked at his brother, as if to argue, but nothing came out. Ally took the bag of money and guns, gave Simmy his passport from it, and left without looking back. He knew that the plan he told Simmy, the escape through an east coast port, was a non-starter and that Simmy might well tell the cops anyway. He needed to set off elsewhere, where he had an outside chance of success. Ten minutes later, he had reached his parked-up Vauxhall and left the city with all the anonymity he needed to flee towards Mharisaig.

What Ally didn't realise at that time, was that Police Scotland were approaching him at pace from more than one angle, and that he was in the deepest shit possible. His nefarious activities in Aberdeen aside, Ally was now their hot prospect as a man with a grudge against Robert McBride. Indeed that very day had he not been forced to go on the run, he would have been interviewed for his whereabouts in four high-profile unsolved cases, one in Aberdeen, one in Edinburgh and two in Mharisaig. Ally was also unaware that Rhonda had told the cops about the Astra and they were already checking live traffic cameras, which detected it travelling cross country, with one at a T-junction capturing a clear picture of his face.

All this put Ally Quinn as the prime suspect with Police Scotland, easily overtaking the previous favourite, Adam Darnow.

While Ally drove west, the police were already busy processing the rest of the Quinn gang in Aberdeen, having brought in as many officers as they could to root around their various properties. The Quinn mob, their known associates and many other contacts were being hauled into custody at an astounding rate.

Ally had the radio on while he drove, but the media were not yet permitted to report on the ongoing arrests, he correctly surmised. He was four miles outside Mharisaig when he realised that a blue light was followed his car. Speeding up, he forced the Vauxhall to its limit until something made a rather drastic noise under the bonnet and he clattered to an ignominious halt just before the turning into the village. The cops skidded to a halt at the front of his car, blocking him in, before emerging apprehensively, and then retreating inside again as Ally waved a handgun at them.

'Get out the car.' Ally instructed as he knocked on their window with the pistol, pointing at the driver, who looked like he was going to pass out.

They emerged from the police car, hands in the air and blethering to Ally the usual crap he expected. Two young cops, just laddies really and all Ally needed was for them to leave him in peace to get away. Unfortunately the sound of more sirens could be heard echoing through the pass, so all Ally told them in no uncertain terms to run or he'd put a bullet in them. They scarpered at a fair rate over the field and lost themselves in a copse of trees before Ally realised that the smartarses had taken the keys to the cop car with them, and now he was on foot.

A five-minute jog later, Ally was round the back of a formidably grim-looking manse, walled in and set back from the village. There were lights on inside and one car parked at the back door, so Ally reckoned that this would be as good a place to try and hide as any. His only hope was to go to ground, make himself hard to find until an opportunity presented itself and he could escape, maybe even in this handy vehicle. These hopeful plans in place, Ally Quinn struggled over the wall and landed in the back garden of Ruaridh Nolan.

The Killer and Adam Darnow

Two days later and I'm readying to leave my parents' cottage, heading back to Inverannan to get away from the insanity that Mharisaig has become. This recent turn came about after being shunned by my fellow denizens of the village, largely because of their media-guided preconceptions about my involvement in the murders. These were heavily fuelled by the national press in their two-day sequences of articles before, I assume, the cops told them that it was a live investigation and that they weren't exactly contributing to their efforts.

The other reason for me leaving is that Anna has finally succumbed to the guidance of her mother, who quite reasonably has had me marked down as a scoundrel for some time. She called on me at the now-renovated cottage for a last afternoon, and on leaving gave me her goodbyes and a maybe-catch-up-when-all-this-blows-over breakup speech. This left me feeling somewhat abandoned, a taste of my own medicine perhaps or Anna had just inevitably come to her senses over me. Maybe she used me and always meant to discard me, or was just pretending it was like that to make it easier on me, but I doubt that.

So, with my community avoiding me, my lover abandoning me, the press impugning me and the police hassling me, I feel have no option but to leave Mharisaig yet again, this time to never return.

I had ventured to the pub last night to meet with Niall and let it be known that he'd have to find somewhere else to live, the cottage is getting locked up and I'm off into the wide blue yonder again. It was easier to break to him than I thought, as Niall admitted that his conversations with Liz had actually taken place and trial reconciliation was to be attempted, alongside his feared Couples Counselling. I bought a couple of last rounds for the regulars, although they were also less friendly than normal too. So it was that even my drinking ties were cut, quickly and with little goodwill. Niall didn't even come back with me to the cottage, went in to Liz's instead and I sauntered along the roadside unaccompanied as light dwindled in this month of long Highland days.

So I wake up alone again, my last day in my parents' cottage. There's not much to do, and I loaf around and sit in the garden until the afternoon when Niall drops in to pick up his things. We head into the living room to avoid the heavy rain shower which is all too typical of the Highlands in spring.

'How's it going?' I ask.

'Fine so far, although I've been doing the dishes and not lying on the sofa, you know, being helpful.'

'That can't last mate.'

He agrees.

'See you later then.'

'Aye, see you then. You OK on your own here?'

I tell him that I'll be fine, nothing to worry about and he nods, a sad expression playing across his features.

With that, Niall is gone too. He doesn't know it yet, but I'd placed an envelope of cash inside his rucksack, which might help smooth his relationship situation, for a time.

I watch TV and make dinner, then a while later I get my running gear on and set off through the village to a few unfriendly gazes, not that I care. The run clears my head and I go farther than I intended to, returning as the last of the twilight fades. Walking into the living room, I stand panting and looking at the pinboard which Niall and I compiled, the names and the lines connecting in a surreal web of murder and suspicion. Right beside that, I look at my not-to-scale sketch of the cottage and surrounding area, the lines of sight from just outside and farther back.

It's time to see what will happen when I walk outside, I think.

Putting the living room and hall lights off, I open the front door and walk to the gate, open it and stand leaning back on the newly installed fence which forms the short front boundary of my parents' cottage. Folding my arms, I stare into the darkness and wait. After maybe three minutes, a movement straight ahead catches my eye. A branch shakes and suddenly a dark clad figure rises and stands looking at me, across the few yards of the single track road. He's hooded, the rest is hard to see in the cloudy night but there's a significant knife in one hand and something else in the other. I'm calm and could stay like this for a while, the exquisite pause before imminent violence. He seems to be content to savour the moment too and, while I consider speaking, I refrain lest I ruin the moment for both of us, hunted party though I am. My thoughts turn to escaping, running, to see if he could match me, but he probably could, hadn't been a problem with McBride or Broony, not an advisable tactic, so I lean on the fence, waiting until he boils.

His first step is made, directly towards me and I don't move. A second, slow like he is prolonging an approach or maybe giving me time to run, to be scared, but I don't give a fuck, not here and not for this Bheulach. I notice his other hand holds a black truncheon, or cudgel or something, and I hold up my hands to show that I am unarmed. He raises both arms and here we go, I think.

In the shortest time, he lunges at me with the cudgel and I feint with a dropped shoulder and leap to the other side, a move I naturally deployed playing football to send some cumbersome defender the wrong way. Before I move out of his way, I extract from the hedge my two-pound hammer with my left hand and a sword of Niall's provision with my right. I back off to let him see the changed odds and he pauses, the need to slaughter me perhaps tempered by the threat I now present to him. His kill urge must be strong, for he comes towards me and I swing the sword to maintain some distance and raise the hammer in case he rushes into the gap I leave.

He leans back and we are interrupted, lights from the field and my helpers have sprung too early to my defence. I need to stop him from escaping now, and I'm sure he will understand his altered position. My sword, a genuine replica claymore Niall assured me, is heavy but not an ornament, and it's this that I go with, making a series of left/right downward hacks towards him until he realises that he's fucked and I'm better armed than him. Right when I reckon I'm on him, he springs forward like a bloody cobra and sinks his knife in my armpit, which is not only sore as fuck, but makes me drop the claymore. The lights are almost on us, he thrusts the knife at me again but I knock it away with the hammer and on the backswing from that, hit him on what I think is his cheek. It bounces off and the next thing I know it all goes dim and I am on the roadside grass, seeing a pair of black trainers disappear along the road as voices surround me.

A few minutes later, I am hauled into the kitchen and Niall and the lads are trying to get my t-shirt off to see the damage. There's a load of blood but it's not hit an

226

artery, we have a medical kit for this very purpose and after some swearing, I've got a line of adhesive tapes to hold the wound in place. Unfortunately, the bastard has escaped and our ambush has failed, but even though he hardly flinched, I must have made a mark on his face with the hammer, it certainly didn't glance off. The fucker must be made like the Terminator.

Niall sends the others home after we demolish a bottle of malt between us and tells me that he will stay.

'Nah mate, this guy is off to lick his wounds. He won't be back tonight.' He nods.

'Adam, why don't you call the cops now? This proves that it's not you, we'll all confirm that and they can get off your case.' I look up at him with all the warmth I feel, but that's probably the painkillers and whisky.

'It's better for me without the police mate, you know that.' With that he leaves, making sure that the latch has fallen and the door is securely locked. I go upstairs and fall into a deep sleep, wakening when an ill feeling comes over me and see a dark figure standing over me, then nothing at all.

The next, confused feeling isn't exactly disorientation, or even fear. My head is hurting like hell and my wrists are in agony, tied behind me. It takes minutes for me to blink my eyes open, blood crusted on my eyelids, eventually freed to let me look at my assailant before me. This looks bad.

My vision is blurred, but it's him all right. He's doing the standing still thing again, nothing in his hands but I can see that damn sharp knife sitting on the kitchen counter beside him. Me, I'm on one of the wooden kitchen chairs from the charity shop, hands held tight behind me by what feels like cable ties. My armpit wound is also giving my hell, so I take a moment to remind myself that pain is just electrical impulses to my brain, and they can be overcome. He glances around to perhaps ensure that the situation suits him and that's my moment. The daft fucker didn't tie my ankles and with a surge from my core, I throw myself forwards and my head strikes him hard in the stomach, sending him back, hopefully winded, and me backwards to the floor, the crappy second-hand chair disintegrating as I go.

I get up and grab the knife from the counter, reaching it around, thankfully slicing the now-loose cable tie without cutting myself and getting the blade into my right hand. He's up and looking at me, and I see that his face covering has a black-on-black skull motif, like a Halloween mask. He picks up a chair leg from the mass on the floor and it looks like he's not a quitter, fair play to him. I reach down and get one too, then have a bit of a swing at him, but there's not much room in the hallway and my reach is inhibited by the armpit wound. I stab at him, which is better and he backs off, swinging to keep a distance. He's opening the door behind him, using his spare hand and I lumber towards him as he reverses. Perhaps I should recognise that I've been twice injured and have poor vision and chuck it, close the door and barricade it, but I'm after this fucker now for better or worse. We're outside and he seems to have the same opinion, moving around like he's ready to come in for the kill, so we're on.

We fight like that for a while, him landing hits with his chair leg and me with mine, I'm jabbing and slicing with the knife too, catching him three times but this inhuman shit doesn't flinch as I would have. The cut in my armpit is hurting more know, even with the adrenalin of the fight. Blood is dripping continuously down my arm, onto my hand and the ground, which no doubt is why he's persevering. The moon has decided to reveal itself, so we're at least well lit for the scrap. He thumps me on the face with the table leg but I swing the knife about to keep him back until I get my balance back.

I let him see that I'm weary, the old rope-a-dope my trainer in Glasgow used to call it and it works, he swings in again for the finish and I skelp him forehand with my chair leg and slice his hand when he defends himself, a proper cut that he can't ignore. He drops his weapon and I hammer him on the neck with the chair leg and am about to finish him with the knife when he drops low and runs at me, taking me in the midriff and sending me backwards with him on top, crashing into my new fence. I bite the bastard hard into his neck and he screams, pulling away with difficulty and leaving me with a chunk of his flesh in my mouth and the metallic taste of blood. He's keening and reeling about, holding the wound and I grab the knife and chase him, but I'm too weak to catch him or whatever and away he goes at a loping sprint, leaving me panting on the roadside.

A car approaches and I wonder if it's the police but it's not. I'm standing with the knife in one hand, blood and skin dripping from my mouth after the neck bite, drenched with sweat and blood as Anna and her mum drive past, slowing but understandably, not stopping.

Ally Quinn Incognito

Ally Quinn dreeped down from the top of the wall, landing on soft mossy grass to the rear of the house. The dim, verdant shade from the overgrown trees helped to cover him until he could scurry forward to the only entrance he could see, a green-painted wooden door with an old-fashioned circular metal doorknob. His breath was coming fast as the sounds of sirens became louder, from perhaps four vehicles. Quinn knew that the search for him would be immediate and that staying hidden here, somewhere in this old house, could be his best chance at staying free. The door opened inwards, the light just enough to reveal a proper old country house, musty and without modern fittings. He was in an unlit hallway, racks of boots and coats to his left and what looked like the kitchen straight ahead. Turning right, he opened a narrow door which revealed a plethora of household boxes, bags and what appeared to be fancy dress costumes, for which purpose Ally had no idea. Removing his shoes and clearing the wet marks with a jacket, he then retreated into the mess of this little room.

It took him less than ten minutes of silent re-arranging to construct a crawl space, behind dusty boxes and using a tea-chest to consolidate a two-foot wide gap where he lay under a layer of redoubtably odorous hats, coats and dresses. Ally was confident that he'd left no visible marks in the dust to show that he'd made a den at the back of this storage room. If the police made just a cursory inspection of the room, he'd be fine.

So it was that Ally Quinn fell asleep amongst the dusty coats and dreamed while the police swarmed over the lower part of Mharisaig, waiting on the armed units arriving. Cordons were set up at the main road, plus the

230

two minor roads which come into the village from the other side and even the forestry tracks to the north. Residents were roused from their peace and houses checked, including that of Ruaridh Nolan, although the slumbering Quinn didn't even hear them come and go. It was first light when Ally wakened and, contrarily, he felt better than he had in ages, although this may have been partly due to the reduction in the levels of alcohol and cocaine in his system. He lay for the whole morning, wishing that he could put his phone on to find out what was going on, but he knew that silence was his best friend. By the afternoon, hunger was biting at his stomach and the need for the toilet was becoming pressing too, so out he must needfully go.

Ally pulled himself silently over the tea chest and towards the door. He could hear the muffled sounds of someone else in the house, so slipped his FN pistol from his jacket pocket and, with it loaded and the safety off, emerged to view the hall. The noises were ahead, so he progressed along, opened the kitchen door and stood looking at the open-mouthed man as he chopped what looked like red peppers.

'Who the fuck are you?' He asked Ally, one of those plummy Highland voices which sounds English.

'Never you mind that boy, put the knife down on the bunker and back off.' Ally gestured him to retreat from the kitchen worktop.

'Get out of my house. The police are just outside. One shout and they'll be here.'

'Aye, and one shout and your fucking head will get blown off. Shift.'

Ruaridh Nolan placed the knife on the counter and walked two steps back. After a brief tussle, he was tied to the wooden kitchen chair with only a bruised cheek to show for his half-hearted resistance.

'You got a mobile phone son?' Ruaridh looked ready to ignore his question, but a stare from Ally persuaded him to defer any conflict until an opportunity presented. He nodded towards the back door.

Ally strode to the doorway and extracted the phone from the green Barbour jacket pocket, topmost of the few on the rack. He then checked the other two downstairs rooms for a landline, but it didn't look like there was one. Throwing the mobile into the toilet bowl, he then returned to the kitchen.

'Good lad. Keep the heid and I'll be out of here shortly and you can get back to whatever it is you do.' Ruaridh nodded. Ally shoved a dish cloth into the younger man's mouth, then left him be for a time while he investigated the rest of the villa.

A quick check confirmed that they were alone in the rambling property, so that was fine. He couldn't see any police presence outside, but knew that they'd be patrolling so he had to make sure that the big laddie downstairs was well confined. After this recce, Ally sat down in a room at the back of the house, opening the laptop he found on the low table.

'Let's see what's happening.' He told himself, opening a new tab and searching for the Aberdeen local news. The internet connection flickered in and out, but soon he accessed the headlines which he knew would be there. Simmy and the others had been arrested, major drug haul for Police Scotland, a manhunt for the gang leader in the West Highlands, covered by the Courier, BBC and STV as well as a shedload of others. The link with the Mharisaig murders and the Edinburgh one was also a main topic in the press, at which Ally went cold and his chest tightened. As if this wasn't bad enough, his face was plastered all over the papers and the internet so any chance he had of escaping into a crowd had just dissolved.

Still, the new Ally Quinn was not a man who gave up easily in the face of misfortune. He had access to a car, weapons, money and with luck and good timing, could still make it southwards to where anonymity was an easier prospect. He needed to keep this guy under wraps while he got away, and he pondered over whether just to go back into the kitchen and finish him, but there was no pressing need for that, not yet. Ally knew Mharisaig well enough by now to see that this house was well along from the entrance road to the village, so the police blockade of the village might be farther back, letting him through. He also knew that the murders around the village had been up on the other side, so if the cops thought it was him and that he was back for a last visit to the murder site, they'd be up there.

After fixing some food under the gaze of the now-furious Ruaridh Nolan, he settled back down at the laptop to check out some other options for his escape. Ally memorised the road network, such as it was, seeing that he had a few choices of which to take, depending on whether he made it away from Mharisaig unfollowed.

He exhausted his analysis eventually and lay back on the sofa with the laptop on his stomach, clicking on a few of the folders to see what his captive was all about. It looked like he was something of a young professional, chartered accountant, whatever that meant, and from Stonehaven no less. There was a Spotify account with music which Ally had never heard of, not that his tastes were likely to be same as a guy in his mid-twenties. He opened a couple of photo folders, which were of the family variety and predominantly featured Anna

Berkmann, which made Ally sit up with a new degree of interest. Further folders showed what appeared to be stalker-level interest in the young woman and he was about to go to the kitchen to find out what the fuck was going on when he noticed a sub-folder titled *McBride*.

Inside were snaps he hadn't seen of Robert McBride and a few that he had seen before, when they dropped out of an envelope in his Aberdeen home and into his lap, that momentous night.

The Police Come Around

I am sitting, leaning my back on my nice new fence when the police arrive, then the ambulance, which I'm kind of glad about. The adrenalin has left a while ago and I am getting cold. Hands are moving me and I feel an oxygen mask being placed over my mouth and then don't feel anything until I wake up, in what smells and feels like a hospital, so I reckon that I'm probably in Fort William. I don't open my eyes, but think for a while and remember, and wonder. I suppose that Anna called 999 after she got home, which was decent of her. It doesn't take me too long to organise my thoughts and if all goes well, my days as a suspect are over. There won't, hopefully, be any public knowledge of my earlier, failed ambush on the serial killer, but everything after that would appear genuine, unplanned and easy to recount when required. I might come across as a bit of a lunatic, especially the vampire neck thing, but that's better than doing time for murder.

Sure enough, my first visitors are indeed of an official nature. I deign to engage any legal assistance and just lay out what happened, as best I can remember. They seem disappointed that I can't identify the culprit, which seems a tad harsh in the circumstances, but otherwise they are competent, detailed and non-judgemental. I'm genuinely knackered, so it takes another two interviews over the four days I'm in hospital before the constabulary is satisfied that I have nothing further to add, remember or admit. For my part, I have some choices to make and some action to take.

After they decide that I'm as patched up as I can be, I respectfully refuse their further assistance and walk alone from Belford Hospital, taking a circuitous route to a

B&B, where I sign the visitor book with another name and pay cash in advance. I've not been followed, I'm sure, and a few hours watching from the window of my room confirms that no-one is outside. The cops had kindly brought me my essential things from the house and the next morning I awake feeling much stronger, walk into town to get a new phone or two, and to arrange the next part of my recovery.

I dine out that evening, at a hotel outside the centre, in case my enemy is watching. Again, I pay cash before leaving and walk to the B&B without seeing the figure I'm avoiding, until I'm ready again. It's obvious to me that he won't quit. He'd have done it earlier, done it that night when my trap failed. He was injured, cut, slashed, bitten and hammer-struck and still he didn't give up until he absolutely had to, so he was a determined psycho, but so am I, when needs be.

My assault has been widely reported in the media, the excellent team at the hospital had agreed to bring me the newspapers and it was all good, especially when I noticed that the piece in the rag of Ms Aston had taken a complete U-turn, written by another hack without bias against my good self. It also looked like Niall and the others had kept out of the limelight as I'd hoped, they did well enough but now is the time for professionals. I make my calls, outline the necessary arrangements and the next morning, leave the B&B in a taxi, the return to my cottage in Mharisaig given the all-clear by the cops, forensics done and dusted, as it were.

My cuts are fine now, I've always been a quick healer and the best part of a week is enough to let me move freely, but with care. On arrival, my car is still where I left it and the house locks, as requested, are changed by Niall. My new keys open the locks to reveal a much tidier and less blood-soaked scene than I left. I drive to the shop, to let it be known that I'm back and two locals even deign to ask how I am, and I reply politely, that I am well and that everyone must be pleased that I'm not the serial killer they thought I was. I'd called Niall to let him know what was happening and Anna to thank her for calling the ambulance. She was fine, but no offer to visit. My unholy visage of that night may be hard to wash from her memory, I think. I call Inverannan to speak with Gillian, but she won't come to the phone, which I thought might be the case. Since I had become the focus of the story, almost all the newspapers had at some point mentioned my relationship with Anna, so I was just going to say sorry and have a nice life, or something pathetic like that. Anyway, I can't do anything about that, fretting over mistakes is no way to get the job done.

When I get back, there's a package waiting for me in the agreed place, under the bin beside my driveway. I take it inside and open it, and for the first time in a while, I'm properly armed and ready, and it feels as good as it always did. I rest for the next two days, at home and exercising a little, until I can move in the way which I need to. The cops visit me twice and drive past god knows how many times.

The next day, I rise, prepare and go for a run, through the village, up past my rented cottage and into the forest, which the police have expressly told me not to. I carry my running backpack, which has water, a cereal bar, and a banana. I take the route past which Broony turned, then up to where McBride ended his days and back down the same way. After my first run, I stand in my living room, listening to the police sermonising to me about staying where they can protect me, and me telling them exactly when and where I'd be running if they wanted to follow me and offer protection, which they demur. I repeat my run twice a day, at the same times, for four days and each day the cops, increasingly exasperated, give me shit about it when I get back to the cottage, even searching me, the untrusting swine.

As nothing happens, they stop trying to persuade me not to, and stop following me, so I know that it will not be long. The sixth day onwards, my running backpack has water, a cereal bar, a banana and my handgun.

On the seventh day, which was incidentally my estimate of his return to visit me again, I set out before twilight as usual for my second run of the day. Up towards the Crags, I feel that I may not be alone. I'm almost exactly at the spot where Robert McBride met his maker when I stop and turn. Tattered Police tape still marks the area where Robert fell and not long before then, I had passed the track leading to where Broony's guts once decorated a gravestone. Standing with my back to the Crags, I watch a black-clad figure that I knew, in my heart and head, was still around, slow from his run and walk towards me.

Ally Quinn's Last Stand

Ruaridh Nolan could hear the sounds of the keys on his laptop as Quinn clicked away for the best part of two hours. It had taken a while, perhaps his psyche couldn't process the awfulness of it, but eventually, Ruaridh had to accept that the man he had tormented with the photos of cuckolding was now in his house and that was just the way it was. He almost peed himself at the thought of this thug finding the photos on his laptop and redoubled efforts to loosen his bonds. The ropes at his wrists cut appalling, obviously Quinn was one of those coastal types who knew knots, but he persevered as time was short. His favoured right hand was eventually free and from there, he removed his ankle fetters. Unfortunately, this freedom coincided with his captor finding the offending photos and, having lost his temper, barging into the kitchen to see Ruaridh about to take flight.

'Bastard!' shouted Ally, with a red-faced anger which usually bode ill for the subject. He leapt forward at Nolan, who was half out the other kitchen door and was trying to get it closed behind him. They struggled for a few moments, one on each side of the door and holding the handles to lever it open and closed. The antique doorknob was not up to this kind of pressure, so with a click, the metal cracked and both men flew backwards in their respective rooms, giving Ruaridh the opportunity to get through and lock the stout wooden door which connected to the dining room. Ally, having left his pistol back beside the laptop in haste, went back for it and resumed his pursuit in earnest.

'Who the fuck are you?' Ally screamed through the door. 'You sent me those photos, what the hell is going on?'

Although being still largely in charge of the situation, Ally Quinn felt a kind of dizzy madness coming over him, the feeling that cosmic forces were conspiring to make his life a tangle of insanity and failure, and he didn't like it one bit. He wanted to shoot the lock away, but that would bring the cops, so not an option. There wasn't time to wait, as this guy could get out of a window and alert them, so something had to be done. Quinn ran back the way he came, out the back door and around just in time to catch his quarry halfway out through a sash window.

Ruaridh looked up at him and uttered a whimper before being struck, once and firmly, by the butt of Ally's pistol. His body dangled from the frame for a short time until it was dragged back indoors by an increasingly paranoid and enraged Ally Quinn.

It was almost dark when Ruaridh wakened, blood caking the side of his face and with a headache the like of which he'd rarely before experienced. He was tied to the chair again, but this time even more securely and with a rope around his neck, attached to the old pulley, which in better days his mother had used for drying clothes. He flinched as he realised that his assailant was sitting in the twilight shadows across from him, drinking from a bottle of whisky, which on closer inspection was his prized 18-year-old Glengoyne. Quinn set the bottle down on the floor and approached Ruaridh, kneeling in front of him and staring at him, as if to try and identify him.

'OK son, who are you to me? I've been through yon laptop and you've no secrets left, just explanations.'

Ruaridh stiffened at the voice, the lilt of Doric slowed down slightly to help a non-Aberdonian understand his intent. His shoulders slumped and he forced himself to meet Quinn's gaze.

'I was trying to fuck up Robert McBride. He was living with my cousin Anna, I just wanted rid of him. I followed him to a pub and the guys there told me who your wife was, who you were and I figured that you would give him a doing if you knew that he was…seeing your wife.'

Quinn went back to his chair, brought it forward to sit close in front of Ruaridh.

'Aye, that makes sense. It caused me a lot of bother though, a lot of grief, ken. Maybe it did me good though.' He seemed to Ruaridh to be talking to himself.

'Where would I be if you hadn't sent the letter, that's what I've been thinking about?'

Ruaridh shrugged.

Quinn's eyes widened at this perceived snub, this shrug of indifference, and he pulled the rope at his side with some strength, lifting Ruaridh and the chair a few inches from the floor, stretching his neck and the thick knot at his throat closing his airways. Moments of agony later, Quinn lowered him back down, Ruaridh retching, straining to get oxygen back into his lungs.

'You know where I'd be? Probably still working the rigs, still getting messed about by Rhonda, so maybe you done me a favour boy, although you didn't mean it like that, did you?'

Ruaridh could just about focus on Quinn, those dark, mean eyes piercing him with barely suppressed rage. He knew that he would die here in his mum's kitchen unless he could act, somehow. He tried to speak, but the rope had squashed his neck, so at first attempt only a gurgle came out.

241

Quinn rose and went for the bottle, sat back down and took another decent swig of the Glengoyne, which was almost half-empty now. Ruaridh took the momentary gap in Quinn's attention to free his right hand, the chair having buckled slightly when it landed after the near-hanging. The space this created in his bonds was then enough to release his left hand, with not much more than an indiscernible wriggle.

One thing which Quinn did not intuit from the laptop was that Ruaridh, although not in an organised-criminal way, was maybe a bit of a psychopath himself. Indeed, the rage which drove Ally Quinn was now being overtaken by the rising fury of the sedentary Ruaridh.

'So, how much do you know about my wee trips to Mharisaig?' Quinn stared, close, into his captive's eyes.

Ruaridh, almost free and ready to get a grip of Quinn, paused and looked in complete incomprehension at him.

'Like, do you think I killed McBride, the other laddie and that?'

Ruaridh shook his head slowly, and Quinn could see a face etched perhaps with both confusion and, he thought wrongly, fear.

'Maybe you set this up, got me to come to this shitehole and get McBride for you?'

If he was about to go further into these meanderings, Ruaridh didn't need to hear. The slightest turning of Quinn's attention to place the bottle on the floor gave him an opportunity, and he took it. Ruaridh grabbed Quinn by the hair, smashed his head downwards and onto his knee, breaking his nose and stunning him enough to allow Ruaridh to wrench himself into a chair-restricted standing position and get on top of him.

242

Quinn was struggling for all he was worth, but Ruaridh was the younger and more vigorous of the two. Pummelling the back of his head inexpertly was wearing down his opponent, so he kept on doing that. At the very moment Ruaridh thought that Quinn was beaten, he felt a bee sting in his leg, letting out a yelp as the sting went straight into his leg, just above the knee. He looked down and there was a little knife sticking out of his leg and no bee at all. It was much sorer than he initially thought too, and so was the swinging punch which the rising Ally Quinn hit him with as he rolled Ruaridh off from his back. Ruaridh pulled the knife out, it was just a wee short thing, but by far the sorest thing he'd ever felt. Quinn skelped him a full punch in the face and back he went, but he kept consciousness and the knife, so when Quinn loomed over him, he sprung forward and gave him the knife back in his shin, right into the bone.

Ruaridh watched Ally Quinn jumping back, then falling as his leg gave way to the pain. They both lay, intermittently groaning and swearing at each other until Quinn righted himself to a sitting position, which impelled Ruaridh to do the same, propelling himself backwards to lean on the kitchen unit, opening the drawer above him and scrambling with his fingers until they clasped on a knife. Still bleary, he held it in front of him to show Quinn that he was armed, but was met with nought but a laugh. Ruaridh looked at his knife, which was actually a potato peeler. He laughed too, and threw it aside and groped around the drawer until he found a serrated bread knife, which still made both of them laugh again, but at least it was potentially a usable weapon and god knows, the next one could be a whisk or something, so he settled on the bread knife for now.

'All right son, we've done each other enough damage for now.' Quinn told him softly. 'Whatever your game is, it's not doing me any good. I'm wanting away and I'll need your car.' Those mental wee eyes stared at Ruaridh again, and although he wasn't scared, he didn't really fancy a knife fight with a rope-muscled gangster, so he nodded.

'Keys are over there.' He motioned towards a glass fruit bowl on the kitchen unit, sans fruit.

Quinn struggled to his feet and reached for the keys.

'I need you to stay quiet till I'm gone son. I'll leave your car somewhere, the cops will find it and you'll have it back. It's that or we go for it again, alright?' Ruaridh nodded and felt so tired, the blood was pumping from his leg, at a rate similar to his opponent, who seemed much less fazed by his injury than Ruaridh.

Ruaridh watched as Ally Quinn limped towards the back door. He listened as the car started and heard the crunch of driveway stones as it reached the high front gate, then a pause and the sound of his car pulling away sharply. Minutes later he took off his trousers and started to patch up his wound with tea towels and sellotape, rising as he heard the sirens passing his window, presumably in pursuit of the wounded gangster.

Outside, Ally Quinn had got into Ruaridh's car, blood leaking at a steady rate from the little cut on his shin, not his first stab wound but definitely a sore one, he thought. His heart, without the aid of his usual medicine which was back in his flat in Aberdeen, thumped audibly to him and he forced himself to breathe slowly until he felt well enough to go on. He got the gate open, but he felt like shit, wished he had some antacid tablets as he had heartburn too and he was sweating from every pore.

He knew that there was a chance of using a side road to get away, had the memory of the Google map of the area to keep him right. If he went about a twenty-second drive back towards the entrance to the village, there was a right turn before that which would take him away, east and towards higher ground. This unsealed road would eventually meet a single-track proper road leading almost directly south and towards the main road, past where any roadblocks could be expected, although that was guesswork for now. As he drove away, he left the headlamps off, so the dim moonlight glimpses on the cloudy evening had to suffice.

Reaching the turn, he kept the car in second gear, quiet as he could and rolled onto the rougher surface. Instead of the unimpeded route he expected, Quinn was looking at three recently-placed barrels blocking his way. Almost simultaneously, blinding lights shone on him from more than one source. He could see the blue lights now, men emerging from vehicles and shouts, noises, so he got his pistol and opened the door, face soaking by sweat and unable to move freely for the pain in his shin. He leant on the roof of the car, steadied himself despite his left arm being pretty useless for some reason, and emptied the entire clip in the direction of the cops, who scattered and retreated, making him laugh, but the pain in his side and chest stopped that. Ally Quinn got back into the car and dropped the gun at his feet, still aware of the lights but all else uncertain. The car radio was still on, he hadn't noticed it before. He tried to think of who it was, maybe a Britpop band he remembered from such a long time ago, but he couldn't get the name. A bullet or two zinged into the car through the metal of the passenger door, but he barely noticed as one made a mark on the top of his leg. He smelled petrol and thought that this might be a problem, then a flicker of fire arrived behind him, and he wondered if he should get out in case the petrol tank caught fire, but Ally didn't feel well at all. His heart made an agonising, final spasm

and with that, Ally Quinn's short but eventful
renaissance was over.

The Mharisaig Murderer

The figure stands, legs planted apart and with a dark rucksack on his back. He takes a long knife or machete from it and has what looks like a black tyre iron in his other hand. We stand looking at each other for some time, yet again, until he starts towards me. A crossbow dart hits him in the right leg, taking him down, then another dart in his right arm neutralises his immediate threat to me. Four khaki-clad men emerge from the shadows of the pine trees, kicking away the weapons from their silently recumbent target. I walk towards them, my small group of trained killers surrounding the beaten amateur. I nod at the first man, a good comrade who had worked with me many times over the past two years. He reaches down and pulls the mask away, the other men holding the flailing arms to let him.

His face mask is removed and as I knew, it's Allan Douglas, who made such a grand job of the cottage. I gesture and my men kick the shit out of him, to make transportation less of a struggle and give them reward for their days of waiting. Then the lads remove the darts from his limbs and drag him through the woods to their 4x4, left waiting the next row along, and throw him into the open cargo bed. They have identified a remote and disused bothy about three miles away, which amusingly enough, is owned by the company which employed Robert McBride. Soon, Allan is taken inside and tied to a chair, much as he'd done to me. He's stripped and as he regains consciousness I can see the vivid wounds which my teeth made on his neck, angry and unhealed still.

He is at the start of a long night of questioning, although I can't stay for that. Before I get a lift back though, I take some painful bladed revenge on young Allan Douglas, first for Broony whom I didn't like and then for Robert McBride who I didn't know.

Cleaned up, I get dropped off back at the Crags and run to the cottage, having left my pistol with the lads and a promise to see them on my morning run at the same place. The cops give me a friendly wave when I get home and then I shower, put my clothes in the hottest wash and sleep all night like an innocent. I wake early, desperate for my run, but I must wait till the appointed time. It's raining like it only can in Scotland and my run is harder for the fact. The 4x4 is where it should be and soon I'm Allan Douglas' last visitor.

'Morning, Allan. You're not looking good, it has to be said.' He's sitting in the middle of the plastic-lined left side of the bothy, temporary lights giving the interior a weirdly medical feeling. His formerly fresh and serious face is puffy, bruised and sporting the criss-cross of cuts which I inflicted the previous evening, by way of letting him know how it feels to be cut with a sharp knife.

'Did you get any sleep son?' He looks up at me through a haze of pain. I think he's trying to tell me to fuck off, but it doesn't come out like that at all.

He's too far gone to have an actual chat with, so I turn to Vernon for an update.

'He's a tricky bugger, that's for sure. He broke about an hour after you left.'

'What's his gig then, is he a serial killer right enough or a consultant?'

'He's a lone nutter, picked his victims after looking about for people worth killing. He knew you personally though.' I look at Vernon's craggy features in something akin to surprise.

248

'I've never met him before.'

'Maybe not, but he knows you. His dad and him worked up at Inverannan. They had a verbal agreement with Galloglas to build a road network, a jetty or something and a ton of other construction. When you guys bumped Galloglas, they were fucked, went bust and his dad pegged it not long after. Seems that he tried to find the Allantons but couldn't, so you were the next best thing. He more or less followed you from Inverannan to here and was ready to offer himself to help with your cottage until he could get you.'

Well if this isn't yet another fucking oddity from my old life. I knew, by a process of elimination that Allan Douglas was one of two suspects. The other one, I'd thought of too harshly given his now apparent innocence, but no actual harm was done, so all is well.

'So, what's the deal with the ritual stuff, all the crosses cut in and the guts out?'

'He wouldn't say at first, but then we gave him the gear. It's a power thing, he fucking loves it. Doesn't think it's a proper kill unless he's done it the way he likes.'

'Amazing. I'm starting to think that we're doing the general public a massive favour by taking this guy out of commission.' I tell them. The lads' nod in unison.

Vernon hands me a piece of paper, which he tells me that Allan had in his rucksack. It's beautifully calligraphed, almost like a section from a handcrafted bible of old.

Psalms 58:10 ~ The righteous shall rejoice when he seeth the vengeance: he shall wash his feet in the blood of the wicked.

Vernon explains. 'His plan was to leave one like this at each of his kills. Babbled on about a right few other quotes while he was under the influence. The lad seems properly devout, if you don't take into account all the murders.'

I look at him for some explanation, but he doesn't even raise his head. I shrug at Vernon and he returns the motion. Time is passing and I need to get back, my cops will be worried if I'm late.

'Well Allan, I'd love to hand you over to someone more qualified than me, who could spend years finding out what makes you tick, maybe write a thesis on you. I can't do that unfortunately.'

He looks up at me with battered eyes and I can see the hatred burning within. The lads move away from the immediate area.

'I don't know what fucking weird gratification you got from all this Allan, but go to hell knowing that you failed with me and I couldn't give a fuck if you ever lived or died. That's how unimportant you are.' I see a flash of anger in him, give him my best cheeky grin, point the silenced gun at his forehead and pull the trigger twice.

'Job done lads, you have my thanks again. Payment will be made through the usual channels.' I hand the weapon to Vernon and remove the long gloves I'd donned. I get hosed down outside, which is fucking freezing, and then get dried with a towel and jump into the 4x4 for a lift back to whence I came. My last look back and the boys are clearing up. Soon they will be ready to take Allan Douglas on his last trip to the machinery which will render him, fit for porcine consumption.

I had, back in Fort William, arranged this scenario with some of my employer's former comrades, a costly exercise but highly successful. Not only have I resolved the issue of being targeted by the individual personally, but also exacted revenge for Broony, McBride and the guy that the crazy fucker killed in Edinburgh, plus whoever else he'd murdered and countless more he'd no doubt had gone on to fillet across the country.

As I run back downhill, I ponder on the major revelation, which took my lads a night of cuts, drugs and dentistry to glean, that Alan Douglas had been contracting for our business in Inverannan, before its conversion to legitimacy. He must have been ready to build the road to the new harbour, the mooring itself and probably umpteen other jobs, all off the books and paid for with our plentiful cash reserves. Our abandonment of these projects I suppose must have left him bankrupt and, as they weren't actually employees, they were somehow missed then and later when we wound up the old Portfolio activities. Couple that to a psychotic fucking murdering personality issue and there we have it, young Allan Douglas, the best Serial Killer that no-one in Scotland will ever know about, except me, four ex-squaddies and a team of large pigs who are about to get some minced murderer for their dinner. If caught, he would have blabbed about me to the cops too, of that I have no doubt. He must have been well aware of the business of Inverannan and even if little evidence is left up there, it would be awkward, to say the least, to have anyone official start investigating, even at this late stage. So Alan, talented builder and surveyor, has ended up in the best place for all concerned, but mainly me.

Aftermath and Afterwards

I'm not the good guy. I'm also not keen on being the bad guy. I can't go back to Mharisaig or Inverannan and right now I can't be arsed meeting anyone else that I have ever known. Each time I go back anywhere, it all goes wrong. I'm not Adam Darnow from Mharisaig anymore and I haven't been for a long time, I was just able to act him, to pretend I was him.

It took me several days to finally get away from the questioning, the cops, the media and all that. It turned out that a proper Aberdeen gangster, Ally Quinn, had died that same night in a great, old fashioned shootout with the cops, on the road just outside Mharisaig. The news media had reported that his wife had provided enough evidence on Quinn to bust his organisation, his cohorts and to confirm that he was actively seeking Robert McBride by way of cuckolded revenge.

The papers gave a lurid description of Quinn's death, when after exchanging fire with the armed police unit, all the exertion and drama had reached a crescendo when the petrol tank of his stolen car blew him and it to pieces in a rather spectacular explosion. He will remain, despite never being convicted except *in absentia*, the eternal main suspect as the serial killer. My own scuffle with the actual serial killer, coupled with the alibi of being abroad at the time of the Edinburgh murder and the lack of any tangible evidence, blood or other forensic matter to connect me to Broony's demise, means that I am not in the frame, now and forevermore. Quinn's movements in the past few weeks will forever appear shrouded in criminal mystery, so from what the cops have suggested it's their intention to at least attempt to place Quinn at the scene of every unsolved murder on their roster. For me, he was probably someone who liked to watch the whole thing unfold, maybe even tried to figure out for himself who the serial killer was.

Allan Douglas, now he was the main man but for reasons various, he couldn't fall into the clutches of the authorities. All he is now is a missing person like hundreds of others, who won't ever turn up. He wasn't on the radar of the cops and for his own reasons he wasn't even a registered business, just doing my cottage work with his former tradesmen off the books, cash in hand. I don't even know where he lived, or what his life outside serial killing entailed.

I knew it was him though, although not at the start why, or his motivation or indeed anything else about him.

The turning point was after I'd spoken with John Allanton about tactics, before I moved back into my parent's cottage after Allan Douglas had completed his building work. John had told me to keep my own counsel, talking to my friends as if someone else was listening, all the time, and that gave me the thought. Who had I met recently that I didn't know before? Who had happened into my life and what were they doing there?

I wondered to myself what the killer had in mind. He would certainly be watching me. Had he installed listening devices, as John had perhaps suggested? These took me a while to find, but when I did, I left them in place. They helped let me set both traps, although I should have got Douglas the first time. I definitely shouldn't have involved Niall and the others, but I didn't know for sure that I could tackle Allan Douglas myself, and events proved that I couldn't. I then spoke to the cops in my living room, telling them the route my run would take and them telling me not to go, that they couldn't protect me if I left the main roads. My hunter, listening, would surely plan to reach me there, and so it proved.

The last thing I had to do in my home in Mharisaig was to dispose of these minuscule listening devices, all but embedded in the plaster at the side of the smoke alarms, so diligently fitted by Allan Douglas, master builder and psychopath. I reckon that he wanted me alone, like the guy in Edinburgh and poor Broony, to slice me up for whatever weird gratification that would give him. He needed to make absolutely sure that Niall or Anna, I suppose, were not with me and he had uninterrupted time to work on me, which even in my capacity as a bit of a psychopath myself, gives me the right shivers.

Locking up my parents' cottage for the last time, I drive down to the village and say my final goodbyes to Niall in person before I leave, giving him another five grand for a last thanks to him and his crew. We have a hard talk about the need for silence on anything he may suspect I have done. I say I'll keep in touch but will I fuck.

Anna, I speak to on the phone from the village hotspot but she is just really glad to see the back of me if I'm reading it right. The whole incident has pissed her off completely and I am given the impression that I could take my misanthropic carcass elsewhere with no regrets, and that Mharisaig is a better place without me. I agree wholeheartedly, although this could easily be said of anywhere that I live.

The last thing that Anna asks me is why Robert McBride had Ruaridh's number in his phone, and I tell her that it was perhaps the only other link McBride had to Anna, if her mum died, and Robert McBride loved Anna like I never would. She cries, at that.

I start up the car and plug the phone in to charge. I look in my rear view mirror at the village shop receding in the distance as I leave for the last time. Swinging right at the main road intersection, I see the police tape still blowing loosely in the wind where Ally Quinn breathed his last. Each piece of evidence would be in a warehouse in Aberdeen by now, I suppose. There's one final visit for me though, before I head south to lose myself in London.

Slowing to a stop and bumping my car onto the roadside verge, I get out and look up at the prominent villa, set back and enclosed by a stone wall. The gates are open, and I can see the back of a dark-coloured estate car parked behind the imposing building. The façade is grubbier than I remember, its' asymmetrical design as unpleasant as I always thought. The window frames need painting and weeds grow all over the driveway and the once-neat shrubs are now huge and overgrown. Old Mr Nolan and his wife must have left a while ago, but I knew from Anna that Ruaridh still came here, was meant to be keeping it in good order. Knocking on the door, I hear a shuffling sound of Ruaridh Nolan coming to answer me.

The ancient paint-cracked door creaks open and Ruaridh looks at me with more than a hint of surprise.

'Hi Ruaridh, heard you've been through the mill.'

'Yes. What do you want?' The emphasis on *you*, as if some unspecified blame lay with me.

'I'd prefer to talk inside Ruaridh. I think we do need to talk, don't you?' He nods, then turns and leaves the door open for me to follow him.

255

It's been many years since I've been in this house, maybe it was even as long ago as Primary school. There's a memory buried somewhere that someone got hurt and we had to come back here with them.

'Did I come here when we were kids Ruaridh, when someone got hurt?' I ask him.

He turns and looks at me. 'Yes, my wee brother fell from a tree swing over at the woods. You carried him here after it. My mum thought you were a fucking hero.' I'm detecting some antipathy towards me, must be a family thing.

He gestures towards what looks like the worlds dustiest antique sofa. I sit, a cloud of light stoor surrounding me as do.

'What exactly do you want Adam? I'm just getting ready to go home.'

'Where's home Ruaridh? Not here?'

'Stonehaven, I work there.'

There's an atmosphere in the room, and it's not all down to the dust.

'What's the script with you and Anna?' I ask him, straight. He blushes and looks set to burst.

'I don't know what you mean. She's my cousin, and anyway it's damn all to do with the likes of you.' His fists keep clenching, so I keep going.

'How much do you love her Ruaridh? Is it enough to boot Robert McBride off the top of the Crags?' His eyes are protruding, face crimson and both fists are clenched, so I sit forward and get ready in case he takes a run at me.

Ruaridh calms himself and seems to be regaining composure.

'I love her more than you ever could, you bastard.'

'I don't doubt it. My track record on that front is very poor.' He snorts at my comment as if it was rhetorical. I go on.

'I don't hear any denial about McBride, so I'm going to take that as an admission.'

This time, he looks at me with increased seriousness.

'Ruaridh, what I really want to know is whether you were killing Robert McBride up there, or were you killing me. So, which is it?'

We hold each other's gaze for some time before he answers.

'McBride'

'Why?' He turns and opens a cabinet, taking out a bottle of whisky and a glass, gesturing to me to see if I want one, but I shake my head.

'He messed Anna about terribly. He really was the worst sort of low-life. Drugs, drink, stupidity, weakness, he was just a waste of space.' He takes a deep slug of the whisky and I notice that his hands are shaking badly.

'So how did it go down that night? He was only in Mharisaig en route to see Anna, so where did you come across him?' Another glug and his whisky is finished, so he pours another, even larger than the first.

'Oh, I was already in Mharisaig for one of my wee visits. I can be over here after work and back in the morning for a 9 am start, as long as there are no roadworks. It's better at weekends though, I get more time to myself here.'

'And what is it that you do when you're back here? Do you go to the pub? I seem to remember that you were the life and soul back then.'

He laughs, but mirthlessly. 'Yes, I suppose I was. It's just that now, all our friends are gone, all the interesting ones anyway, so nobody here is on my wavelength any more. We catch up at reunions, although you don't seem to be anywhere to be found by all accounts. Why is that Adam?' There it is, his first question back at me, so he's getting bolder with the whisky.

'I'm not on social media Ruaridh, can't be bothered, too busy with other things.'

He snorts.

'Yes, Anna had some impressions on that front which she shared with me, when she got back from London and told me that you'd been horrible to her.'

I leap out of my chair, knocking the glass from his hand and grab him by the throat with my right hand, pushing him against the wall. His hands try and pry mines away, but he's angered me and strong as he is, I'm stronger.

'You haven't fucking seen me being horrible Ruaridh. But if I think for a moment that you show any interest in me or my life after I leave this room, I promise that you will.' With that, I throw him to the floor and sit back down. Retching, he gets back up and stands behind his chair, trembling and looking as if he is deciding if he has enough bottle to try and fight me.

'Sit fucking down.' I tell him, and he does. I give him another moment to gather his composure.

'Ruaridh, for reasons that you don't need to know, I couldn't give a fuck if you killed Robert McBride and got away with it. Well fucking done. I do know that you are a total weirdo, so stay away from Anna and let her get on with her life. She's had me, Robert McBride and you, so she deserves a chance to spend some time with someone better than the three of us.'

The colour is ebbing from his face now and perhaps he is resigned to the truth in what I'm telling him.

'I'm going away now Ruaridh. You should sell this fucking mortuary of a house and stay away. I'm sure it's healthier in Stonehaven than whatever it is you think you're doing here. Also, don't even Google my name after this, let alone come near me, understand?'

He switches mood in an instant and leans towards me, livid anger on his face. His voice is strained with emotion, louder maybe because of the whisky.

'You don't know anything about me, Darnow. I want what's best for Anna. You, McBride and whoever else, I'm not interested unless you try and hurt her again. That's what McBride was going to do, and I saw him when I was watching you. I thought it was you for a moment but when I followed him, I realised it was McBride, going to see Anna, if you would believe it.'

'Did you lose your temper Ruaridh?'

He laughs, loud and harsh.

'Perhaps a little bit. He ran away though, straight over the crags, the useless shit. I was going to bury him somewhere up there, off the tracks, but I couldn't after he'd fallen, so I just came back.'

'Did you take the money from him?' I ask.

Ruaridh bristles, perhaps he's fine with being a murderer but doesn't like the implication that he's a common thief. After an awkward pause, he nods almost imperceptibly.

259

'Well, I don't know how you should do it, but that money belongs to Anna and she should get it back to her. That, and it's evidence that could incriminate you, so don't let the cops find that, or anything you used, OK?'

He must be wondering why I'm giving him advice and to be honest, so am I. Time to go.

I stand and he does too.

'So that's it, is it?' He asks. I nod and walk to the door, but he follows me. I think his alcohol intake is influencing his behaviour.

'I've always hated you.' He tells me, apropos of nothing.

I shrug, leaving the room, but he limps after me into the hallway.

'You're not getting out that easily, you bastard!' He grasps a solid looking walking stick, which he swings at me, but I drop my shoulder and move the other way, so he misses and spins around, barely keeping upright. I punch him solidly in the centre of his face and he crashes into the umbrella stand, spreading the floor with its contents. He thrashes about on the parquet floor for a few moments while I watch until he calms himself, lying there with hatred in his eyes.

'Look Ruaridh, I need to be somewhere, so calm yourself down. Just think yourself lucky that you've got away with murder with no suspicion. Not everyone does, you know.' He watches me from his recumbent position and I can see a rivulet of blood running down his leg and onto the wooden floor.

I open the door, moving a couple of umbrellas as I do.

'You know, you remind me of him.' He shouts after me. I make a gesture that suggests that I don't know and I'm waiting for him to tell me.

'Quinn. That gangster who broke in, the one the police think killed McBride, Brown and the other man. He had that manner, the same one you have.'

Meeting his stare, I give him a little reassuring smile.

'No Ruaridh, that's no comparison at all. He was a criminal, a murderer and a drug dealer. I'm a property developer, that's all.'

I take a last look at Ruaridh Nolan as I close the door to his family home softly behind me. It's a long trip down south and I have a meeting arranged with John Allanton. He has a proposition for me.

Printed in Great Britain
by Amazon